KISSING IN THE KITCHEN

Karen went to Steve in her kitchen. They stood very close, her head on his shoulders. He smelled of cold weather and newly cut wood and fresh sweat. She kissed him lightly on that place where his cheek became his jaw. "Thank you," she said. "I don't know what I'd've done without you."

"You're most welcome." His lips met hers. They were gentle. They were giving, understanding. "I'm not finished," he said against her lips. "But most of the light is gone. Alex said I could return the chain saw tomorrow." He kissed her again, and held her close. "Lady," he murmured, "you grow big trees at your house."

She smiled. "I can tell."

He held her close and carried her with him again into that silent waltz. She closed her eyes and let herself follow. Let herself feel. Let herself move as one with him. . . .

Books by Annie Smith

HOME AGAIN

AUTUMN LEAVES

Published by Kensington Publishing Corporation

AUTUMN LEAVES

Annie Smith

ZEBRA BOOKS
Kensington Publishing Corp.
http://www.kensingtonbooks.com

ZEBRA BOOKS are published by

Kensington Publishing Corp.
850 Third Avenue
New York, NY 10022

All Kensington titles, imprints and distributed lines are avail-
able at special quantity discounts for bulk purchases for sales
promotion, premiums, fund-raising, educational or institu-
tional use.

Special book excerpts or customized printings can also be created to fit specific needs. For details, write or phone the office
of the Kensington Special Sales Manager: Kensington Publishing Corp., 850 Third Avenue, New York, NY 10022. Attn.
Special Sales Department. Phone: 1-800-221-2647.

Zebra and the Z logo Reg. U.S. Pat. & TM Off.

First Printing: November 2003
10 9 8 7 6 5 4 3 2 1

Printed in the United States of America

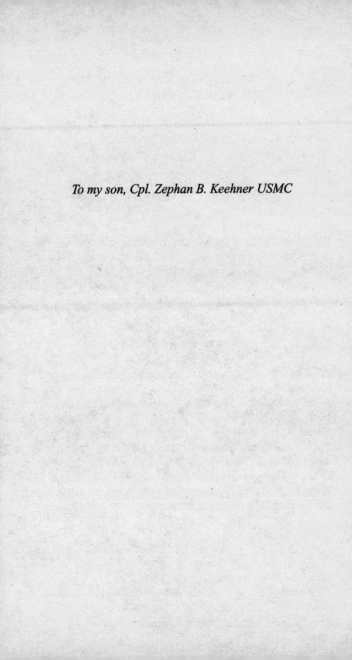

To my son, Cpl. Zephan B. Keehner USMC

ACKNOWLEDGMENTS

Several years ago, my older son announced he had joined the Marine Corps and in four weeks he would leave for boot camp at Parris Island. My son has never understood the tactical value of timing. Two days earlier I had had surgery and my emotions were not quite stable. Also, at that time, our country was actively bombing Iraq. I didn't know much about the Marine Corps, just what I'd learned watching *Full Metal Jacket,* which hardly inspired confidence. It would be, I am sorry to admit, a serious understatement to say I was somewhat less than supportive. I was, in fact, furious with my son.

Two or three weeks after my son left for boot camp, the husband of a friend of mine suggested I read a book titled *Making the Corps.* I am always looking for a few good books, so I checked it out and read it. That book healed my self-imposed psychosclerosis. (Thank you, Jim Ebbatson, for challenging me to test my attitudes with a little dose of reality. My attitudes failed. I grew.)

Watching my son graduate from boot camp, and now knowing a little of what he had accomplished in order to do so, was one of the proudest moments of my life. In January of 2003, I visited Parris Island, where they make Marines, once more to do research for this book. While I was there, my son received his deployment orders. While I was finishing this book, my son was in Iraq. In a letter home, he wrote he had a job to do, and he was going to do it. I am more proud of him than words can ever express.

Thank you to Cpl. Ryan N. Hanes and his dog Basco; Sgt. John N. Knight, Marine Combat Instructor of Water Survival; Drill Instructor SSgt. Theresa Marzluf; and Cpl. Eric R. Lucero and Lt. Tammy L. Megow of the Parris Island Public Affairs Office. More than simply background information you all reminded me why I am so proud to be a Marine mom. Without knowing it, you helped me through the dark days when I was glued to CNN. You are all *truly awesome!*

I thank Pvt. Megan Stiner and her mother, Vera Pierstorff, who shared part of their very special day.

Thank you to Vonzell Johnson, Drew Schwartz, and Broderick Harper who talked to me about boxing. Thank you to Lennox Lewis who changed my attitude about boxers, Wayne "The Pocket Rocket" McCullough who changed my attitude about boxing, and Micky Ward and Arturo Gatti whose first fight was truly breathtaking.

Most of all, my most heartfelt thanks to my husband, Mark, who reminds me to always look on the bright side of life; my younger son, Justis, who brought me Pink Lady apples when I needed them; and the dogs who are part of my life, Ch. Nab's Kelda Wallis CD HIC who has been my best friend for sixteen years, her daughter, Dove, who eats anything not nailed down, our Newfoundland Sweetbay's Caledonia who learned how to open the refrigerator, and Lily who really is a perfect pet.

A portion of my royalties supports the Newfoundland Club of America's work to rescue Newfoundlands.

Write to me at Annie Smith, P.O. Box 30401, Columbus, Ohio 43230.

Chapter 1

"Let's go, dogs!" Karen Matheson held the back door open as her small herd of four Newfoundlands thundered past her and out into the yard. She followed them outside and lowered herself onto the step. She was worn out. She leaned back on her elbows and raised her face to catch the light summer breeze.

Her dogs were beautiful. They were everything Newfoundlands should be; with their glossy black coats and bright eyes, they were happy and healthy. Three of them were her foster dogs, until she could find forever homes for them, but she could not have loved them more than if they were her forever dogs. They bounded and gamboled and gallumphed. They played with tug ropes, snuffled at the row of hollyhocks that lined the fence, and excavated a corner by the garage—always hopeful of unearthing a long-forgotten bone. All except Brian Boru, her very own and most beloved geezer dog. He did his business and then ambled over to her to promote himself some attention.

Karen held the sides of his big head in her hands. Up close, his muzzle and cheeks were now more salt than pepper. His dark brown eyes were cloudy and dimmed with age. "I love you, Bri."

Brian swished his tail and drooled. Then, with a great gusty sigh, the old guy lowered himself to the step beside her.

Karen gazed at the dogs in her backyard. Her dogs were safe, and all was well with the world. Karen was at peace.

Squealing brakes in the driveway shattered that peace. Katie was home.

Karen closed her eyes and tried to hold onto the peace. Nope.

"Well, Bri, I should go see if she's in her human mode."

Brian grunted.

"You can stay out here, if you want," Karen told her elderly dog.

Brian wanted to stay. She wished she could stay outside with him.

Why, she asked herself, was it easier to deal with other peoples' teenagers than with her own?

Karen went into the kitchen to peer into her Crock-Pot. At least dinner would be good. Katie might be more sociable after beef stroganoff—her favorite. Karen filled a pot with water and set it on the stove to boil. She pulled a bag of noodles from the cupboard. She looked at the noodles. Should she call Katie, or should she wait for Katie to make the first move? The noodles, in their plastic bag, didn't have an opinion. The noodles huddled together passively on the counter.

Karen went to the bottom of the stairs. "Katie," she called. "Please come help with dinner." She didn't wait for an answer. Instead she watched the pot until it boiled, and then poured in the noodles.

"So, Mom," Katie said from her stance in the doorway. "What do you want me to do?"

Now *that* was a loaded question, thought Karen. But Katie was speaking of the immediate, not the whole. More importantly, she was speaking English, and to her mother, politely. When training dogs, Karen always rewarded appropriate behavior. Much of the time the same rules worked with kids. "Thanks." Karen nodded her head toward the refrigerator. "Would you please do the salad?"

"Sure," Katie said casually, as if everything between them was fine. She opened the refrigerator and pulled out the vegetables. She grabbed the cutting board and knife.

Karen could pretend to be casual, too. "A woman from Buffalo called today," she told her daughter. "Her Lab recently died and she's interested in adopting a rescued Newfoundland."

"Does she sound like a keeper?" Katie whammed the knife down and vanquished the poor cucumber.

Karen nodded. "Someone who had a dog who lived to be fifteen is doing the right things—assuming what she said is true. I gave her the web address and she said she'd print off the application and send it in to the national coordinator. She'll see how her references check out." She rummaged around in a cupboard until she found the strainer for the noodles.

The screen door slammed. Karen sighed. "Ferry let herself in again."

Katie set the salad bowl on the table. "That dog is too smart. She's a regular canine Houdini."

"And here she is! Hello, Ferry girl," Karen greeted the brilliant dog. "You certainly look pleased with yourself."

Ferry wandered over to Karen to lean against her legs, looking up sideways, a sparkle in her eyes. Karen slipped her a raisin.

"That dog has you trained, Mom. She lets herself in and you reward her." But Katie said it with a grin, teasing. "She's pleased because she performed the ultimate escape. She escaped her first family. Wretched people." Katie punched out the lights of an imaginary foe.

Karen blinked at her daughter. "You sound fierce."

"I am fierce. They don't deserve dogs." Katie narrowed her eyes and threw herself into a fighting stance. Ducking and weaving, she gave the air a series of punches. "Let me meet them in the ring and I'd show them my jabs." She added her jabs to the punishment. "I'd teach them to be responsible dog owners"—another couple of punches—"and finish them off with a neat left hook!" She threw her arm up in victory. "Then Michael Buffer announces, 'Undisputed Underdog Champion of the World, Katherine Eleanor Matheson! Matheson!' And the crowd goes wild knowing the underdogs of the world are safe."

"You know violence is never a viable answer."

"Well, it's how I feel. And you always say feelings are always valid."

Karen frowned as she tested a noodle for doneness. "When you began going to that gym, you told me boxing was a great way for you to work out and get in shape."

"This isn't boxing," Katie said. "This is personal."

"How did responsible dog ownership become personal?"

"Just is."

Karen shook her head. She felt helpless. Doctor, she told herself wryly, heal thyself, and thy family. Thing is, she didn't know how. Katie had changed. It was more than graduation from high school. Her gentle child had become full of some sort of secret anger. She had turned into a shadowboxing stranger, who stuck a chin-up bar in the doorway to her bedroom, and who spent her free time watching *Starship Troopers, Full Metal Jacket,* and *Rules of Engagement* over and over until Karen wanted to scream, "Who are you, and what have you done with my daughter?" She poured the noodles into the strainer, turning her face from all the steam. It all started with that paper Katie had written for her senior history class.

Suddenly, Katie sank down in the middle of the kitchen floor and held out her arms to Ferry. "She has such an expressive face, doesn't she?" The big dog padded over to her. "Ferry the hairy Houdini," Katie crooned.

Karen never tired of seeing her daughter with her arms wrapped around a dog. A girl and her dog—it was a beautiful thing. Katie might be going through her angry-at-the-world teenage phase, but she loved dogs. She was at home with dogs. She was at peace with dogs. She understood dogs. Karen knew her daughter would ultimately be okay. "Dinner's ready. Let's eat." And after a pleasant meal, she added silently, we will discuss your plans for college.

Dinner *was* pleasant. Katie made a serious effort to be agreeable. Katie was spreading it on thickly. A little too thickly. Karen wondered what she was up to. She didn't wonder too hard, though; she wanted to enjoy her daughter's good company while it lasted. It lasted through dinner, through clearing the table, through doing the dishes. But, Karen thought as she squirted dish detergent into the Crock-Pot in the sink, would it last through another round of college-talk?

"Mom, snap out of it. Your cell phone's ringing."

"Answer it for me, will you please?" Karen said.

"Matheson's Home for Wayward and Needy Newfoundlands," Katie said into the phone. "Oh, hi, Jess. No, we're finished. Mom's battling with a Crock-Pot." Katie listened. "Sure, I'll tell her. Bye." Katie hung up the phone. "Hey, Mom, Jessie said we're getting a new dog to foster. She said Melissa wants you to go over to the clinic as soon as you can."

"New dog?" Karen scrubbed at the cooked-on gunk on the Crock-Pot.

"Yeah. Jessie said they didn't know much about her, except that she's in pretty bad shape. Melissa's working on her now." Katie divided the leftovers into plastic containers. "I can finish up here, if you want to get over there."

Karen tried to keep the surprise out of her face. "Thank you."

"So put down the scrubber. I'll finish the Crock-Pot and start the dishwasher. Go put on dog clothes and get out of here."

Ten minutes later Karen was ready to leave. "I don't know

how long this will take," she told Katie. "You know how it goes."

Katie snorted. "This is only, like, the gazillion and fifty-eighth foster dog you've brought home, Mom. I know the drill." But she grinned.

"Are you going to be home this evening?"

"I'm going over to the gym for a while." There was a note of defiance in her voice.

Katie knew how Karen felt about any kind of fighting, and Karen was well aware of Katie's boxer rebellion. She gripped the doorknob. "If I'm not back before you leave please put all the dogs in their crates."

"Mom," Katie said in her most aggrieved voice. "You don't have to remind me."

"Habit."

"Do you want me to bring in an extra crate from the garage and set it up in your room?"

"That would be lovely, thanks."

Karen arrived at the Hartley Veterinary Clinic in record time. She let herself in the back door, trotted down the hall and peered through the window in the door that led to the surgery.

The dog on the table was thin to the point of emaciation. Melissa bent over her, stitching up a long gash in her side. Someone, probably Jessie, had shaved whole sections of the dog; much of her was down to bare skin.

Karen opened the door a crack and called, "Can I scrub and come in?"

"Sure," called Melissa without looking up from the dog. "You know where everything is, and you know the routine."

So she scrubbed her hands with Melissa's "vetty soap," as Angie called it, pulled a sterile gown over her jeans and

T-shirt and pushed her way through the door. The smell of dirty, sick dog slammed into her like a truck.

Melissa looked up from the dog long enough to toss her a grim look. "You feel like playing foster mom to a horribly sick Newfoundland for a while?"

Karen moved swiftly to the table to see the dog. Bunches of shaved spots showed off scars and scabs and bruises and flaming red oozy spots. "Sure."

"Assuming she makes it long enough to come out of the anesthesia, that is. She might not. She's in pretty bad shape." She nodded at the IV needle in the dog's front leg. "Antibiotics and electrolytes. She has a fever. I trimmed all the dying tissue from around this gash and irrigated it. She has a raging infection I assume is from a couple of old abscesses gone bad. I opened them up and drained them, flushed them out so they're nice and clean and can heal. Here, here, and over here on her neck. She appears to be highly malnourished, and she smells like unholy hell. Better hope I never meet the damn people who let her live like this."

Melissa never swore. Not even that time when Hugo ate his way through her CD collection.

"What do you know about her?" Karen swallowed. She wanted to gag from the smell, but if Melissa could stand it, so could she. Karen put her hand on the dog's head. The dog's skin was hot with fever. She wanted to give something to the dog, to try to psychically infuse her with healing. Even if she didn't completely believe in all that heal-yourself-with-mother-nature stuff, enough of it had rubbed off from her own mother so that she needed to give the dog a loving touch— something the poor thing probably hadn't had much. Karen silently said the prayer of St. Rochus, another legacy from her mother.

Melissa took another careful stitch before she answered. "Not a lot. Frank Schmedlapp brought her in. Said if I asked no questions he'd tell me no lies." She tied the thread in a neat knot. "I told Frank I'd fix her up, but no way was she *ever* going back to wherever she came from. And I would never let her be stuck in a kennel and kept as evidence until some legal battle was finished. He told me that he marked her as dead on the official papers. He told me I could give her to you to put her up for adoption—as long as she went to a good home and his name never came into it. I told him I'd have to tell you where I'd gotten her, and he said okay, but no one else." Melissa shot her a quick grin. "I'm pretty certain she's an illegal alien, not supposed to be here."

"You mean that officially she was found on the side of the road and some kind soul brought her to you. Of course I'll take her. I'll foot the bill, whatever it takes. You know that."

Melissa snipped the piece of thread. "Among other things, it'll take massive doses of antibiotics."

Karen looked down at the poor remnant of a dog, held together by Melissa's skill and thread, with a big chunk of luck. Currently, she and Katie shared their home with four Newfoundlands, three of them fosterlings, up for adoption. This dog, if she survived, would be number five. This dog would require serious nursing care, which translated into serious time. This dog needed a permanent home, a forever home, not temporary boarding, not foster care. However, finding the best forever home for a *healthy* dog was a lengthy process. Finding the right forever home for a sick dog was . . . She stroked the poor head. "I won't list her with Rescue," Karen found herself saying. "I will keep this dog." She stroked the head again. Suddenly, the sick dog smell wasn't as unbearable as before.

Karen ran through the songs that sang in her mind, searching, searching, until—

"She's my dog, and her name is Bridgit O'Malley," she said. "I've been saving that name. She deserves to be named after the most beautiful song in the world."

"Play it for me sometime," Melissa said.

"Sure." Tears welled up in Karen's eyes and she ran her hand lightly down the dog's back. The coat should be glossy and black. What was left unshaved was thin and brittle, and along with skin and bone, Karen felt bumps and lumps and billions of matted clumps. She drove her fingers through the ruined hair, parted it. She found more scabs and more scars. What had this poor dog endured? She gently lifted a lip to look at Bridgit's teeth. They were worn down and covered with plaque. Her gums were the light color of a dog in shock, rather than healthy red. "It's going to be okay, Bridgit," she whispered in the sleeping dog's ear. "Melissa will fix you right up, and I'll take you right home."

She kept one hand on the sleeping dog, on *her* new dog, while with the other she stroked Bridgit's poor head. If Bridgit didn't make it, if she died, at least the last thing she'd feel was the touch of a loving hand.

Chapter 2

Steve's mission for the evening was simple. Attack the paperwork. Subdue the paperwork. Conquer the paperwork and make it secure. His dislike of everything involved with the paperwork was irrelevant. There were bills to pay and supplies to order. Let's get motivated here! Lock and load. Yeah, he thought, give him his old rifle and he'd deal with the paperwork.

Maybe he could entice Lennox to destroy it. Lennox was highly motivated to carry out acts of destruction. Where was that dog? Steve glanced around his office.

Lennox crouched in the doorway, on high alert. The dog's body quivered, stretched as tightly as a drum.

"Hey Steve, you here?" Katie Matheson's voice shot across the darkened gym.

Lennox leaned toward her voice.

"Get her," Steve whispered to his dog and rolled his chair back so he could watch.

Lennox hurtled through the gym, weaving and dodging the equipment, a silent stealth missile, intent on the girl in the doorway. Lennox leaped up in the air, his front legs straight out. He rammed her. She plopped down on the floor with an *oomph!*

Lennox jumped on her.

The girl giggled. The dog wiggled. Peals of laughter filled the gym.

"Let me go," she gasped through her laughter. "Let me go, you doofus."

"That was a legal knockdown," Steve called. "You weren't ready for him. No use whining about it."

"I'm not whining," the girl gasped. "Lennox, that tickles!"

Lennox wagged and wiggled and tickled. Lennox loved Katie Matheson. Katie Matheson loved Lennox.

"So what brings you here this evening?"

Katie's giggles and laughter slowed until she lay gasping on the floor of the gym. "I felt like a mere visit with you and Lennox." Katie pushed up to her feet. She dusted off the seat of her pants and jogged across the gym to him. Lennox, wagging his tail, trotted along beside her.

He raised his eyebrows. "A mere visit?" Katie was a deliberate person. She didn't do *mere* anythings.

Katie dropped down on the worn couch and pulled Lennox up next to her.

Steve knew all he had to do was wait. Katie would talk to him when she was ready. He looked at his dog on the couch, flat out on his back, waving his front legs, entreating Katie to rub his belly.

Katie stuck her face in Lennox's face. "What," she asked the dog, "are you two going to do when I leave for boot camp?" She jerked her head back. "Gross! He stuck his tongue in my mouth!"

Steve tried not to laugh. "I've warned you about that."

She scrubbed her mouth on her sleeve. She glared at him. "You think it's funny, don't you?"

He nodded. "Yes. I do. Lennox thinks it's funny, too."

The black dog's lips had fallen back to reveal his strong white teeth. His teeth looked vicious, but his eyes were full of delight. Lennox knew exactly what he'd done. Lennox had a sense of humor.

Steve felt like smiling also. Now he knew why Katie was

here. "About boot camp," he said. "Does this mean you've told your mother?"

She dropped her gaze. She looked at Lennox. "No."

Steve sighed. "You have to tell her. When you sign those papers, your recruiter will go with you to talk to her about the whole thing. If you're right about her reaction, it wouldn't be nice to spring it on her without any advance warning."

"I know." She looked up at him again, her expression sincere. Then her eyes glinted in that wicked way. "You want to tell her for me?"

"Me? Hell no. Your mom scares me. She looks at me as if she hates my guts."

Katie shook her head. "It's not personal. She doesn't hate you. She hates any kind of aggression. She believes in Peaceful Solutions to Every Challenge." She made a face. "I know I really have to tell her myself. I was going to tell her tonight—but I wanted to wait until after dinner because she's much more reasonable when she's not hungry. But, then she got a call from the vet's to come pick up a rescue dog."

"You think you were saved by the bell? You should know better."

"I know. A fighter," she recited in a singsong voice, "cannot be saved by the bell in any round including the twelfth and final round."

"This is your final round."

Katie bent down to rub noses with Lennox. She nodded. "Yeah." Then she asked, "Do you think I'm ready?"

"What do you think?"

"I think I am. I have to give Sylvie notice before I quit working for her. But I don't want to do that until after I tell my mom, because she and Sylvie are really good friends, and Sylvie has the best intentions in the world but she isn't very good at keeping secrets."

Steve studied the girl in front of him. Last January, when she'd first come to his gym, she told him she wanted to get into shape so she could be a Marine. She was thin and blonde, and looked sort of fluffy. He'd assumed she was some silly teenage girl with a misguided sense of glory in the uniform. He'd decided if he made it tough for her—give her a taste of what she'd have to do to be ready for boot camp—she'd realize her mistake and give up. He was the one who had realized his mistake, and he was glad he had. "You have heart, Katherine Matheson. You'll make a fine Marine. I'm proud of you."

She turned red and hid her face against Lennox.

"Katie." He waited until she looked up. "Go home and tell your mother. That's an order."

"Melissa's finished," Karen whispered to her newest dog. She perched on a stool grabbed from the lab.

"She probably can't hear you," Melissa said. She pulled off her gloves and dropped them in a biohazard container. She pulled off her gown and tossed it in the laundry hamper. Then she stretched her arms over her head and arched her back, slowly twisting from side to side. "I used to be able to stand over a surgery table forever. Now, after only four hours, I need to work out the kinks. They lied. This is one place where I'm *not* getting better. I hate this getting-old business."

"They must've been speaking metaphorically. *We* are getting better, but our *bodies* are getting older."

Melissa reached for her stethoscope. "How conveniently they forgot to mention that part."

Karen watched her friend listen to Bridgit's chest. Melissa's eyes looked straight ahead at nothing, a look of concentration on her face as she moved the flat part of the stethoscope to various parts of the dog's front and back. Finally she looked up and smiled. "She sounds good. Surprisingly, she has a strong heart."

"A courageous heart. A brave heart. It's probably gotten her through a lot," Karen said wryly.

Melissa checked the hanging IV bag. Then she folded her arms across her chest and considered the dog. "Combing out all those mats will take an ice age. She's endured so much already."

Karen thought. Combing monster mats out of a dog was never fun, especially dogs who weren't used to being combed. Of course, if they were used to being combed, it would mean they *had* been combed, and if they *had* been combed they probably wouldn't have monster mats. "Let's shave the rest of her. Right now, while she's still under, so it won't be stressful for her. And if there are any ugly spots under the mats we can deal with them."

Melissa nodded. "Good idea. You want to do it? Or do you want me to run upstairs for Jessie? I think she's back from dog school."

"I'll do it. She's my dog. My responsibility." She wrinkled her nose at the thought of what was probably lurking under all those mats.

Melissa plugged in the clippers and handed them over. "All yours. I'll be back in a bit. When you're finished, we'll move her to the recovery area. You can sit with her there until she wakes up."

When Karen was finished, the dog looked even skinnier and more pitiful than before. The floor around the table was covered with filthy stinking matted dog hair. "Oddly enough," she said to Melissa when she came in, "she didn't have any fleas."

"Probably couldn't get past the mats," Melissa answered.

"Heartworm test?"

"All done. Negative."

Karen bent down close to her dog's ear. "Good girl," she said softly.

Bridgit didn't hear her.

* * *

Late into the evening, Karen, still in the clinic, stroked the dog's head and softly sang "Bridgit O'Malley" over and over. Karen had no illusions about her singing voice, but she didn't think Bridgit would care, even if she were awake.

Jessie, from her small apartment upstairs, brought down some iced tea. She handed Karen a tall glass and settled down beside her.

"Thanks," Karen said. After all that singing, the cold tea felt soothing to her throat.

"You missed the big excitement at dog school this evening."

"Yeah, what?"

"It was all over the six o'clock news. Dog-fighting ring over in Madrid. This afternoon the Humane Society and the police did the bust. Frank Schmedlapp did good."

Dog-fighting ring? Karen looked down at the dog. At Bridgit who'd had several abscesses, which were most often caused by puncture wounds from bites. The logical conclusion was easy to come by. No. On the official papers the dog Bridgit used to be was listed as dead. That dog did not exist. This dog was Bridgit and Bridgit's life started here and now. New name, new life, new pack. Karen wasn't going to sully the newness, the promise, with thoughts of what had come before. Those thoughts would create anger, and Bridgit did not need any more anger or fear in her life. Karen would not give the past any power over the present, or the future. So, at last she said, "I'm glad. The Humane Society did do good. Say, Jess, thanks for teaching my class tonight."

"Not a problem. Tanner asked me to have you call him about the CGC class. You're still going to teach it?"

Karen nodded. "I plan to. It's a fun class. I hope there are enough dogs signed up."

"I'm sure there will be. It's half full already. Word is spreading to sign up now or forever hold your leash. Say. I saw these really cool bumper stickers that would be perfect on your car. They say—"

"No."

"You're still philosophically opposed to bumper stickers."

Karen glanced at Jess. "People should be paying attention to the road—not reading bumper stickers."

Jessie stroked Bridgit's head for a moment. "You want something to read?" she asked. "I've got the new Lisa Scottoline. Real page-turner. Have you read her? I like her, but she needs to put more dog stuff in her books."

Karen chuckled. Jessie was not subtle. "No thanks. It's actually sort of pleasant being with her and watching her breathe."

Jessie nodded wisely. "Ah. You're doing the bonding thing."

"Yup. Sort of like when Katie was a baby."

Jessie snorted. "Katie has never been quiet. She is a mover. A doer."

Karen smiled. "Yeah. My kid can do anything."

"As long as her feet are on the ground. Hey. Maybe in a previous life she died by falling off a cliff. That'd explain why she's afraid of heights."

Karen smiled tolerantly at her friend. "Maybe so."

Now Jessie nodded at the dog. "M'liss said you're keeping her."

"She's been through too much already to try to find a good home for her."

"It'll be good for you."

"What will?"

"Keeping her. Katie'll be leaving soon for college—assuming that's what she's actually going to do. It'll be good for you to have a high-needs dog to sop up your mothering instincts."

Karen chuckled. "Which one of us is the psychologist?"

Jessie shrugged. "I've known you for a long time. Some of

that book learning's rubbed off." She struck a pose. "I'm not a real psychologist," she intoned, "but I play one on TV." She dropped the persona. "Bridgit is a high-needs dog if I ever saw one. She's perfect for you."

Was Jessie right? Karen wondered. So what if she was? She shoved the thought aside. "This is not about me," she told her friend. "This is about this dog."

"Of course. *Everything* is about dogs. You don't have to convince *me* about that." Jessie paused. "But some of the small parts of the big picture are about people. And I think this little bit of one of the small parts is about you."

Chapter 3

At last the paperwork was secure. Steve, with Lennox sitting in the backseat, drove home. The summer sky still held a hint of light. Steve took Lennox in the backyard and looked up. Too much ambient light to see stars. Then he noticed Lennox sniffing suspiciously at something in the grass. "Leave it," he told his dog. Lennox looked up at him. Steve went to him and found a half-empty beer bottle had been thrown over his fence. Nearby was a second bottle. Someone had thrown beer bottles a couple of times before, but not for a while, and the last time—when the bottles had broken—the police weren't much help. Steve dumped the beer bottles in the trash, found his flashlight and spent an hour going over every bit of his yard to make sure there wasn't anything else that could hurt Lennox. Lennox thought this was a great game.

Inside the house, Steve's phone rang.

"It's me," his sister said.

"Hi, me," he said.

"That's so lame and so old."

"So are you, Maisie May."

"Cute, Stevie Steve. You're so cute. Hey, cut the fun stuff, you need to be serious now. I called you a couple of times earlier this evening but you weren't home. Did you see the news? A dog-fighting ring was busted today. Over in Madrid. The news media people were their usual ratings-hungry sharks in a feeding frenzy. They gleefully made a big deal about warning viewers that the pictures they were about to show were graphic and some viewers might find them disturbing— but the dumb idiots showed them anyway. Knowing they were inflammatory. Inviting people to be inflamed. And then, they even pointed out exactly what was in the pictures. What idiots. Friend of mine up here blames Disney for what happened to cockers. I blame the news media as much as the drug people and the dog fighters for what's happened to Am Staffs."

"Someone threw a couple of beer bottles into my back yard. I found them when I got home this evening."

"Low blow."

"Probably hoped Lennox would hurt himself."

"You and Lennox watch your backs," May said. "And watch the late news. It's on in a couple of minutes. I've told you before and you didn't listen, so I'm telling you again, you should take Lennox to get his Canine Good Citizen title."

"Maybe."

"No maybe about it. Course, the idiots who throw bottles probably wouldn't recognize a CGC if they tried. Still, it couldn't hurt and it might keep the bureaucrats off your backs. Is there a class near you?"

"I know who to call to find out."

"If not, let me know. You can come up here. We're not as far away as you think we are. You haven't been up to see us for weeks."

Steve hung up the phone. He looked at the clock. "Whaddya think, Lennox? Is it too late to call Jessie?"

From his spot on the couch, Lennox sprawled on his back, all four legs in the air, his head dropped over the side to watch Steve upside down. He wagged his tail.

Steve sighed. "You're right. I'll call her in the morning." He sank down on the couch next to his dog. Lennox grinned at him and wagged his whole hind end. Steve rubbed his belly with one hand and felt around and under the cushions with the other. Ah! He held up the remote. He flicked the TV on.

The lead story was the dog-fighting ring. The anchor mentioned the number of American Staffordshires in the viewing area—admitting Am Staffs, as they were called, weren't *really* the same as pit bulls, not anymore. And here in Ohio, owners of these dogs must have high fences, and keep their dog on a leash at all times to prevent them from being a danger to society. The implication was clear that these dogs *were* a danger. Steve snorted in disgust. Just as May had said, the anchor warned the viewers that "these pictures may be disturbing," but they showed them anyway. The pictures *were* gruesome, Steve thought. Anyone who remotely cared about animals would be incited to riot.

Lennox's heavy breathing turned into loud snoring. Upside down, with his belly exposed, his hind legs splayed, his lips falling away from his gums, snoring. "Yeah," Steve said to his sleeping dog. "You're a real danger to society." Lennox woke up enough to thump his tail a time or two.

The next day, after Lennox took him for his morning jog, Steve called Jessie. "Do you have a Canine Good Citizen class at your dog school?"

Jessie said there'd be a class starting soon at the pole barn, in a couple of weeks on Thursday nights at eight, but it was full. "Do you want me to squeeze you in? There's always a no-show, so I'll put you down. That way you can count on it instead of being on a waiting list."

"Don't—"

"It's no problem. Here, let me check something. Good. Lennox is all up to date on his shots. I'm writing myself a note to send you a registration form. But you have to fill it out and return it right away. Karen's teaching the class."

"Karen?"

"Karen Matheson. You know. Katie's mom."

Katie's mom hated him. Maybe this wasn't such a good idea.

By the time Karen went into the kitchen Friday morning, Katie was gone. There was a note on the table. *Mom, I took the dogs out and fed them breakfast. I'm out running. Please be home this evening after supper—we have to talk, and there's someone I want you to meet. Love, Katie.*

What's this? Karen wondered. Who was this someone she wants me to meet? Suddenly, she had a very bad feeling about this. Karen remembered one morning, eighteen—no it must have been nineteen—years ago, when she said to her mom and dad, "There's something I need to tell you." Karen's stomach clenched. She did not need this now. She shoved away her cup of tea. She was not going to think about this now. She had a new rescue dog to take care of.

She opened the crate next to her bed. "Good morning, Bridgit. It's a beautiful day in the neighborhood. Let's go outside and appreciate it."

Bridgit wasn't sure about this.

Karen promised her she'd have a good time.

Bridgit heaved herself to her feet and allowed Karen to lead her outside into the yard. "Let's learn about going potty," Karen said. Bridgit gave the ground a few perfunctory sniffs, then squatted. "Good girl," Karen said with calm approval. She stroked the poor shaved head. Bridgit didn't care. Karen took her back inside. Karen checked her wounds. Everything looked as good as could be expected. No redness, no puffy swelling. "These are antibiotics," she told the dog. "You have to swallow them. This won't hurt." She popped the pills down Bridgit's throat. Bridgit didn't protest.

Karen felt uneasy about leaving Bridgit home alone this first day.

She glanced at the clock. Someone was usually in the office by now. She dialed the phone. Sure enough, Theresa answered.

"I got a rescue dog last night," she told Theresa. "She's in really bad shape. I'm going to be late this morning."

"Do you want me to have Vicky cancel any of your appointments?"

"Oh, no. Not that late. I need to make sure she eats something, and deal with the other dogs and take Bridgit out one more time so she can pee before I leave. I don't think she's ever been a housedog, so I'm not sure how long that will take. Maybe half an hour or so."

"We'll be here," Theresa said.

Karen put Bridgit back in the crate in her room, along with a small amount of dog food moistened with chicken broth. She closed the door so Bridgit could eat in peace.

The other dogs knew a new dog was in the house. They could smell her. Smell the stink of her, Karen thought. After a potty trip, the dogs assembled, in pack order, their heads and noses pointing to Karen's bedroom door. They knew something was in there. Karen reached for her camera and took a picture.

"She's in isolation right now," she told them. "We don't know what bugs, if any, she's carrying. I don't want you guys to get sick, too."

Ferry, who had recently bullied her way to the head of the pack, and therefore was sitting right next to the door, gave her a quick grin, as if to say, "Don't worry about us, Mom, I have it all under control."

"Ferry," Karen said in all seriousness, "I am the pack leader here. Do not forget it."

Ferry swished her tail and lowered her head apologetically.

"Now, c'mon, dogs! Crates!" She said the word briskly. The dogs picked themselves up off the floor and padded off agreeably down the hall to their room and their individual crates. Karen gave each dog a top-of-the-head kiss and then latched the doors to their crates.

Ferry gave her a classic Innocent-Me look.

Karen considered her for a moment. "I'm not falling for that one," Karen said with a chuckle. She snapped three bungee cords across the door to Ferry's crate. "You shouldn't have pretended to be so innocent," Karen told her. "You were hoist by your own petard."

She closed the door to the dog's room.

Karen went into her bedroom and knelt by Bridgit's crate. "Let's see how you did with your breakfast, Beautiful Bridgit." She kept her voice calm and pleasant. Bridgit hadn't done anything. The food in her bowl had not been touched. "You have to eat, sweetie, to get big and strong again." She led Bridgit into the kitchen to find something the dog would eat. Bridgit decided a spoonful of peanut butter would be okay, but that was certainly not enough. Karen opened the refrigerator to see what might be tempting to a dog in serious need of nourishment. Bridgit finally accepted a couple of bites of leftover stroganoff.

Karen wanted to spend the rest of the day bonding with her newest pack member, this very needy new pack member. "I can't. I have to work for dog food," she told Bridgit as she shut her back in the crate. Bridgit ignored Karen. She carefully lowered herself down, facing the back of the crate. Karen sighed and shut her bedroom door.

"Guard the house," she called to the dogs. "I'll be back at lunchtime."

With a lead heart, Karen drove away from her house, away from her dogs, to beautiful downtown Hartley. Karen's office was in what the city optimistically referred to as the Historical District. The renovated Victorian house sported bright white gingerbread trim that looked great, but was a pain in the neck to keep clean. Now, she noticed the trim would need to be painted soon. She added "trim" to her never-ending mental list of chores.

That morning, doing paperwork at her desk, Karen glanced at her clock, then looked out the window. Yup. Right on time. Steve Songer and his dog jogged down the street.

Theresa appeared and looked over her shoulder. "Yum! Short shorts and a tight T-shirt. And the body to go with 'em. Vicky!" she called over her shoulder in a loud whisper, "You should see this!"

Vicky trotted in to add her oohs and aahs. "Those legs! I love summer! Karen, what kind of dog is that?"

"American Staffordshire."

"Looks like one of those pit bulls."

Karen thought of Bridgit. "They're related."

"I wonder if it's mean."

"Katie knows him. The dog. She thinks he's great."

"Katie knows him?"

"The guy, Steve Songer, he has that gym over on Carmel Street. Katie started going to the gym." She didn't want to explain Katie's interest in boxing. "Exercise class."

"I can see why." Vicky sighed. "That guy has one gorgeous bod."

"Katie's only eighteen," Karen said. Then she thought, *I* was only eighteen. She thought of all those evenings Katie spent at the gym. *Mom, there's someone I want you to meet.* Karen narrowed her eyes as she watched Steve jog down to the corner and turn onto Whyte.

"Maybe I ought to go to that gym, too," Theresa said. "I could use a workout."

"We could go together," Vicky said.

"You two do that. I'll stay here and finish my paperwork." Steve was out of sight so there was no reason to keep looking out the window.

At noon she went home for lunch. She took her dogs out while she ate a quick lunch of leftover stroganoff. Then the others went back in their crates and Karen took Bridgit out for a pee. Maybe when Bridgit was well again, she'd bring her to the office. Teenagers usually responded to dogs.

She took a good look at her newest dog. Still no puffiness around the wounds, that was good. Her color was better, also good. Physically, she was good. Emotionally she was not there. Bridgit's lethargy might be a result of the massive infections, but she might be the kind of dog who shut down when faced with stress. Karen sighed. Whatever the cause of her depression, Bridgit needed some heavy-duty self-confidence boosters. But carried out with great subtlety so as not to stress her more. "I'll be back at dinnertime."

Late that afternoon Katie called her at work. "Hi Mom. I'm at Abernathy's. I'll make us baked taties for supper if you want."

Karen was touched. "That would be lovely. Thank you."

"You want everything on yours?"

"Everything and extra sour cream. But we have cheese at home."

"Okay. By the way, I met our newest inmate. She really stinks. What happened to her?"

"Someone found her on the side of the road and dropped her off at Melissa's."

"Yeah, right," Katie said in a voice that told Karen she didn't believe this fiction. "Whatever you say. Anyway, I took her outside for a few minutes. Without the other dogs, don't worry. She pooped. I called the clinic and Jessie said they hadn't run any tests for parasites yet, so I picked it up in a zippy bag and ran it over. Jess did the microscope thing and she's full of roundworms so I got the medicine and gave her the first dose. I hope you don't mind."

"Mind?" Karen was genuinely touched. "Not every kid is willing to take dog poop to the vet's. Thank you. That was so thoughtful."

"That's me," Katie said cheerfully. "I'm in the dairy aisle now. Gotta go. See you at supper."

Karen stared at the phone in her hand. I love you, Katie, she said to herself. Katie was one great kid. Katie was the very best. What would she do when Katie went away to college? Except it was getting late in the year to expect to get in. *There's someone I want you to meet,* Katie's note said. Karen's stomach clenched.

As promised, Katie had supper under control when Karen arrived home. Her dogs, sans Bridgit, swarmed around her with tails and tongues swishing. They followed her to the kitchen. When Karen sat down Ferry shoved in front of Brian. Karen gushed over the younger dog then sent all the dogs outside to run off some energy. All but Brian. "C'mere, old guy." She held her arms out for her oldest dog. He tottered over to her. She put her arms around him and leaned into him. She was home. She was with her dogs. She closed her eyes and sat, content to simply *be* with her oldest dog. Most of his days he spent asleep now, and he sometimes wandered down the hallway and got lost. He didn't hear well anymore and she wasn't sure how much he could see. He had given her his complete devotion for ten years, almost eleven—a long time for a Newfoundland. She knew her days with him were coming to an end. It made each moment all the more precious.

The screen door banged. "I set up supper on the picnic table," Katie said. "It's too good a day to miss a second of it."

With her arms still around Brian, Karen said, "Thank you. I mean it."

"Taties'll be out of the oven in a couple of minutes, and we have salad with goodies from Grandma's garden and some new dressing she made. I went over this afternoon," Katie said. "And Abernathy's had great-looking corn. It's all shucked and ready to go into the pot." Katie was rubbing the charm on her necklace.

"One of these days you're going to worry that charm right down into nothing," Karen told her.

Katie dropped her hand. "It's silver. It should last a while."

Karen couldn't put her finger on it, but something was not right. It might have been the way Katie's gaze didn't stay on one thing for more than a second, or the hint of a nervous giggle in her voice. It put Karen on guard. Something was up.

One of the kitchen chairs, loaded up with heavy books, pressed against the front of the refrigerator.

"What happened?" Karen pointed.

"Ferry figured out how to open the refrigerator," Katie said. "She discovered the refrigerator contains lots of good things to eat. In fact, a veritable smorgasbord for an inventive Newf."

"It won't take her long to learn how to move the chair aside."

Katie nodded. "I had to get the cheese out. That dog sat right here and watched very carefully to see how I did it. I swear if she had opposable thumbs she'd be dangerous. Oh— I took Bridgit out a little bit ago. By herself. She did her thing, I told her she was the most brilliant dog in the world, but I don't think she believed me. I brought her back inside. She's in her crate asleep now."

She reached into the pot with the tongs and pulled out an ear of corn. She carefully drew a long black dog hair off it and wiped her hand on her jeans. "Hot," she said with a grin. She slid the corn onto a plate. "Supper's ready," she announced with a grin. "Go wash your hands."

After supper, Katie did dishes. Katie hated doing dishes. Karen listened to Katie's chatter as she scraped plates and stuck them in the dishwasher. It was nervous chatter. Karen watched her with narrowed eyes.

The doorbell rang.

The younger three Newfs thundered toward the door in a barking black flood. Brian slept at her feet. Katie looked suddenly stricken.

"Expecting someone?" Karen asked.

Katie wiped her hands on the towel. She bit her lower lip. "Um. Yeah. Mom, please go into the living room." She called to the dogs to hush as she hurried down the hall to the door.

Karen felt a sudden chill. The other shoe, she thought, was about to drop. She made herself take a deep breath to compose herself.

"Mom," Katie was in the doorway with a young man in an immaculate uniform. "This is Sergeant Newland. My Marine recruiter."

The young man stuck out his hand. "Hello, Mrs. Matheson."

It wasn't a shoe that dropped. It was a damn ugly boot.

Chapter 4

"Come in." Steve held the door for Jim Tate and his girl-friend du jour. This one, like the others, was softly rounded with curly brown hair and a nice smile. "Fights are almost ready to start."

"I can't believe I'm actually going to watch boxing," she said with a slight giggle. This one giggled, too.

"Bojado's fighting tonight. He's great." Jim told her. "You'll like it. This is Lennox. Named after Lennox Lewis who is the undisputed heavyweight champion of the world."

"I agree with you," Steve said, "but it *was* disputed."

Lennox did the gentlemanly host thing. The girlfriend pet-ted him. He wagged his tail.

Steve led them into his living room.

The doorbell rang and Steve headed back to the door. "Jim, you know where the sodas are in the refrigerator."

Soon Steve's living room was crowded with his students, some accompanied by girlfriends or younger brothers, or buddies. All were ready to worship at the Church of "Friday Night Fights" with Max Kellerman and Brian Kenny in the studio, and Teddy Atlas with Bob Papa ringside. Tonight's fights, Max announced, came from the Mohegan Sun in Un-casville, Connecticut. The main event was a fight between Emanuel Evans and Luis del Rio. But first, a rematch be-tween junior welterweights Francisco Panchito Bojado and Frankie Santos.

"Hey, where's Katie?" one of his students asked.

Jim shrugged. "I saw her earlier today. She said she had something important to do tonight."

"More important than boxing?"

"Guess so."

"She'll be here tomorrow night," Jim said. "The McCullough Barrera fight. She won't miss that. She's been talking about it for weeks."

"Shhh! The ringwalk is starting."

In Uncasville, Mexican music erupted out of the sound system. Bojado, his face shadowed by the hood of his robe, and his corner men made their way down the aisle through the cheering crowd and into the ring. Jim nudged his girlfriend. "Bojado had his first professional fight when he was still in high school. Imagine being a professional boxer at our age."

The girl looked suitably impressed. "He's cute!" she said when Bojado's hood was thrown back.

"That's why they call him the Baby-Faced Assassin," Jim said. "He almost always wins by knockout."

Karen felt as if the wind had been knocked out of her. After Katie dropped her bomb, the professionally pleasant recruiter did his utmost to impress upon her what a wonderful life Katie would have in the Marine Corps. The Corps was highly committed to taking care of its own. Katie would be encouraged, even expected, to excel. He showed her some *National Geographic*-quality photographs of squeaky clean young women and men wearing immaculate uniforms. Karen flashed on images from the war against Saddam Hussein. There had been nothing squeaky clean about those pictures. They were shown on television, unedited, with all the sweat and grime intact. War was the newest reality television.

Sergeant Newland gave her an information package, including a video and a booklet describing a training program that would, he promised, help Katie with her IST, the Initial Strength Test all recruits were required to pass. Of course, Katie was in such great shape already, Sergeant Newland enthused, she wouldn't have any trouble.

Karen thought of all the hours Katie had spent swimming and jogging, using the chin-up bar in her bedroom doorway, at Steve Songer's gym. Her daughter, she realized, had been working toward this for a long time. Karen made the sort of polite noises one made when one was paying attention. She took the information packet and pretended to look at it, pretended she found it interesting. She glanced up at Katie. Katie stared back at her.

After a while, Katie and the immaculate uniform left. Karen was alone.

She opened her mouth to say something—she had no idea what—to Katie, but Katie wasn't there.

Brian shoved his head against her knee. She automatically petted him. Then she dumbly noticed Brian had hauled himself up on the couch next to her. From far off she heard the kitchen door slam. She got up to check and found Ferry had let herself outside. Dinnie and Heck stood looking forlornly through the screen. Karen opened the door and followed them outside. She sank down on the porch step.

How had this happened? Why hadn't Katie talked to her about this? She always thought she and Katie could talk about anything.

After a while, she brought the dogs back inside, put them in their crates and shut the door to the dog room so she could take Bridgit out. Bridgit shuffled down the hallway after her, lethargic, showing no enthusiasm. She followed Karen outside, sniffed around without much interest, squatted on a likely spot. "Good girl, Bridgit!" Karen remembered to keep her voice deliberately calm. The dog stood up, her head hanging. She was the picture of defeat, of hopelessness, of emotionally going to a place beyond the possibility of caring what happened to her.

Stress, Karen thought. The first night of dog classes she always talked to the class about the different ways dogs coped with stress. Some dogs became hyperactive and bounced around, other dogs became sluggish and tired. When faced with a sluggish dog, Karen told the owner to take the dog for a short walk, get the blood flowing, balance the brain chemicals so the dog could learn more easily. Right now, Karen understood exactly how those dogs felt. She and Bridgit could both benefit from a short walk, get their blood moving, balance their brain chemicals.

She pulled a leash from the hook inside the door and stuck a couple of zippy bags in her pocket.

"Hey, Beautiful Bridgit, we're going to walk." It would be a very short walk because Bridgit wasn't up to more than a block or so. "It'll be good for us both," she promised the dog.

With neither enthusiasm nor protest, Bridgit allowed herself to be led out the gate.

Why the Marines? Of all things, why them? She and Bridgit walked to the end of the block, turned around and walked back again. Once they were back inside, Karen pulled her thoughts up short. That was enough useless pondering right now. Right now, Bridgit needed a bath. This would probably be her first bath ever. "Don't worry," Karen told her. "We're old pros at first-time bathers."

Bridgit didn't protest the water, or the shampoo. Or the gentle toweling. Bridgit allowed life to be done to her, without life touching her at all. Karen put Bridgit in her crate and went out to put her arms around her Tree, press her forehead against the rough bark and gather strength from the Tree, as she had innumerable times in the past, as she would innumerable times in the years to come.

* * *

She drove to what used to be the edge of town. Now it was in what Roger called the mere outer rings of the Hartley galaxy. She drove up her parents' street. When she was in high school, cows grazed and gazed over the fence at her house. Now the old cow field was a new subdivision.

She parked her van in her parents' driveway. She gathered Bridgit's leash and patted her leg to encourage the dog to climb down out of the van. "Here we are. You can do it. That's right. Good girl." She stooped down and gave her dog a brief hug. Her dog was, as usual, unresponsive. "Someday you'll feel safe enough, Bridgit." Bridgit didn't care.

Karen led the dog up the wide steps to the wider porch, past the jungle of potted plants and the porch swing, up to the oversized welcome mat. The painted flowers dancing around the doorway, once so bright and cheerful were faded now, the colors softer, muted by time. Karen immediately felt better, just being here.

"Mom!" She stuck her head in the door. "Where are you?"

"Come in, dear! I'm in the kitchen!"

Of course. Where else would her mother be? Unless it was in her garden, or in her sewing room. Karen led Bridgit through to the back of her mother's house.

Her mother had her hands deep in a sink of suds. Her mother thought dishwashers were a waste of electricity. Yes, her mother was the same hippie she'd been in high school.

In one flowing motion, her mother rinsed a bowl, set it in the dish drainer, wiped her hands and stooped down to hold out her arms to Bridgit. "Who is this?"

"This is Bridgit."

"Hello, Bridgit. I'm your Grandma Susannah." She sank down cross-legged onto the floor and crooned to the dog softly, stroking the shaggy head. "What happened to her?" her mother asked, in the same tone of voice so Bridgit wouldn't be disturbed by a change of tone. Karen's mother loved dogs, too.

"I didn't ask."

"Where did you get her?"

"Jessie called me the other day. Bridgit had been dropped off." She felt guilty not telling her mother the truth.

Her mother ran soft fingers along one of the scars on Bridgit's side. "They don't know where she came from?"

Karen shrugged. "They prob'ly do. I told them I didn't want to know."

Her mother finally looked up from the dog. She smiled at Karen. "Well, then, we'll consider her a gift from Saint Rochus, patron saint of dogs and those who love them." She turned her attention back to Bridgit. "And a wonderful gift you are, too."

Bridgit showed little interest.

"She's been hurt bad, this one, hasn't she?" Her mom put her cheek down on top of Bridgit's head, closed her eyes and rocked slightly back and forth, whispering to Bridgit all the while. Karen knew, without hearing the words, her mother was reciting the prayer for animals. She whispered along,

> *Hear our humble prayer O God, for our friends the animals, especially for animals who are suffering, for animals who are overworked, underfed, and cruelly treated; for all wistful creatures in captivity who beat their wings against bars; for any who are hunted or lost or deserted or frightened or hungry; for all who must be put to death. We entreat for them all Thy mercy and pity, and for those who deal with them we ask a heart of compassion and gentle hands and kindly words. Make us, ourselves, to be true friends to animals, and so to share the blessings of the merciful.*

Leaving her mom to Bridgit, Karen finished the few dishes. She filled the kettle with water and set it on the stove. She pulled a tea ball from the drawer and a box of tea leaves from the cupboard—her mother didn't believe in tea bags, either. She steeped the tea in a fine china teapot, an odd juxtaposition to the heavy earthenware mugs, but that was her mother. Karen bent down to smell the late-blooming rose stuck in an old green pickle jar on the table.

"You're still an old hippie, Mom."

Her mother smiled beatifically. "The world could use a few hippies again."

"Why?" Karen poured tea for her mother.

Susannah left Bridgit to sit in her rocking chair with her constant knitting in her lap and take the proffered mug. She leaned back in her rocking chair and sniffed the tea aroma. "Our time, the hippie era was a time of idealism, of hope. We truly believed we could change the world by living lives of peace and love and cooperation. Living with Mother Nature instead of against her. Making love, not war. As the poster said, war was not healthy for children or other living things. It's still true today."

"You were naive." Karen was surprised at the accusation in her own voice.

Her mother gazed at her with that inscrutable look of hers. "Maybe so. But being naive is more optimistic than being jaded. The world needs optimism more than cynicism, don't you think? If you didn't believe in hope, if you didn't believe there was something better, you wouldn't work with teenagers, and you certainly wouldn't rescue dogs."

Quickly, before she lost the words, before she chickened out, Karen said, "Katie joined the Marines."

There. It was out. She'd said the words. Now they were real. She couldn't pretend that since they'd never been said it couldn't be so. "She's leaving for boot camp next week."

Her mother was silent. Her mother looked at her for a while. "When our children grow up, they often do things that surprise us. Sometimes we get mad at the things they do. But they have to make their own choices."

"What about the times their choices are just plain wrong?"

"Wrong for whom?"

"Quit being the Queen of Serene! I'm upset. Be upset along with me!"

Her mother chuckled. "You can't raise children to be eagles and then get angry when they don't turn out to be sparrows."

"Quit quoting Eleanor Roosevelt. It doesn't help."

"I thought it was appropriate." Her mother sounded amused, in her patient-mother sort of way. "And it wasn't Eleanor. It was one of the other Mrs. Roosevelts, one married to the other Mr. Roosevelt. Edith."

"Well, it still doesn't help. Sounds like you're telling me it's my fault."

"You raised Katie to make her own choices. She's made a choice. You don't have to like it. But you absolutely have to support her in it."

Chapter 5

Once more his living room was full of his students and their friends. Katie, to his surprise, brought Jessie, who hunkered down and pulled Lennox onto her lap. She looked right at home in the middle of a bunch of kids waiting for boxing.

"When I was a kid I watched "Friday Night Fights" with my dad," she explained. "Besides, I was the one who introduced Katie to *Rocky*. Only the original one. After that they went downhill."

"Yeah," Katie said, "and you started—"

"—I started you off watching boxing movies," Jessie cut Katie off with a glare. Katie grinned back with unrepentant impudence.

Steve wondered how things had gone with her mother.

Katie shushed everyone when Jim Lampley welcomed everyone to HBO's "Championship Boxing." Tonight, from Las Vegas, a long-awaited, much-anticipated bout between Marco Antonio Barrera and Wayne McCullough. Next to Jim stood Larry Merchant and a grinning George Foreman.

Katie cheered for George. "I love listening to George talk about boxing."

The undercard fights were decent, and one was even pretty good. When Jim Lampley told the television audience that the cut over the fighter's eye was caused by an accidental head butt, one of the young men in Steve's living room muttered that it was caused by an accidental butthead and the girls giggled.

Steve kept an eye on Jim Tate. How did he watch a fight? Fighters, or ex-fighters, tended to be like passengers in a car; they slammed on the brakes, too. When Steve watched boxing, part of his mind analyzed the fight. He found himself mentally moving with the men in the ring, dodging, weaving, his muscles tightening to throw a punch. He became part of a great fight. Jim, who someday might be a great fighter, shifted slightly in his seat, his attention focused on the television, all but ignoring the girl beside him. Steve nodded to himself. Jim Tate was part of this fight, too.

After the last undercard, while Steve was in his kitchen to pull out the last round of drinks, Katie came in and leaned against his counter. "I told her."

"Was it as bad as you thought it would be?"

Katie nodded.

"What was?" Jessie stuck her head in the door.

"Last night I told my mom I had signed up to become a Marine."

"Cool!"

Katie looked surprised. "You mean it?" she asked.

"Of course. Marines are important. They've done great things."

"Good," Katie said. "You can work on my mom. She is somewhat less than impressed."

"I bet that's an understatement," Jessie said.

Finally, from one of the big casinos in Las Vegas, the fighters started their ringwalks with all the pomp and ceremony of a big show. In Hartley, someone made a last call for soda refills before the fight started. From the middle of the ring, Michael Buffer—"With that velvet voice!" Jessie exclaimed—announced it was time to rumble!

"Tonight, fighting out of the red corner," Michael introduced Marco Antonio Barrera. And out of the blue corner, from Belfast by way of Las Vegas, Nevada, Wayne "The Pocket Rocket" McCullough. Katie led the loud cheers. "Tonight's fight will be refereed by Joe Cortez."

The fight fans in Las Vegas roared their approval, and Steve's living room crowd erupted in cheers—Joe was a favorite ref. Michael Buffer held the mike while Joe Cortez spoke his final words to the fighters. He wanted a clean fight. "Obey my commands. Protect yourselves at all times. And remember, I'm—"

"Fair but I'm firm!" the crowd of young people chorused along with him.

"Show some respect, you guys," Katie said in an older-sister tone of voice. "Remember what George Foreman said. The referee is the most important man in the ring, other than the fighters."

"Well, duh," someone said.

The bell rang. The fight was on.

Sunday afternoon the telephone rang. It was Colleen Martini looking for Katie. Katie wasn't home; Karen told Colleen she'd leave a note for Katie to call. What she wanted to do was to scream to Colleen, "Did you know about this? Did she talk to you about this?" But she didn't. She liked Colleen. Colleen was going to go to Ohio University in the fall. She scribbled Colleen's name on a piece of paper and impaled it on the bulletin board next to the phone. The telephone rang again. This time it was Sylvie. "Jean-Luc wants you to bring the dogs over for a visit."

Karen took Ferry and Dinnie next door to visit with Jean-Luc. It was more than a visit, it was a gathering. Melissa and her dog, Hugo, Sally and her dog, Maxie. And Jessie with puppy Sagan.

Except for Jessie, her friends all offered suitable words of support and understanding. They patted her shoulder, told her everything was going to be fine. Sylvie said Katie had told her the same thing that morning. "I'm going to have to learn to clean my own house!" she wailed.

"Well," Jessie stood in the middle of Sylvie's living room with her hands on her hips. "I think Katie being a Marine is great." That got their attention. "Marines were with Charles Wilkes when he first mapped The Ice, you know, Antarctica, back in the 1840s. And it was a Marine pilot who first flew across The Ice. Marines get to do cool things—no pun intended."

They all stared at Jessie.

"Oh," she said, "and Drew Carey was a Marine. And John Glenn, and Leon Uris, and Montel, and Burt Reynolds. And," she added as they continued to stare at her, "Bea Arthur."

"Bea Arthur?" Sally said. "The 'Golden Girls' Bea Arthur?"

"Yes." Jessie was firm. "She was a Marine."

Karen glared at her. "That's such a real consolation, Jessie."

"Good." Jessie glared back at her. "I'm glad to be able to help."

"Knock off the terrier act," Melissa told them. "We all know you're both strong women. Besides, you're confusing Sagan. She thinks you might really be mad at each other."

Jessie dropped her glare. "Oh, Sagan, baby," she immediately threw her arms around her puppy. "Karen and I aren't mad. We're best friends. And best friends can say things to each other that ordinary friends and acquaintances can't."

"That's the truth," Sally said.

From the back of the house, The Baby Boogaloo let out a howl. "He's awake!" Sylvie said. She trotted off to fetch her child.

"I need a baby fix, right now," Karen said. She followed Sylvie down the hall. "Let me do it."

Sylvie stood in the doorway as Karen picked the baby out

of his crib and changed his wet diaper. She held him close and started the automatic Mommy Rock, shifting her weight from one foot to the other, making soothing noises. Holding the baby felt so good. Letting your children go didn't feel good.

"I hear you have a new dog," Sylvie said.

Karen gave her the Bridgit basics.

"Sounds like she'll need a lot of care and emotional support. It'll be good for you, what with Katie going off. You have a high-needs dog to take up your time and energy."

"Jessie said the same thing. You all been talking behind my back?"

"Great minds think alike."

Karen dropped a kiss on the baby's head and breathed in his clean baby smell. She wished Katie were this small again so she could keep her safe. Karen carried the baby down the hall. Sally held out her arms. Karen let him go.

"What's new in the life of the Boogaloo?" Sally asked.

"We're taking him to New Jersey this fall," Sylvie said. "To visit Ray's foster family."

"Do you want me to take care of Jean-Luc for you?" Melissa asked.

"No thanks. They invited Jean-Luc, too. Can you imagine that?"

"Sure. They obviously have lots of sense."

Chapter 6

Katie made herself scarce for the next two days, leaving before Karen was up and coming home to change clothes and run off again. Katie was avoiding her.

Monday morning, from the front porch, Colleen Martini called, "Good morning!"

"Come in, Colleen," Karen hollered back. "Katie's upstairs. Say, where are you two going this bright and early?"

"Cedar Point. For the last time as carefree high school students. We're going to ride the rides till we get sick."

"Really? What a lovely way to spend the day."

"Except Katie. She won't do the roller coasters or the Ferris wheel. You know, her acrophobia. So the rest of us will do those. Katie gets to wait for us and hold our purses."

"Designated purse holder, eh?"

Katie clattered down the stairs. "Bye Mom," she gave Karen a quick cheek smooch. "Back late."

And she was gone. Just like that. Abruptly, finally, gone.

In the morning, Karen woke up feeling tense. As she got ready for work, she felt on edge, as if she waited for a storm. She made herself a cup of herbal tea. Her mother swore by it, but this morning, it didn't help.

When she arrived at work, Vicky handed her a pink message slip. "The doc from Planned Parenthood called. She asked you to please return her call."

"Thanks. Did she sound like it was a rush or a rush-rush?"

"Ordinary rush."

The door jangled open and Theresa rushed in. "Good morning everyone!" Theresa had that trying-too-hard, brittle, bright bravado in her voice that meant she hadn't had much sleep.

"Worrying again?" Karen asked her.

"Yes. And I know he's fine. I know worrying is normal, I know it's a normal reaction to an un-normal situation. I know all the psychobabble, but I still worry. I guess it's part of being a mother."

Theresa had been a wreck when her son's army unit was first sent to Iraq. She'd stayed glued to CNN. *I'm his mother, she'd said. We wipe their eyes and kiss their boo-boos when they're little; we make sure they wear bike helmets and eat their green beans. Our lives are devoted to taking care of them, keeping them from hurt. Now they're in the middle of fighting a war—the most dangerous thing—and we're not there to take care of them! Don't worry, she'd added, I know this is an emotional reaction, not a logical one.* Karen had handed her the box of tissues and was glad she'd had a girl, glad she'd never know what it felt like to send a child off to war.

Boy, she told herself now, life sure fooled you. At least Katie wouldn't be sent into battle. Even the Marine Corps didn't send women into battle. Did they?

"Katie signed up with the Marines."

Theresa and Vicky dropped their mouths in stereo. "She did what?"

"She wants to be a Marine. She told me Friday night. She leaves for boot camp on Sunday."

"How are you feeling about it?" Vicky's eyes were full of compassion.

"I am so angry at her I could spit."

Theresa gave her a brief hug. "I know exactly how you feel. But it'll get better, you'll see."

After work she walked Brian down the driveway to the mailbox, which was about as far as he could go these days. She pulled out a clump of mail and told Brian what a smart Newfoundland he was to get the mail. He wagged his tail and together they ambled back to the house. Karen ruffled through the mail and pulled out a letter bearing an ominous-looking return address. It was from the Marine Corps commander. It was a general letter to parents, thanking them for raising children to join the Corps. For raising children to become cannon fodder, Karen thought sourly. She tossed the letter aside.

The Planned Parenthood doctor and Karen played phone tag until the next afternoon. Karen was it. "She's seventeen," the doctor said. "She's a sweet kid, but her parents are a trip."

"Not supportive?"

"Not at the moment. Sometimes parents come around at the last minute and surprise me. So far, these parents have not surprised me."

"Sure," Karen said. "I'll see her. Let's keep the usual arrangement; let them think I'm a contractor and I'm part of your service fee."

"You certainly won't get rich if you keep seeing these girls gratis!" the doctor said. It was an old discussion between them.

"I don't do this to get rich."

"I know. You do this for the girls. And Karen, you have my deepest respect."

The long day was finally over and Karen could go home to her dogs. Her dogs kept her sane. Her dogs kept her going when she wanted to crawl in a hole. Her dogs made her take the time to stop and see the world. She took out the dogs and watched the world with them for a while. Until she felt better.

In her kitchen she stared at the glass on the counter. Katie had left her glass on the counter with half an inch of milk in it to curdle and stink. She knows better than that, Karen thought. She knows I hate it when she does that. Katie seemed to be getting on her nerves a lot lately. Karen almost looked forward to Katie leaving. Then she felt immediate guilt. I didn't mean it, she silently cried.

The *Hartley Herald*'s front page was given over to dog fighting and Hartley's proposed breed-specific legislation. Karen read the article. She dropped the paper on the kitchen table and stared out the window at Bridgit in the backyard. Intellectually, she knew breed-specific legislation was wrong. But looking at Bridgit—emotionally, she wasn't sure. She had been wrong about a lot of things recently. She'd been wrong a long time ago, too. The phone rang.

It was Jessie. "Seems like the Hartley village idiots are sending letters to people who own pit-type dogs. That was sure fast. I think they've had these letters ready to go for months. This dog-fighting thing gave them the excuse. As if those dummies in the city building would know a pit-type dog if they met it on the street. Friend of mine, down in Columbus, got a black-and-white Cardigan puppy, took her for a walk and some idiot stopped her to ask if the puppy was a pit bull. Stupid jerks. Making laws about dogs when they don't know squat about them. Idiots."

"Well, we elected them."

"Don't blame me. I didn't vote for any of them."

"Next election you can do your best to vote them out."

"That's not going to help the dogs now. But. You, as someone well-versed in dogs, as a strong member of the dog community, you can do something about it."

"What?"

"You can go down to the city and offer your services as an evaluator."

"As a what?"

"You can evaluate any dog they think is a pit-type dog. You can be the single voice of sanity at the city hall."

"I don't think so. I'm teaching the CGC class, that's about all I can do right now while Bridgit needs so much."

"C'mon, Karen. You owe it to the brotherhood of dogs. You are in a unique position right now to really do some good. You have to do it."

"Not a good time for me."

"Important events rarely come at a convenient time for us."

"It's not a matter of convenience."

"What's it a matter of then?"

"It's just not a good time. Besides, how many pit-type dogs could there possibly be here in Hartley?"

"Probably not a lot. But those people are so stupid, any dog, not even necessarily mixed breeds, could come under suspicion of being pit-types. I mean, that idiot in Columbus thought that Cardi puppy was a pit, and Hartley has as many idiots as Columbus. No dog will be safe."

"Why don't you volunteer? You're an animal professional."

"Nope. I work for a vet. They might see it as a conflict of interest."

"Why don't you call Tanner? He has better credentials than I do. He's a professional. For me it's a hobby."

"I did. He said he'd think it over. He told me to call you. He said you owed him a big one and besides you had the paper training."

Karen squirmed. "That's low."

"Yup. Here's one even lower. What would Katie say if she knew you had a chance to help Lennox and you refused?"

"Lennox?"

"You know Katie adores that dog."

"Yeah, I know."

"Well, pay attention. Katie also adores Steve."

Karen sputtered. "He's old enough to . . ."

"Calm down. Don't be ridiculous. She doesn't adore him that way. She thinks he's her big brother, or her uncle or something. Katie has more sense than to fall in love with a man old enough to be her father. And Steve has too much honor."

"A boxer? Honor?"

"Yes. Honor."

"How do you know what kind of friends they are?"

"Because I know both of them, that's why."

"How do you know Steve Songer?"

"Because he brings Lennox to our clinic. And because Katie's invited me to go over to his house to watch boxing along with a bunch of his other students. He also retired from the Marines a couple of years ago."

Karen was speechless. Her mouth dropped open but no words came out.

"She said that when she told you she wanted to be a Marine," Jessie continued, "you weren't overly thrilled. Steve's spent a lot of time over the past several months helping your daughter get into shape for boot camp."

"Boy," Karen said sarcastically. "That sure makes me want to help him even more."

"If you knew him you really would want to help him. I think you'd like him, if you gave him half a chance. And I think you'd love Lennox too."

Karen looked down at the dog at her feet. Bridgit's cuts were healing, and soon the stitches'd be falling out. She was gaining weight. Her coat was beginning to grow back into soft bristles. "I don't think I could. You know what happened to Bridgit."

"Let me remind you, *you* don't know what happened to Bridgit. You told us you didn't want to know, so we didn't do anything to try to find out. So don't go telling me you know what happened to her, because you don't, and I know it."

"I have a pretty good idea."

"That's not good enough. Karen Matheson, we've been really good friends for a really long time, but I never knew until now that you're a racist."

"The word racist doesn't apply to dogs."

"Why the hell not? It's the same thing. You need to get in touch with your inner warmonger. You might learn a thing or two."

Chapter 7

In the mail, along with junk, which was tossed, and a couple of bills, which were filed, Steve received a letter bearing the official Hartley Village letterhead. The city government was informing him of their new breed-specific legislation. From now on, all pit-type dogs would be banned from the city. They were sending a copy of this letter to all Hartlians who currently owned pit-type dogs. According to county dog-license records, Steve owned an American Staffordshire dog. This fit Hartley's criteria as a pit-type dog. If he wanted to keep his dog, Steve had the right to have his dog evaluated and the city would review his case. If he wanted a list of individuals the city felt were qualified to evaluate his dog, he was to call the city offices during regular office hours.

Steve threw the letter down in disgust.

His phone rang. It was Jessie. "Just wanted to warn you, Hartley's village idiots are sending out letters to all owners of anything even remotely resembling pit-type dogs."

"Thanks for the warning. I got mine today."

"They called us to ask questions about certain client dogs. As if we'd help them with their canine nazi tactics. Get this: They go through dog-license applications—you know those forms you fill out every year. They pull out all the Bostons, bulldogs—even Hugo, what idiots!—boxers, Rottweilers, which are not pit-type at all, by the way, Am Staffs, and bull-terriers. Staffordshire bullterriers were on their list but I don't think there are any in Hartley, and then, get this, *then* they pull out anything that is listed as a terrier mix. I suppose being half cairn is enough to convict you in this town. Toto, too! Miss Gulch is alive and well and living in Hartley."

"Your sources are unimpeachable, I assume."

"I cannot reveal them, but, yes. He is unimpeachable. Oh. The reason I called you, other than to warn you, is to tell you Karen Matheson will evaluate Lennox if you want. She's on the city's approved list."

"Karen Matheson? She hates my guts."

"She'll get over it. Let me explain. A couple of days ago she got a rescue dog who—no. On second thought, I can't break my vow of silence. But I *can* tell you this dog was in seriously bad shape. She had a lot of bites on her face and other parts. You're bright, you can figure out for yourself what this means. Anyway, when she was brought in—excuse me— dumped off, we didn't know if she'd make it. Karen feels very protective toward this dog."

What Jessie didn't say told him as much as what she did say. "Sounds like when it comes to Lennox, she might not have an unbiased opinion."

"Yeah, but I've known her for a long time. She believes in fairness more than almost anyone I know. Almost as much as she believes in dogs. She'll be fair if it kills her. Besides, she knows Katie adores Lennox, and Katie has grown up surrounded by dogs, so her opinion means something. Anyway, when Karen is being a heavy-duty rabid peace-monger, I remind myself she's the daughter of the original Earth Mother hippie and so it isn't her fault."

"In other words, what, you threatened her?"

"Yeah." Jessie sounded quite cheerful. "I did."

That night, someone threw a paper-wrapped rock into Steve's window. Steve smoothed out the paper, a copy of a grainy newspaper photograph of the results of a dogfight. Scrawled across the picture, in heavy red letters, was a clear message —*We don't want your pit bull in our town.*

"I feel all mixed-up inside," Katie told him as they jogged along the park path. It was early morning and the humidity hadn't hit yet. "Excited. I'm really excited, but I'm also nervous."

Lennox trotted along between them, the tags on his collar jingling in perfect rhythm. Steve's dog, like Katie Matheson, could keep going forever. He, however, was getting old. He didn't like it.

"Scared," she said. "I'm scared."

"What are you scared of?"

"Failure."

"You won't fail."

"Why not?"

"For one thing, your drill instructors won't let you fail."

"Because God has a hard-on for Marines?"

He chuckled. "You've been watching *Full Metal Jacket* again. I told you, that movie is not an accurate picture of boot camp. Some things have changed."

"They haven't tried to turn it into a kinder, gentler boot camp? It's still tough?"

He chuckled. "So I hear."

"Good." Then she asked, "What if I fail?"

"You won't. The only way you can fail is if you give up. You're strong. You have heart. You won't give up."

"What if I do?"

"You won't. But if you get to the point where you feel like giving up, think of the first Micky Ward and Arturo Gatti fight." He thought of it himself. He kept jogging.

She nodded. "Yeah. I see what you mean. Ward Gatti One. Okay."

"You've been doing your workout, right?"

"Yeah. Haven't missed a single day."

She was sure one determined kid. She had heart. What she didn't seem to have was a typical teenage life. "That's what you've been doing all summer? Working out? No end-of-summer parties? End of high school ritual stuff?" But she wasn't a typical teenager.

"Not really. A group of us went to Cedar Point. And I've been cleaning house for Sylvie Novino, but that's not really work. This past week my goal has been to stay away from my mom."

"She's still that mad?"

Katie nodded. "Yes, she most certainly is."

"You talked to her about it?"

"Nope."

"Then how do you know she's still mad?"

"I know my mom."

At noon, after he'd spent the morning working out with some of his boxers, Steve showered and changed. He told Mary Lou he was going out for a while and asked her to keep an eye on Lennox. He walked over to the city building, and followed the receptionist's directions through the winding hallways until he came to the administrative offices. He pushed open the frosted-glass door and found himself facing an ancient woman who, evidently, was the junior lackey. She stared down at him over the rhinestone-encrusted half-glasses perched on the end of her overly long nose. She asked his business. He thought she looked more like a caricature than a real person. He explained he'd received a letter from the city, but Lennox was a registered American Staffordshire, not a pit bull. He was proud of his calm demeanor in the face of her obvious distaste.

She whipped a sheet of paper out of the ready file folder in front of her and thrust it at him. "This is the list of approved people who will assess your dog. Any fees incurred will be paid by you, not the city."

"My dog is not a pit bull," Steve repeated. "My dog is an AKC-registered American Staffordshire. He comes from a line of top show dogs. Here are his papers." Steve held out the official AKC document. He waited for her to take it. She didn't stoop so low.

"I have no knowledge of such things. I can only tell you, that this is the list of city-approved evaluators. One of them can give you an official evaluation. You must bring that evaluation to the city."

There were terrific things about living in a small town, Steve told himself. Micro-minded city lackeys were not on that list. No, they were on a very different list. "This letter says pit-type dogs. American Staffordshires are not pit dogs. Have not been for years. The AKC has never registered pit dogs."

The lackey sniffed. "You must have your dog evaluated. Then the city will consider your request. If you choose not to take this route, you are, of course, free to move elsewhere."

When he arrived back at the gym, Mary Lou was working with one of the few female boxing students. "How'd it go?" she called.

"We have a lady present. I cannot give you an accurate answer." He pulled on his favorite pair of practice gloves and let the heavy bags have it.

The answering machine blinked merrily. Karen pressed the button. The first message was for Katie from the impeccable Sergeant Newland. He asked her to call him about arrangements for Sunday. The machine beeped. Next was a message for her, from Katie who said she was eating out with Colleen, then they were going to watch a video. She'd be home late, don't wait up. *Beep!* The woman from Buffalo said she'd e-mailed her application to the national rescue coordinator. *Beep!* The national rescue coordinator said she'd received an application and was checking it all out and how was Dinnie doing?

Karen made a mental note to call the coordinator back. She quickly saw to Bridgit, had a quick supper, took the other dogs for a quick potty, and it was time for Karen to leave for dog school. She looked at the dogs. They looked back at her. They knew she was getting ready to leave. They wagged their tails. She still looked at them. They wagged their tails harder. She brought Ferry with her. Ferry was an excellent traveler, and an excellent example for the puppies to try to emulate.

This was the last puppy kindergarten class for the summer session. At the end of the hour, she gave each puppy owner a ribbon and a certificate and encouraged them to register for the next series of classes. She told them she would miss them. It was the truth. Karen hadn't had a puppy in her house for a long time. She watched them leave, feeling a little wistful. Puppies were like babies, brand new and precious; every new lesson learned was a cause for celebration. It had been a long time since Karen had had a new baby in her house, too. She looked down at Ferry. "But I have you, and you're pretty great, too." Ferry knew she was great.

Karen took Ferry through some basic heeling exercises. Ferry smirked at her as if to say, this is child's play, give me a few locks to pick and I'll show you what I can do.

"Ferry, heel."

When she got home, Katie's car was in the driveway and her bedroom lights were off.

Friday night, Karen ate her supper solo. Again. Katie was out. Again. Karen dripped in the humidity of an Ohio

summer. She ate outside, balancing a plate on her knees
while three dogs sat in front of her watching her every move.
Brian slept in the shade; Bridgit stood next to the fence,
staring out. What did Bridgit see? What did she look for?
When would Bridgit look inside the yard, when would
Bridgit look at her? Karen thought. "Like you three guys,"
she said. "Watching me and drooling. Give it up. You had
your supper."

But she relented. It was too hot to eat. She broke her leftover pizza into dog-bite sized pieces. She tossed bites to the
three at her feet, then woke Brian enough for him to have his.
Then she went to Bridgit. "You want some pizza?" She held
out the bite of pizza. "It's for you. Go on. You can have it. You
sure? Okay. Well, then, maybe next time." This dog was certainly not motivated by food. "What can I use to motivate
you?" Karen asked her. Bridgit did not answer.

She took her plate into the oven-hot house. No. Ovens were
dry heat. Ohio in the summer was a perfect imitation of a
sauna. Imagine, she told herself, people all over the world pay
money to sit in a sauna and sweat, and you are lucky enough
to sweat in your very own sauna for free, right here in the dis-
comfort of your very own home. It did not make her feel
better.

Karen called Sylvie. "Beach party," she said. "Bring Jean-
Luc and the Boogaloo." Their arms full of beach balls and
towels, they took the dogs—all but Bridgit who by the mere
fact of ignoring them, elected to stay by her fence—to the
very back part of the yard for a swim in Karen's pond. Karen
loved her pond. It was big enough for dogs to swim in the
summer and deep enough for the goldfish to survive in the
winter. The dogs loved her pond, too. They threw themselves
into the water with reckless abandon.

Baby Louis squealed in delight as Sylvie dipped him in
and out of the water. "My little merbaby," Sylvie said with

pride. She held him on his tummy on top of the water while
he smacked the water with his fists.

Even in the middle of the thrill of canine Marco Polo, Ferry
kept watch to make sure Sylvie kept the Boogaloo's face out
of the water.

"Let me have him," Karen said. She called Ferry to her.
"Let's swim with the baby," she said. She held Louis next
to Ferry. "Hold on, little Boogaloo," she told him. He flailed
his arms and somehow managed to grab onto the fur on
Ferry's neck. "Good boy," Karen told him. "Even if you
don't know what you're doing, you're doing it quite well."
She supported his body while he kept a vice grip hold on
Ferry's coat and Ferry swam around and around the pond
towing the baby. Karen sang "Ferry Me Over," the song
Ferry was named for. "Ferry is ferrying him over to Caledonia," she told Sylvie. "Ferry, you're a ferry!" The
Boogaloo kicked and grunted in his excitement and lost
his hold on Ferry. She stopped swimming on a dime and
turned around to nudge at him.

"Good, Ferry girl!" Sylvie called to her as she threw a ball
for Jean-Luc. "You know, Karen, that dog is a gem. I think
you should keep her, not adopt her out. Keep her and do competition obedience with her, or train her in water rescue. She's
terrific."

"No." Karen looked toward the house, where her newest
dog pressed against the fence. "I'm keeping Bridgit."

"Keep them both. You can have three permanent full-time
dogs."

"Brian's so geriatric, and Bridgit's so needy, and Ferry has
such a mind to keep engaged, I don't know if I could do them
all justice."

Late that night, Karen woke to the sound of thunder and
rain. She felt like thunder. She felt like rumbling and grum-

bling and crashing and bashing. She went back to sleep and, in the morning, the grass was damp, but the humidity had left.

Karen spent the day doing dog chores. Katie was, of course, off somewhere. This was the last day they had to spend together, and she was off with her friends. Karen frowned at the chair in front of the refrigerator.

Sally and Maxie, her new dog and constant companion, stopped over after supper. They wandered out to Karen's backyard. Karen snapped a leash on Bridgit. Bridgit had to follow her to the big swing. She settled down, her head on her front feet, facing the fence.

Karen gushed appropriately over Maxie. "What a perfect dog you are," she said. Maxie took the compliment with her usual grace and poise before settling down at Sally's feet. Maxie, like all the other dogs, ignored Bridgit.

"Look!" Sally held out a clump of something for Karen to see. "It's a baby blanket! I made it for the Boogaloo." Sally beamed. "Mrs. Wilde has been helping me and I finally learned how to knit!"

"Good for you. Mrs. Wilde has been trying to convert you since we were kids. What made you decide to finally take her up on her offer of knitting lessons?"

"Well, you know, I have that shawl Deb started for my birthday present. She died before she could finish it. Her mother-in-law sent it to me. It's sort of symbolic, I guess. I'm raising her son, and I'm finishing a shawl she started."

"I suppose your house will be overrun with yarn now," Karen teased. "The cats'll love it."

"Maybe. We'll see."

Karen chuckled. "No doubt about it. You are a person of extremes. I foresee wall-to-wall shelves of yarn in your house very soon. You jump into things with both feet, Sally. Look at how many boxes of Thin Mints you buy every year. You have every one of Mel's movies. And you started out with three cats, then you inherit one dog. Not content with only one, now you have three, even if one of them is Tanner's. You don't do things halfway. You never did."

"And the goldfish."

"What about the goldfish?"

"Micah decided since we had three cats and three dogs we needed three fishies to balance it all out. So I took him out to the fish farm and he picked out a goldie. Really pretty black moor. We'll have to see if he stays black. Micah named him Flis after a sled-hockey player."

"Three is the magic number?" Karen teased. "For Christmas you'll have to knit at least three sweaters, or afghans, or pairs of socks or something."

"Maybe I will."

"You're serious."

Sally smiled. "Yeah." She smoothed out the rumpled baby blanket in her lap. "I know this isn't great knitting, but Mrs. Wilde says you get better with every stitch you knit. And it feels good to make something for someone. I sort of understand why Deb knitted things for her friends all the time. Mrs. Wilde says when you knit you take part in a tradition that goes back to practically before written history. It's like there's this great big current of knitting women. Deb was part of it, your mom is part of it, and Mrs. Wilde, and Connie. Now I'm part of it, too. And it'll go on and on and on into the future and someday our daughters' daughters' daughters will be part of it. It's like passing the torch."

"My mom says the same kind of thing." Karen held out her feet, in her most comfortable Birkenstocks and a pair of mom-knit socks. Whatever knitting had done in the past, now it seemed to have given Sally a boost of self-esteem.

"I know. I see your mom all the time at the yarn shop. We sit and knit and talk together. Why didn't she ever teach you to knit?"

"She did. I used to knit. I haven't done it for a long time

though." Karen sat in the evening air, swinging on her porch swing with one of her best friends and she thought about that long time ago. Maybe it was because it was the end of the evening, or because her life was changing, or because she was depressed over Bridgit, and upset with Katie, or because Sally had recently experienced a monumental loss. Whatever the reason, Karen felt the words well up within her and spill over the wall into the open night air. "The summer after I graduated from high school, while all my friends were waiting to go to college, I was waiting to have my baby. I didn't want to go out much, and besides, how much fun is a seriously pregnant teenager? I mean, it's not like I could get excited about new clothes, and giggling over boys, and all of that. I was hot and uncomfortable. Here was this baby growing inside me and none of the girls who had been my friends could at all relate, not even a little bit. A year earlier a girl in school had gotten pregnant, but she ended up marrying the boy. I didn't even have that."

She reached down to stroke Bridgit's head, more for her own comfort than for Bridgit's. Bridgit didn't move. Karen thought of the isolation she felt the summer she was pregnant with Katie. "Mom brought out some baby blanket patterns, and she took me to Mrs. Wilde's shop. I saw this yarn and immediately fell in love with it. It was soft and warm and fine, silk and cashmere, I think, and much more expensive than anything I'd ever worked with before. Totally impractical for a baby. Mom put a dozen balls in the basket and took it up front and paid for it. Just like that. She said my baby deserved to have the best." Karen wiped her eye on the sleeve of her old T-shirt. "I'd never knitted anything as complex as that blanket. One time I got stuck and I couldn't figure it out. It was as if the pattern was suddenly written in Chinese. I accidentally dropped a whole bunch of stitches and then I started crying. Mom calmly picked my knitting up from the floor and fixed it for me and got me back on the pattern. She didn't get angry at me or anything. I don't think I could have done it without my mom."

The two friends sat in the swing in silence, two dozing dogs at their feet. Bats swooped swiftly through the dark sky, following some pattern of their own.

"I've never heard you say anything about that before." Sally's voice was hushed. "About being pregnant with Katie."

"Yeah, well, I wouldn't not have had Katie for the world, but my experiences of being an unwed teenage mother were not a high point of my life."

"So you leave tomorrow," Steve said.

She nodded. She drew her elbows in and sort of shook for a moment. "Yeah. This is it."

"You've trained hard. You've prepared yourself. You're ready to enter the ring."

"But I'll be alone. I won't have you in my corner."

"Okay. Here's something for you to think about." He focused for a moment. He drew himself up tall, proud, as if he was still a drill instructor. He would speak to her formally, to convey the respect he had for the Corps. Soon, she would understand; she would have that respect, too. "When you get off the bus and you step onto those yellow footprints, that will be your first step toward becoming a member of the world's finest fighting force—the United States Marine Corps. You will be connected to all of those who have stood on those footprints before you, and all of those who will come after you. You won't go through this process alone. You'll be part of something bigger than you can imagine. Your drill instructors will remind you of it constantly. No matter what you might think to the contrary, your drill instructors will be in your corner. Every step of the way."

For a moment, she was under his spell, and he knew she

felt the magic. Then she snorted. "Yeah. Like Hartman was in that guy Pyle's corner."

"Yeah," he grinned as he imitated her tone perfectly, "like *Full Metal Jacket* is really real."

"Yeah," she grinned back at him. "Like Lee Emery wasn't really a real drill instructor so he really didn't know what he was doing in that movie."

"Yeah"—he could keep it up too—"like I wasn't either. In fact, I really wasn't even a real Marine, so I'm really talking through my hat. Excuse me, through my cover. By the way, don't ever refer to a drill instructor's campaign cover as a Smokey the Bear hat. That will put you in very deep trouble."

She chuckled. "Okay. Subject change here. Did you watch the evening news last night?" she asked him. "You know that dog-fighting ring over in Madrid? The Humane Society and the cops tracked down some more of them. Busted them."

He glanced at Lennox, wiggling on Katie's lap; the dog's mission was to scrub her face.

"Some of the dogs were in such bad shape they had to be put to sleep. The rest are in custody. It's not good for the dogs, but it's good they caught the guys, isn't it?" She slid Lennox onto the floor and took up a boxing stance. She shadowboxed a few punches. "If I'd been there I'd've punched their lights out." She danced a few steps. "I'd've shown them what it's like to really fight." Pow! She let loose against an imaginary foe.

"Boxing is not personal. I've told you that again and again."

"But fighting dog-fighting is personal." She threw a few jabs followed by a punishing right. "Someone hurts dogs, they have to answer to me." There went a neat left hook. Too bad her opponent was only a figment of her imagination. She was winning this round.

"I thought your mom took care of the hurt dogs of the world."

"She's a major pacifist; she takes care of the hurt dogs. I want to take care of the people who hurt them. Take care of them so they'll never hurt another dog again." She threw a punishing blow to the body of her imaginary opponent.

Suddenly Steve wished he had a chance to know Katie's mother. He'd like to know a woman who could single-handedly raise such a terrific young woman, a woman who cared passionately about the underdogs of the world.

"Like Lennox. If anyone ever hurt him I'd track them down and punch their lights out." She demonstrated. Then she dropped to the floor and pulled Lennox onto her lap. "You're such a mushy dog," she crooned.

"My dog is not mushy."

She tossed him a disgusted look. "He is a great big mush. He only looks fierce. Sort of like Superman in reverse."

"Now I'm really offended."

She grinned. "I doubt it. But you *would* be really offended if I told you I think *you're* really a great big mush, too."

"Yes. I would be."

"That's why I've never told you I think you're really a great big mush." She looked pleased with herself. Then, she said, "Thank you for helping me get ready to go."

"You're welcome."

"I mean, you've become someone I consider a friend. If I get through boot camp—"

"When."

"—it'll be partly because you helped me."

"It'll be because you did it."

"Couldn't've done it without your help."

"Couldn't've done it without your heart."

She rolled her eyes. "Hey, Lennox, why can't I give this guy a sincere compliment?"

"So you're all packed?"

"Yup. Six white sports bras and six plain white cotton undies. All new. And I have my list of addresses of people to write to." She closely examined the hair on Lennox's head. "Thanks for letting me write to you. I figure I'll need someone who'll understand. You know. I'll write lovely sweet letters to my mom telling her I'm fine and being all positive and stuff. I'll write to Colleen about how fun it all is. Then I'll write you the truth about stuff and you'll understand."

He narrowed his eyes at her. "Why don't you tell your mother the truth?"

Katie separated the short hairs on Lennox's back and peered closely at the skin. Steve started to tell her Lennox did not have fleas, but he knew Katie wasn't looking for fleas. She was evading him.

"If I tell her how tough it is, she'll worry. She doesn't need to worry about me."

"You're still not letting your mother know how you really feel, are you?"

"It's not that," Katie said.

"It *is* that."

"I don't want to worry her."

He looked at her until she looked up at him. She met his gaze for the briefest second before she returned her attention to Lennox. "Don't look at me like that. She has enough to worry about right now. She has this new high-needs dog."

"You can't protect her, you know."

"I'm not trying to protect her. Well, maybe I am. But it's always been just the two of us. And the dogs, of course. And I keep thinking if she thinks I'm okay and everything then maybe she'll be able to have her own life. You know. Meet some nice man and fall in love. Roses and chocolates and the whole thing. I don't think she's ever had that."

Chapter 8

All too soon it was Sunday. Bridgit's last day of antibiotics, Karen thought, and the day Katie leaves for boot camp.

"Are you sure you really want to do this?" Karen asked Katie when she finally wandered, yawning, into the kitchen.

"I'm sure." Katie moved the chair in front of the refrigerator to get out the orange juice. Ferry hustled over to observe this chair-moving process.

"Don't you think college would be better? I know it's too late for one of the big schools, but I'm sure one of the community colleges—"

Katie set the orange juice pitcher down with a major thump, almost a slam. Juice sloshed over the side of the pitcher and onto the counter and dripped down onto the floor. Dinnie reached it first.

"Mother. I have signed on the dotted line. It would be a federal offense to back out. I will not try to get out of it. I don't even want to get out of it. There is nothing you can do to change my mind. Even if there were, it's too late."

"What did Sergeant Newland say to make you think this was the best choice for you?"

"What makes you think it isn't?"

Karen started at the reasonable tone of her daughter's voice. Then Karen stared at Katie, standing straight and tall before her, suddenly confident. Her daughter was sure. Her daughter had certitude. Her daughter had become someone else altogether.

Karen sank back in her chair. Katie looked like—why had she not seen it before? The young man Karen met eighteen, no nineteen, years ago in the Columbus airport during an unexpected blizzard. The young man Karen had fallen completely in love with, spent a glorious night with, and never seen again. The young man who was Katie's father. He had the same confidence and certitude. But she'd never seen him again. In the morning he was gone. On the pillow next to her, he'd left her a strip of three photobooth pictures of the two of them, and one small black medallion, an eagle and globe and anchor, tucked carefully into a little white cardboard box. When Karen returned home, when the snow was plowed from the highways, she kept his face in the front of her mind, always. She waited for him to arrive on the doorstep. After all, she'd carefully dropped enough hints so he could find her. But no matter how many sweet dreams and wishes, and then furious rants, and finally desperate pleadings she'd mentally sent to him, he never knocked on the door of her parents' house. He never returned to carry her off to his castle in the sky. And as much as she'd resented him for this, she also loved him for giving her the greatest gift of all. Now, the only reminder of him in her life, the only thing she cared about, was her daughter. She looked so very much like him. "I love you, Katie."

"I love you too, Mom."

Katie went off to see her grandparents one last time, and went out for one last Mexican dinner with Colleen. Finally she came home, and disappeared upstairs. Karen heard the shower running.

At exactly six o'clock there was a knock on Karen's front door. She opened it to the Impeccable Recruiter. He'd come to take her daughter away. Katie would spend tonight in a hotel in Cleveland, then tomorrow would fly to South Carolina, take a bus through a town called Beaufort, and then to Parris Island, where, according to Sergeant Newland, They Made Marines. Karen didn't think that was anything to be proud of. She wanted to shut the door on him. Pretend he wasn't here.

Katie ran down the stairs. "Be there in a second!" and she disappeared through the kitchen and Karen heard the kitchen door bang.

The recruiter was obviously too polite to ask the question.

Karen forced her mouth to smile. She was afraid it was more of a grimace. "Some of the dogs are in back. She's telling them goodbye." How could this young man stand in front of her so sure his way was the best thing for her daughter? She allowed herself to feel the slow burn of anger. Anger would keep her sorrow at bay.

After a few moments of uncomfortable silence, Katie was back. She knelt down and woke Brian gently. Karen heard her murmur something softly to the old dog. Then Katie stood up and faced the recruiter. He looked her over carefully.

"Earrings," he said.

"Oh." She reached up and removed her earrings. "I forgot." She stared at the two small gold earrings in her hand and then dropped them in the pottery jar on the little table next to the door. "Mom . . ." Katie reached for her.

Karen hugged her daughter fiercely. "I love you," she told her.

"I love you too, Mom. I really do. But I have to do this."

"Don't cry." Karen needed to squeeze a lifetime of caring and love into one final brief second.

"I'm not." But she was. Katie smeared her cheeks on the sleeve of her T-shirt.

"Ready?" asked the recruiter.

Katie nodded. She picked up her small knapsack filled, Karen knew, with only a nightshirt and toothbrush and comb, and new underwear. And a paperback, from Jessie, to read on the plane. It seemed her daughter was pitifully armed to go up against the Marines.

"Almost forgot." She set down her knapsack and reached up to unfasten her necklace. She handed it to Karen. "Here, Mom. Please put this on my dressing table. On my dressing table, okay? Don't forget. I'll want to find it when I return."

And Katie left her. Katie was gone. Out the door. To the end of the walk. Into the recruiter's car. The car out of the driveway. The car was far away at the corner of the street. Until Karen, in the middle of her yard, her hand raised like a mock salute to shield her eyes from the sun, couldn't see her daughter anymore. She staggered backward until she found her Tree. She leaned against the ancient Tree. The rough bark pricked her back through her shirt. Her Tree held her up. Her Tree was a constant in her life. Now it was too old, with too many fragile branches to make a good climbing tree. But long ago, she and Katie regularly scrambled up and around all of its branches to the tip-top where they could see forever. "I want to go there someday," Katie once said.

"Go where?" Karen had asked her.

"Go all the way to forever."

Karen found herself in her house, with her dogs wagging all around her, leaning against her, shuffling themselves to push against her, nose her, tell her in their doggy way that they loved her. She loved them too. It was a true Hallmark moment.

She reached out to pet the dogs and realized her fist still clutched Katie's necklace in a death grip. She made herself loosen her grip. She studied the small round silver pendant engraved with the Chinese character for love. It was a link with her daughter—a link she didn't want to break, wasn't ready to break. She fastened the thin chain around her own neck and the pendant came to rest next to her heart.

She felt restless. She felt out of sync. She needed to do something, but didn't know what to do. She reached for a dog comb as she sank down onto the floor. Dinnie rushed up and threw himself on the floor in front of her. He loved grooming. She automatically reached down to draw the comb through his thick black coat.

"Karen!"

"In here, Mom," Karen called over the cheerful woofing of the dogs. Dinnie scrambled to his feet and trotted off after the others.

Susannah gushed over the dogs all the way into the living room. They loved Susannah.

"You look disheartened."

Karen made a face. "That is exactly how I feel. Disheartened. That's not a word most people use anymore."

"Too bad. They should. It's a great word. It describes your face." She reached out to pull Karen into a gentle hug. "Let's go sit on the swing and enjoy the end of the evening."

"What's enjoyable about it?" But she allowed her mother, like the Pied Piper, to lead her, with the dogs trailing, through the kitchen out into the backyard and under the tree to her big swing. The swing was a long-ago birthday present from her brother and hung from a massive branch instead of a ceiling, as the swing on her front porch did.

Susannah settled on the swing and patted the seat beside her. "Sit." Karen obediently sat. The dogs sat, too.

Susannah opened her own tapestry bag and pulled out a plastic baggie filled with dog treats. She made sure each dog received equal portion. Even Brian, and Bridgit who took her treat without interest and ambled over to the fence to stare out. Once the dogs were taken care of, Susannah opened her tapestry bag again. This time, like nesting dolls, she pulled out a smaller version of her bag to present to Karen.

"My knitting bag. I haven't seen this for ages. Where did you find it?"

"In the attic. I figured you'd need it about now."

Karen opened the bag and reached in. She pulled out a set

of double-pointed knitting needles and a ball of soft yarn. "I don't remember this."

"It's new," her mother said calmly. "Katie was over a couple of days ago and she saw that round pi shawl you made for me when you were in high school. She must have seen it a million times, but this time she said she liked it, so I asked her if she wanted you to make one for her, too. She said yes, so I took her to the yarn shop."

Karen let her mother's caring wash over her and through her, filling her with comfort and soothing.

"The shop," Susannah continued, "seems empty without Rowan to greet us and follow us around. You remember Rowan. Connie Wilde needs another dog. Look here at the yarns Katie picked out for her Philosopher's sweater—look at these colors. Aren't they luscious? We also picked out this yarn for you to knit into a shawl for her. I assured her," her mother said with a pointed look, "you would love to knit her a pi shawl."

"Mom, she's just left for boot camp. She's going to be a Marine."

"Yes. But even so there will be times when she'll want a shawl. Marines don't wear uniforms all the time. She'll need a shawl. Especially one knitted for her by her mother. Besides, she said she'd like one and I told her you'd knit it." Susannah put down her own knitting. "Katie is still Katie. She will always be Katie. This isn't the end of her life. A stitch marker maybe, but certainly not the end."

Karen fingered the ball of fine wool, Katie's favorite shade of blue. It would make a lovely round shawl. Hesitantly she slipped the needles out of the plastic case. They felt cool and smooth and familiar.

"Connie's mom sent along the instructions, in case you need them. And circular needles so you'll have them when you get to that point."

"That was thoughtful of her," Karen said. She read the beginning of the instructions. She could almost hear Mrs. Wilde's calm peaceful voice. *Cast on nine stitches and join them in a round. The first round is knitted. For the second, yarnover, knit one all the way around. See? This doubles the number of stitches.* She picked up the end of the yarn and a needle. Cast on. For a moment she was afraid she had forgotten what to do. But her hands remembered. It was like riding a bike. She fell into the rhythm, the soft yarn flowing through her fingers, the beginning of a shawl for her daughter. Her mother's presence along with the rhythm of her needles and the motion of the swing were soothing, like deep, calming, breathing.

"Katie," her mother said, "told us Steve Songer did a lot to help her get in shape for boot camp."

"Yeah," Karen said dully. "Everyone says he's a saint."

"You don't think so?"

All of Karen's calm packed up and left. She dropped her knitting in her lap. "Mom, he teaches kids to hit each other. How is that so great? Oh. And Jessie says he named his Am Staff after some great boxer. Who would name an Am Staff—an Am Staff of all dogs—after someone who makes his living beating people up?"

The look Karen's mother gave her was one of supreme patience. "And you'd love to beat up people like that?" she asked.

"Yeah!" Then she realized her mother was teasing her. "I always tried to teach Katie to look for peaceful solutions. Beating up people isn't a peaceful solution. Neither is becoming a Marine." She picked up her knitting again. There was something she had never discussed with her parents. Now she needed to know. "Tell me about Daddy. Why he went to Vietnam."

"He was drafted."

"Did he want to go?"

Susannah shook her head. "No. He was always a pacifist.

He was strongly against the war. Both of us were. Several of his—of our—friends went to Canada to avoid the draft. Your father wouldn't. His draft lottery number was very low. He claimed noncombatant status and was trained as a medic. He said if he had to go to war, at least he'd save as many lives as he could."

"War changed him, didn't it?"

Her mother knitted several stitches. Then she pointed one of her needles toward Bridgit, who was slumbering on the grass between them. "You know the look in her eyes? The look of having known so much pain that her soul is almost dead? That's what your father's eyes looked like when he came home."

Karen thought of Katie's million-dollar smile. In her mind, she tried to superimpose the look in Bridgit's eyes on her image of Katie. It was an obscenity.

"What did you do?" This was before psychologists and counselors knew about post-traumatic stress. She remembered her high school history classes. Young men back from Vietnam were not hailed as heroes, they were called "baby killers." There were no parades for them. And her mother. "You must have been so young at the time. What were you, twenty-three?"

"Twenty-one."

Karen's thoughts dropped with a thud. Twenty-one was so young, it was practically still a child. Twenty-one was only three years older than Katie. "You were only twenty-one when he came home from Vietnam. Before the golden age of support groups, even." Karen looked at her mother with amazement. "I know what it's like dealing with traumatized kids. You were practically a kid yourself. I can't believe you were only twenty-one. How did you do it?"

"I had the best help in the world."

"Who?"

"You and Roger." Her voice shook slightly.

Karen blinked. That wasn't what she expected to hear.

"His love for the two of you was ultimately stronger than the pain of his memories."

"What about his love for you?"

"He once said I was his life, but the two of you gave him the strength to live it." She put her knitting in her lap and swiped at the corner of her eyes. "Oddly poetic for a man of few words, don't you think? You and Roger made us a family. No matter what had happened before, we were a family. We had to work through it. We didn't have a choice." She smiled to herself. "Even if we'd had a choice, though, we'd have chosen the same." After a moment, her mother said, "You're afraid for her."

"Of course! This is not a safe time in the world for my daughter to go off and be a Marine. At least they don't send women into combat."

Susannah reached her arm out around Karen's shoulders and drew her into a hug. "She'll be fine."

Karen leaned into her mother's embrace. "I hope so," she whispered, as a lone tear spilled over and ran down her cheek.

Her mother stroked her hair in rhythm with the swing. "I know so," she whispered back.

Chapter 9

Monday morning, Karen's eyes felt like sandpaper. She went through the motions of taking all the dogs out, feeding them, doling out arthritis medicine for Brian, vitamins for Bridgit.

She came back home for a quick lunch. Then she loaded Bridgit in her van to take her to the clinic to have her stitches removed. She told Melissa Bridgit was moving better but she was still aloof, depressed.

"I don't know how to motivate her," Karen said.

"If there's an answer, I'm sure you'll find it," Melissa said. "In the meantime, keep up the good work. It's hard to believe she's the same dog." Melissa stooped down. "You're a good girl," she said.

Bridgit was unmoved.

"Are dogs ever autistic?"

Melissa looked up at her. "I don't think so."

Karen took Bridgit to work with her. Theory was, if the dog was with you twenty-four/seven, it would be easier to bond. Karen needed Bridgit to bond. Twenty-four/seven wasn't possible, but she would do what she could.

That afternoon, the seventeen-year-old girl from the Planned Parenthood doctor came to see Karen for the first time. Her name was Candy. She took one look at Bridgit, put her arms around the big dog and cried. And cried and cried.

Karen slid the box of tissues toward her, and she took one, she blew her nose, and then put her arms back around Bridgit. Bridgit sat still and allowed the girl to cry.

Finally Candy had cried herself out. "I'm pregnant," she told Karen. "I told my parents and I thought they were going to kill me. They want me to have an abortion, right away. So they can pretend their life is perfect. That's the way they deal with things. Pretend it didn't happen. Sweep things under the rug and if all the stuff makes a lump in the rug, they stomp on it." She sounded bitter. "The doctor at Planned Parenthood told them before she'd arrange an abortion, I had to talk to you."

"Do you know why she wants us to talk?"

"No."

"I help young people, like you, figure out what's going on in your lives. I help people figure out the best way to deal with things."

"I don't think there's a best way to have an abortion. It's still killing the baby."

"It sounds like you're not sure about an abortion."

"I'm sure," Candy said. "I'm sure I don't want one."

"Do you know what you do want to do?"

"No. But I know I can't kill my baby. No matter what my parents say."

"Then, if you agree, you and I can talk together and over the next couple of weeks I'll try to help you figure out what you want to do."

Candy looked suspicious.

Karen told her, "What you want. Not your parents, not me. What you want."

"Really what I want?"

"Really."

The girl looked at Bridgit. Bridgit looked back.

"Is this your dog?"

"Yes. Her name is Bridgit."

"What happened to her?"

"I don't know. Two weeks ago, someone found her on the side of the road and brought her to the vet's. I adopted her."

The Newfoundland national rescue coordinator called Karen that evening. "The woman from Buffalo checked out. Everything looks good. I think she's a keeper. Give her a call and make arrangements for her to come get Dinnie."

Karen hung up the phone and went to find Dinnie. He was curled up under her dining room table. One of Katie's old slippers hung out of his mouth. "You miss her too, don't you?" She crawled under the table to sit next to him. "You can keep that slipper. She doesn't need it right now." Dinnie shoved the slipper at her without letting go of it. "Yes, you've taken very good care of it. No tooth marks at all. You have a very soft mouth." She looked into his big brown eyes. "You also have a new mom," she told him. "You're going to your forever home. You can even take Katie's slipper with you."

This was what she worked for, what she did. She took in needy dogs, fostered them until they were ready to be adopted and then sent them off with their new moms and dads. She'd done this dozens of times before. This was not new. When she brought Dinnie home last winter this was her goal for him. Then why did she feel so sad? "I'll miss you," she told him. She leaned against his great furry body. He wagged his tail and nudged her head. "You know what? You can take both slippers with you. I know Katie won't mind." She wondered what Katie was doing right now.

"Karen!" Jessie opened the front door. "Sagan and I are here with pizza. And then we're going swimming in your pond."

* * *

Karen called the woman from Buffalo. They talked about
Dinnie for almost an hour. The woman was excited. She said
they had lots of snow in the winter and Lake Erie was nearby.
She said she'd drive down on Saturday. With a heavy heart,
Karen said Saturday was fine. It was official. Dinnie was
leaving, too.

The phone rang in the darkness. Karen blinked, only half
awake, certain it was a dream. The phone rang again. She
groped for it. "Hello," she managed.

"It's me, Mom, I'm here, I'm okay. Gotta go now. I love
you. Bye."

"Katie, wait—" but Katie had hung up and was gone. Gone
again. Now, wide-awake, Karen looked at the clock. It was
two in the morning. She got out of bed and stepped over
Brian, sleeping deeply on the rug. She slung her old ratty
bathrobe over her shoulders. She crossed her bedroom to the
open window. She leaned against the screen and breathed in
the night air. Katie was conceived in the middle of the night
and born in the middle of the night, and now, it was once
more the middle of the night and Karen was awake thinking
about Katie.

From Sylvie's house next door, Karen heard the Boogaloo
begin to cry. Then she heard Sylvie singing softly to her son.
Faint notes of the English hymn, "Jerusalem," the words by
William Blake, floated through the night on the lightest of
breezes. Eighteen years ago Karen was the one singing to a
wakeful baby in the middle of the night while her friends
were off living carefree, unfettered lives. Now, her daughter
grown and gone, all her friends were in various stages of
motherhood. M'liss had a stepdaughter, Sally inherited
teenage Micah, Sylvie just had a baby, and Jessie had a new

puppy which she insisted was the same thing as a human baby and easier to housebreak.

While Karen was ending her role of active motherhood, her friends were beginning their mother journeys. Once more she was out of step. She had crossed a threshold, passed one of what her mother called life's stitch markers. She wasn't sure she liked it on this side. It was lonely. Her house was too big, and too quiet, even with the breathing and snoring and snuffling of all the dogs. It was quiet because Katie wasn't there. Katie would never be there again. College dorms were a gradual weaning away process for mothers; their kids still came back for long weekends and to do laundry before they left again. The Marine Corps was cold turkey.

Brian shoved his head against her leg and sighed loudly.

"You're right," Karen told him, "I can't be lonely with all of you guys." Lonely or not, she was only thirty-six years old. "What am I going to do with the rest of my life?" she asked her dog.

Tuesday, Sally called. "Come over for supper. I made macaroni and cheese. Micah says you have to meet his new goldfish."

"What is this?" Karen asked. "Do all of you have a schedule to keep Karen company?"

"We sure do. How did you guess?"

Jeremy Martini was also at Sally's for supper. He and Micah were the commotion equivalent of ten Newfoundlands. Still, Sally was a kindergarten teacher so she was probably inured to the noise.

Wednesday morning, Karen found herself looking out the window of her office. She liked watching Steve Songer jog by. Theresa and Vicky liked watching him jog by too. "Good thing he does his jogging this early in the morning," she told them, only pretending to be stern. "It would not be professional to drop everything and rush in here in the middle of a session to look out my window, now would it?"

"Looks like a commercial for something sexy, doesn't he?" Theresa said.

Karen made a noncommittal noise.

"Maybe that new chocolate whipped cream," Vicky said. "You see this gorgeous guy jogging by, and then you see some gorgeous babe licking chocolate whipped cream off her finger." She shivered. "He sure makes me think of whipped cream!"

"What does a guy jogging by have to do with whipped cream?" Karen ignored the gorgeous part.

Vicky and Theresa shared one of those looks. Vicky shook her head. "Commercials usually don't have anything to do with what they're advertising," she explained patiently, as if to a child. "They have to do with sex. Haven't you figured that out by now?"

"Oh." Karen watched Steve and his dog. His dog looked so cheerful and friendly. How could a dog like that be responsible for hurting Bridgit? She slammed a mental door on that line of thought. She would not go there.

That evening, Karen heard the distinctive *ringie* sounds of her mom's ancient VW bus.

"You really need a new car," Karen called from the doorway.

"I really like this one," her mother said cheerfully. "We understand each other. Your dad is at his airplane club, so I brought dinner." Her knitting bag was on her arm.

After dinner, they sat outside with the dogs and knit. Susannah looked over at Katie's shawl. "That's coming along well," she said. "Katie will love it."

"Knitting is peaceful. I'd forgotten how peaceful it is."

Her mother nodded. "The rhythm of it, the feel of the yarn. It's very contemplative. You take a ball of yarn, chaos, and bring order to it." She grinned. "I know. I'm an old hippie."

Karen said, "Dinnie is leaving on Saturday. He's going to a forever home."

"How wonderful!"

"Yes. It is, isn't it?"

"You don't sound convinced."

"I am. I really am. It's just that it's so soon after Katie left. I'm losing two of my kids at once."

"Our lives are a constant greeting and leaving."

"That sounds like an old hippie greeting card."

Susannah laughed. "It does, doesn't it?"

Steve went home for lunch on Thursday. He told Lennox to run around outside in the backyard while he ate his sandwich. All too soon it was time to go back to the gym. "C'mon, Lennox! It's time to go back to work!"

Lennox ignored him. Lennox had his nose in something in the yard. Steve headed outside. "Hey, bud, what do you have there?"

Lennox glanced up, guilt on his face. He chewed quickly. Steve reached for him. He swallowed.

"What was that?" Lennox wagged his tail. Steve looked on the ground around Lennox. He didn't see anything unusual. He looked at Lennox. Lennox looked innocent. "I'll believe you this time," Steve said. "Let's go to the gym." He made a motion with his hand and Lennox bounded up and into the house.

Steve saw something white in his mailbox. It was a post-card from Katie with her mailing address. He stuck it in his pocket and whistled to Lennox. Lennox leaped into the car.

Back at the gym, Steve scribbled a quick note and licked the envelope and stuck on a stamp. He called Lennox for a short walk.

Karen caught movement in the corner of her eye. She glanced away from her client and out the window to see Steve Songer and his dog across the street. He stuck something in the mailbox. The light breeze lifted a lock of his hair, making him look young. Now who was interrupting a session to watch Steve Songer? she scolded herself. She anchored her attention firmly back on the session, what was going on in this room, right now. She told herself she didn't care to whom he wrote. But she couldn't get the image of chocolate whipped cream out of her mind.

Mary Lou taught an exercise class of mostly middle-aged women who needed a social outing more than they wanted to get into shape. Mary Lou insisted it was good for the gym, brought in some easy extra money, and besides, she liked doing it. Steve liked it too. He liked the women. The women were cheerful, friendly, and alternately flirted with him and treated him like a kid brother.

When the women were in the gym, the guys kept a leash on their language as they worked the heavy bag, or the speed bag, or each other in the practice ring. The guys were polite to the women who came for exercise class. No one had to remind them, no one made a big deal of it, it was understood. The women were treated like ladies, always.

Steve's first clue that Lennox didn't feel well was after the exercise class. One of the women called Lennox and Lennox stayed curled up on the old rug. The woman looked at Steve, surprise in her face. This was a first. Lennox loved the women.

"That's odd," Steve said.

"Maybe he had a late night last night," the woman said with a smile. "See you later, Lennox. Hope you feel better soon." And she blew the dog a kiss as she left to go outside into the bright summer sun.

After school, Jim Tate showed up for his individual coaching. After the young man warmed up, Steve worked one-on-one with him for half an hour. Jim had the makings of a good boxer. He had speed, discipline, and an iron jaw. Most of all, he wanted it. He had heart. Skills you could teach. Technique and process could be learned. But heart, you either had it or you didn't. Steve would take a student with heart any day. "Good work," Steve told him at the end of the half hour. "Don't forget your cooldown."

"Where's Lennox?" Jim asked.

Steve looked across the gym at his dog. Lennox was still on the rug. Still curled up. Something wasn't right. He climbed through the ropes and ran across the gym. His eyes never left his dog. Lennox did not move.

"What's up?" Jim followed him.

"Something's wrong with Lennox," Steve said. He knelt down beside his dog. "His eyes look odd. And look, his gums are pale."

"He's drooling," Jim said.

Lennox didn't drool. Lennox never drooled. Steve went into his office and grabbed his phone and the phone book. He shoved the phone book at Jim. "Look up the number for the Hartley Veterinary Clinic, will you?" He knelt beside his dog again. He put his head on Lennox's chest to try to hear his heartbeat, but he didn't know what he was listening for.

Jim rustled the pages of the phone book. "Here it is." He read the number.

Steve dialed. He listened to the phone on the other end ring. "Hi Suzette, this is Steve Songer. Is Jessie there? Or Dr. Winthrop?"

"Hi Steve, what's up?" he heard Jessie's cheerful voice.

"Lennox. Something's wrong. He hasn't moved for about two hours, he's drooling, his gums are pale, his eyes look weird."

"Gross!" said Jim.

"And he just vomited."

"You're right. Something's definitely wrong," Jessie said. "How soon can you get him here?"

"Ten minutes."

"See you then."

Steve hung up.

"Hey, man," Jim said. "You take Lennox. I'll clean this up."

"Thanks," Steve said briefly. He carried his dog out of the gym. Jim hurried after him to open the car door.

Chapter 10

"Has he eaten anything unusual today?" Dr. Winthrop asked. She kept her attention on the dog, listening, looking, peering into the dog's eyes and mouth.

"At lunch. I let him outside and he found something in the yard. He swallowed it before I could get it away from him. I don't know what it was."

"How long ago was that?" Dr. Winthrop palpated Lennox's abdomen carefully.

"Three or four hours."

"He shows signs of being poisoned."

"Poison?" Steve asked.

"Who'd poison Lennox?" Jessie said.

But Steve knew. In this world were people who poisoned American Staffordshires thinking they were pit bulls. "One of my sister's dogs once, Lennox's half sister, someone poisoned her. It was right after some great media hype about pit bulls."

"Was she okay?" Jessie asked. "Lennox's sister, I mean."

"Yeah. After a while."

Dr. Winthrop said. "I'm taking Lennox into the back. We'll start some fluids. That'll keep his kidneys working and help flush the poison out. I want to keep him at least overnight."

"Will he be okay tomorrow?"

"Don't know. We'll do our best. He's a strong dog." Dr. Winthrop carefully picked Lennox up. "Let's go, big guy. You're going to stay with us for a couple of days."

Jessie opened the door for her. "Poisoned him," she muttered, "because some dumb idiot thought he was a pit bull? That's a hate crime!"

"Yes," Dr. Winthrop said. "It is." She carried Lennox through the doorway, into the back of the clinic.

"Should be punishable by death," Jessie muttered as she followed the vet. "By slow evisceration with a rusty knife. Wait here," she said over her shoulder to Steve. "I'll be back."

Steve paced the small examination room. He felt like a caged tiger. He wanted to punch something.

Jessie came back to talk to him. "We have him all settled in for a while. We set up a drip and gave him something to soak up the poison. Melissa's with him now." She leaned against the wall as she talked. "It hasn't had too long in his system, that's good. We'll call you in a little bit, when we know more. Will you be at home?"

Steve shook his head. "Gym."

"You should go home." Jessie scowled at him for a moment before she turned her scowl on the chart in her hand. "Okay. I have that phone number here. I'll call you as soon as we know anything."

"Thanks," Steve said. "I appreciate it."

"No prob. We love Lennox. We're charter members of his fan club. Me, and M'liss, and Katie Matheson, and just about everyone who knows him. It's a good thing Katie's not here. She'd start a riot."

"Uh, Jess. I know you're friends with Katie's mom. Don't let Katie know about this. Not now. She has enough to do at boot camp without worrying about Lennox."

She bit her lip. "Oh. Okay. Karen will find out. You know the doggy grapevine around here. I'll tell her not to tell Katie. Hey, don't worry. We'll take good care of him."

* * *

A letter from Katie waited in Karen's mailbox. Karen held the envelope close and studied the return address. It wasn't a normal address at all, it was full of numbers and initials. She ripped the envelope open.

> *Dear Mom,*
>
> *I miss all the dogs. I even miss checking my plate for dog hair before I eat. You will be glad to know I am not pregnant and I don't have flat feet. All the girls have to have pregnancy tests. When we first got here they made us stand on this box to check our feet. Then they gave us new tennis shoes. They say we'll get boots when we earn them. Right now we have to wear these bright yellowish things that look like school crossing guards'. It's sort of embarrassing. I guess it marks us as total newbies. The food is okay. I am not starving. It's basic food. Nothing fancy. No chocolate desserts. The Marines must think chocolate is unpatriotic or something. Give the dogs great big hugs for me. Tell them I miss them. I miss you too.*
>
>

Love,

Katie
>

Karen wandered aimlessly around the house. She picked things up and set them down. She combed Heck for a moment. Dog school was between sessions so she didn't have to rush supper and head off. Didn't have anywhere to be right now. She took the dogs outside, wandered around the yard, and then went back inside.

Karen sat down at her computer to write a letter to Katie. She didn't know what to say. The kitchen door banged. Karen heard Ferry snuffle her way into the living room. She stared at the cheerfully blinking cursor. What do you say to your daughter when she's away at boot camp and you're terrified for her and furious at her and miss her like crazy? Karen had no idea. Finally she closed out her word processor and played solitaire until Ferry rushed to the front door bearing a noisy greeting.

"Karen!" Jessie's voice was loud enough to compete with the dogs. "I have Chinese takeout with me and if you don't call off your hound I'll let her have your half and you won't get any and you'll be hungry and it won't be my fault."

Karen closed solitaire and shoved away from her computer. "What's this?" she asked Jessie. "Tonight's your night for Karen duty?"

"Yeah." Jessie headed into the kitchen. Ferry followed her. Karen followed the dog. Jessie set the takeout bag on the counter. "This was supposed to be Melissa's night, but she wanted to stay at the clinic. We had an emergency. Hey, can we use the fancy plates? They're so pretty with Chinese." She continued to talk while she bustled around Karen's kitchen, pulling out plates and silverware and glasses, not allowing Karen to edge a word in, so Karen opened the door for the other dogs.

Jessie continued her monologue. "You know Steve Songer's Am Staff? Great dog. Don't know if you've heard, but some disgusting pervert, some complete perversion of a human being, tried to poison him. I think it should be classed a hate crime. Ah. The kitchen chair as a lock. Katie told me Ferry had aspirations to be a world-class food thief. I know. You should get some of that industrial-strength Velcro. Put it high enough and she won't be able to reach it. Then you could dump the chair. Oh good. You have iced tea. Anyway, I wanted to report it to the police, but Steve said we didn't have any incontrovertible proof that it was deliberate." She made a sound of utter disgust. "Here. I brought sweet-and-sour chicken, almond chicken, and fried rice, and egg rolls. I was only kidding, by the way, about giving the dogs your half. It would have been too messy to divide equally. Sit. Dinner is served. And you know Chinese, it tastes best when it's hot."

Karen spooned dinner onto her plate. "Thanks. Ferry, don't even think about it." Ferry settled back down, pretending she really didn't have the slightest interest in what was happening on the kitchen table.

"We figured you probably wouldn't cook for just you, and, you know me. Any excuse for Chinese." Jessie counted the dogs in the kitchen. "Where's Bridgit?"

"In the backyard. She stares out through the fence all day. She doesn't react to me at all. If she were a person I'd wonder if she was autistic."

"You sound bummed out."

"Yeah. My beautiful new high-needs dog doesn't acknowledge my existence, my beautiful guy dog Dinnie is going to his new home this weekend, and my beautiful daughter is doing her darndest to turn into a Marine. I think I have a right to feel deserted."

"Oh. That reminds me. Steve said for me to tell you it's really important to not tell Katie about Lennox. He says she has enough to think about without worrying about Lennox. And you know she would. She adores that dog."

Karen thumped her fork down and stared at Jessie. "What nerve," she said. "What gives him the right to dictate to me what I can and cannot tell my daughter?"

Jessie held her hands up in surrender. "Hey, don't shoot the messenger here."

"Then don't bring messages from Steve Songer about what I can and cannot tell my daughter."

"I don't think he meant it like that."

"Well that's the way it sounds."

"He doesn't want to make it more difficult for her, that's all. He's been there. He knows what he's talking about."

"What do you mean?"

"Didn't you know? I assumed Katie'd've told you. Not only was Steve a Marine, he was career military. He retired a couple of years ago."

Of course. That was why he had an Am Staff and taught boxing. He was a professional warmonger. Plain and simple. He'd left the war but the war hadn't left him. "I'm beginning to like him less and less. Okay, I'm sorry about his dog. No dog should be poisoned, regardless of breed. I know Katie likes that dog, and you're right, if she found out she would worry. So I won't tell her. Because I don't want her to worry. Okay?"

"Yeah. Oh." She pulled a wad of paper out of her jeans pocket. She unfolded all the folds and tried to smooth it out on the table. "I called Liz at the library. She looked these up for me. Marine Moms Online is a list you should probably join, and this is the web address for Parris Island where Katie is. Part of the site tells you all about what she's doing and when she's doing it. And some other stuff to help you learn about the Corps."

Karen didn't want it. "Leave it on the table," she said. "I'll look at it later." Maybe it would fall on the floor and Dinnie would eat it.

Friday morning, Karen kept glancing out her window but she never saw Steve Songer on his morning jog. Theresa and Vicky stuck their heads in the doorway, eyebrows raised. She shook her head at them.

Then Karen remembered his dog. She wondered how his dog was doing. She couldn't help it. She cared about dogs. Even Am Staffs.

The early morning gym was empty without Lennox. It was amazing, Steve thought, how one dog, even a busy, energetic dog like Lennox, could fill such a large space. He was not motivated to jog without Lennox.

"How's Lennox?" Mary Lou asked as soon as she arrived.

"How's Lennox?" the guys asked as soon as they arrived.

Steve told them he had been poisoned. Steve told them he was still at the vet's.

Jessie called him midmorning to let him know Lennox was doing better. Melissa wanted to keep him for another day or so, to keep him hydrated.

At lunchtime Jessie knocked on the door to Karen's office. "I called a bit ago and Vicky told me you didn't have a session now, so I brought us lunch. You're supposed to say, 'Jess, that was very thoughtful of you. Let's go in the kitchen and eat.' All work and no lunch makes you grumpy."

"Okay," Karen said with a grin. "Jess, that was very thoughtful of you. Let's go in the kitchen and eat."

Jessie said, "Why, Karen, what an excellent idea."

Jessie waltzed down the hall to the kitchen, spun around and held her arms out to the side. "Read me."

Karen read Jessie's T-shirt. *Haldir lives. I don't care what Peter Jackson says.* "I don't get it."

Jessie looked superior. "That's because you haven't watched *The Lord of the Rings*. Haldir is this really supercool elf. Peter Jackson, the director, *thinks* he killed him off in the second movie, but Peter Jackson doesn't know everything. You can come over some day and we'll watch 'em. How about this Saturday?"

"No thanks."

"C'mon, Karen, you'd really like 'em. I know you would. It's this one very long story about doing what has to be done, no matter the cost. It's about biting the bullet and becoming more than you ever thought you could ever be."

Karen shot her friend a very pointed glare. "I don't like violence in movies. There's enough violence in everyday life. All you have to do is turn on the news."

Jessie shot her an equally pointed glare in return. "Which is a very good reason to *not* turn on the news."

"You're right. I have a choice. I have a choice in news, and a choice in movies. I choose to not watch movies with violence. I don't want to support the people who make them."

"First of all, *you*'re not supporting them. *I* am. I bought the movies. You're an innocent bystander. And also, think of all the great fairy tales. Not the Disney emasculations, but the *real* ones. They're all about ordinary people who confront something bad and overcome it. This is *The Lord of the Rings*. Ordinary people—well, hobbits and . . . others—confront the most evil of all evils. It's such a great story because the stakes are so high."

"They win, right?"

"Yes."

"Then if we know they win, what's the point in watching?"

Jessie groaned. "The point, is what happens to them along the way. And you know what? In times of war our honor and our courage and our greatness are tested. Good movies show this."

"They don't need the violence."

"The violence shows how great the evil is—and makes the honor and courage and greatness more bright in comparison." She looked pleased.

"*Strictly Ballroom* and *The Dish*. Honor and courage without violence."

"But," Jessie sputtered. "They're Australian."

"*Mystery, Alaska*; *Corrina, Corrina*; and *October Sky*. *Shakespeare in Love*."

"Yes, but—"

"*Apollo 13,* and *A Beautiful Mind*."

Jessie closed her mouth. For a mere moment. "They're both true so they shouldn't count. Anyway, Russell Crowe should've gotten the Oscar. He was astounding."

Karen nodded in satisfaction. "True or not, these are all

stories about courage and greatness and honor in times of difficulty."

Jessie thought. "But," she said at last, sure of triumph, "none of them have dogs!"

"The Man Without a Face."

Jessie's face fell. "A dog *and* Mel Gibson. Okay. You win. This time."

Karen could afford to be magnanimous in her victory. She pulled a waxed paper-covered plate from the refrigerator. "For dessert. My mom made buckeyes. I know how you love them."

Jessie eyed the plate suspiciously. "She didn't use carob this time, did she? Or that natural peanut butter? I love your mom, Karen, but those were really, really, really gross."

Chapter 11

"How's Lennox?" the afternoon exercise women asked as they swept into the gym with their cheerful chatter and colorful workout clothes. Their concern for Lennox was genuine; he was an important part of the gym.

He told them Lennox was better, but still at the vet's.

Today, Mary Lou played oldies during the exercise class. The women always liked oldies better than all this newfangled music. Some of the guys evidently liked oldies, too, for some of them sang along as they worked the bags.

The after-school gang also asked about Lennox as soon as they arrived.

Steve told them Lennox was doing better, and reminded them ESPN had preempted "Friday Night Fights."

"Some car thing again?" Jim asked. "There's no boxing because people want to watch cars going fast." His opinion of cars going fast was obvious.

Later that day, Steve went through the gym gathering up gross towels. He ran towels through the laundry at the end of every day. In the ladies' locker room, Steve found a sweater hanging on the hook Katie had called hers for the last nine months. He would have to take it over to her mother's house. He tossed it on top of his desk so he wouldn't forget to take it with him.

* * *

"It's bath time for Dinnie Burns," Karen announced to the dogs when she arrived home from work. "He will be squeaky clean for his new mom." She took the dogs out and changed into dog clothes. She led Dinnie into the laundry room and up the steps to the doggy bathtub. "Good boy." She opened the window to let in the warm breeze. She sang to Dinnie as she lathered and rinsed. After his bath, she rubbed him briskly with a rough dog towel. He leaned against her legs and groaned in pleasure. He looked so sparkly and bright she decided to bathe all the dogs. "C'mon guys," she called to them. "Let's show Dinnie's new mom how beautiful Newfoundlands are."

Brian was last. After his bath she toweled him gently, because she didn't want to knock him over. "When I'm ninety-four," she told him, "I'll lose my balance easily, too." Her T-shirt, wetly plastered to her, was covered with tangles of long black Newf hair, and she knew she smelled of wet dog and shampoo. After all, bathing five Newfoundlands was not a task for the fainthearted. But her dogs were most certainly beautiful. And damp. All the towels in her house were not enough to dry the dogs. Right now, all the towels in her house were in a huge, hairy, sodden heap on the floor.

Hauling a heap of towels to the washing machine, Karen heard a loud knock. The young'uns barked and scrambled down the hall toward the door. Brian joined in, to be part of the crowd more than because he heard anything. Karen wondered who was bringing over supper tonight. She wasn't an invalid, for pete's sake. She kept telling them they didn't have to do the casserole drive thing. She was perfectly capable of eating supper all by herself. Did they listen? No.

"C'mon in!" she hollered. "I'm doing towels!"

The dogs barked.

"Hello," she heard an unfamiliar and male voice call out between barks.

"Good grief," Karen muttered. Great time to greet a stranger. She dumped the towels on the floor and headed for the front door. She swiped at the dog hair on her shirt. It was a lost cause.

"Hello," the voice said again. Steve Songer stood on her porch.

Karen felt suddenly and horribly self-conscious. She was irritated with herself for feeling that way. Sheesh! She had dogs to take care of. Being covered with damp dog hairs and streaks of dog shampoo, and smelling like wet dog was part of living with dogs. She had nothing to apologize for.

"Hello," he repeated. Watching him jog in the mornings, she'd thought he looked yummy from across the street. He looked even more gorgeous close-up.

She felt suddenly limp in the knees. "Hello," she said. She wanted the house to fall down around her. She wanted the house to fall down on top of her. She wanted to press *pause* and rewind. She wanted him held in a freeze-frame until she'd taken her own bath and was groomed at least half as beautifully as her dogs.

"Karen Matheson? We've never officially met. I'm Steve Songer."

"Yes. I know." Karen resented him for looking so perfect while she was at a decided disadvantage. Gorgeous or not, he was nothing to her. She made herself be polite, but she would allow the four big hairy wet dogs to have their way with this new man. "Come in." She shoved Ferry back with her knee and opened the screen door. "They're friendly dogs, but they're straight out of the bathtub wet."

Steve Songer didn't have any qualms about wet Newfoundland. He reached down to pat and talk to the dogs. Of course he was a man after her own heart, she thought sourly. This was Steve Songer, professional warmonger. The man who had helped lead her daughter astray. Why couldn't he be hateful?

He handed her a sweater. "Katie left this at the gym."

She looked at him. "Thank you."

"You're welcome."

She felt he was somehow sizing her up. "Jessie says you retired from the Marines."

"Yes ma'am."

"So you've been through boot camp."

"So I know what I'm saying."

She looked at this man. He and Katie were friends. Suddenly she wanted to know what sort of man Katie called her friend. "Do you want to come in and officially meet the dogs?"

He was still. Then, "Sure. I've heard a lot about them."

She led him into the living room. He dropped onto the floor and held his arms out to the dogs. The young'uns rushed to gush all over him.

"This is Ferry," Karen said. "She's an escape artist. This is Heck, and this is Dinnie Burns who chews on anything and everything. He's going to his new home tomorrow. Over there, in the fireplace, is Brian, who is the most geezerly of the lot."

"I suppose it's cooler in the fireplace?"

He caught on quickly, Karen thought. "Yes. He likes to sleep there in the summer."

Steve made his way through the throng to Brian. He was gentle with the elderly dog. This was a man who understood, who was dog people.

"Would you like some iced tea?"

"Thank you. That would be nice." He was excruciatingly polite with her but she liked the way he looked at her dogs, talked to them. You could tell a lot about someone by the way they interacted with dogs, or didn't interact with them. He followed her into the kitchen. She waved him toward the kitchen table. She poured iced tea. She cut pieces of her mom's lemon bar and set them on a plate.

Finally she said, "Jessie called me. Told me you wanted me to evaluate your dog."

He looked uncomfortable. "Well, the city sent me a letter. Jessie said you would be a good person to ask."

"I have one other dog you need to meet. Wait here." She whistled for the other dogs who all obediently thundered into the dog room and into their crates. They looked expectantly at her. She gave them each a small cookie. "Good dogs," she said.

Then she closed the door to the dog room and went to get Bridgit.

Bridgit followed her down the hall to the kitchen. Her head was down. Karen said, "She's been with me for about two weeks."

She recognized the expression on his face when he saw Bridgit. It was her mom's expression. Steve Songer, like her mother, instinctively knew what to do with a hurt dog. This made no sense. He was a boxer, a former Marine. He believed in fighting—he taught fighting. She must be more tired than she thought.

"Who is this?" he asked, not looking away from the wreck of a dog in front of him.

"Bridgit."

"How is she doing?" He nodded to her many wounds and Karen understood he realized their probable cause.

"Better than she was. I think she might make it, after all. Physically, at least. Emotionally, I'm not sure."

"Katie once told me you named your dogs after Celtic songs."

She nodded. "Bridgit is named after the most beautiful song in the world."

He looked into the dog's eyes. "A beautiful song for a beautiful dog."

How could she not like such a guy? How could she?

After lunch, Karen put the dogs in their crates, all but Dinnie. She took Dinnie out to sit on the front porch and wait for his new mom. Karen kept her arm around him, kept telling him she loved him, and how happy he was going to be.

"You're beautiful!" the woman cried when she saw Dinnie. Dinnie waved his tail and Karen invited the woman in.

The woman fished around in her pocket for a dog cookie and didn't mind when Dinnie drooled on her shoe as he gobbled it.

"He loves to chew," Karen told her. "He loves to carry soft things around. He has a very soft mouth." She pulled out one of Katie's slippers. "These belong to my daughter. She's away right now and he likes to carry her slippers. He even sleeps with them."

The slipper was covered with dried slobber, but the woman took it without hesitation. "It's a beautiful thing," she told Dinnie. "You must love her very much." She held it for him. He took it gently in his great mouth. He was content to hold it.

"He's like a child with a favorite blankie," the woman said.

Karen felt a rush of gratitude toward this woman. Dinnie would have a wonderful life.

She brought out Ferry and Heck who were very beautiful and clean and very effusive in greeting Dinnie's new mom. Ferry especially tried to impress her. The new mom was equally effusive in greeting them. Brian shuffled into the living room, slowly, looking around for the source of all the commotion.

Karen gave the woman a book about Newfoundlands, along with some notes she'd written down about Dinnie; his shoe fetish, his favorite treats and snacks. Also a copy of Dinnie's shot record. "Have your vet call the Hartley Vet Clinic and they'll fax his records." She added in Dinnie's blanket, still warm from the dryer. A small bag of dog food so the woman could gradually switch him over to whatever food she fed her dogs. "And his bowl. And a jug of Hartley water so he'll have familiar water on the road."

"Good," the woman nodded. "He'll be less likely to have a tummy upset from strange water."

All too soon, it was time for Dinnie and his new mom to leave. Karen leaned against her Tree and watched them drive away. Another one of her kids had left for a new life.

"Now we are four," Karen told Brian. The young'uns, Ferry and Heck, and the old'uns, Brian who mostly slept, and Bridgit who almost wasn't there.

Chapter 12

Karen couldn't stand staying in her house a moment longer. She looked at her dogs. Three of them looked back at her. Bridgit needed the bonding time, but Ferry and Heck needed the exercise. She put Brian and Bridgit in their crates, grabbed two leashes and called Ferry and Heck. "We are going to the park," she told them. "We are going to have a good time. We are not going to be gloomy."

Karen loved walking her dogs in the park. They met lots of people. Her dogs loved meeting new people, especially children. What would it be like, Karen thought, to be a toddler in a stroller and come up to a huge dog who towered over you? It would probably be like meeting an elephant. But elephants didn't drool. Did they?

"Hello, Karen Matheson!"

She turned around. The dogs saw him before she did. They wagged their tails and opened their mouths in wide welcoming grins. "Hello, Steve Songer," she said. He wore his short running shorts and a gray T-shirt. *Marines* splashed across the front along with sweat.

"Good time of day for a run," she said.

"Yes. Not as nice as morning, but it'll do." He mushed over her dogs.

"Low humidity today." What was she doing talking about the weather? "How is your dog?"

"He's still at the vet's, but he's doing better. They said they expected him to be able to come home on Monday." He looked up at her. "Which two are these?"

"This is Ferry and this is Heck. Brian is too old to walk much at all, and Bridgit is—" What was Bridgit? Too frail? Too close to dead? "I don't think Bridgit is up to it." No need to explain her dogs to him. She would talk to him, because she was a polite person. But she wouldn't like him. And she most certainly would not think of whipped cream.

He walked the park paths with them. They talked about the breed-specific legislation the city was trying to pass. He told her about his visit to the city. She chuckled at his description of the lady with the rhinestone glasses. He told her he and Lennox would be in her CGC class.

"Where did you get Lennox?" she asked in a deliberately casual voice.

"My sister." He sounded slightly amused, as if he knew exactly what she was asking and chose to not be defensive. "My parents have shown Am Staffs for about twenty years. Lennox is from their line. His parents and grandparents and great grandparents and on and on and on are all AKC champions."

"Oh." She felt properly chastened. "Do you show him?"

"No. I wanted him for a companion. He's neutered," he added.

"Oh," she said again. Talking about neutering wasn't any reason for her to feel suddenly flushed. Dog people often discussed their dogs' testicles, or lack of them. No one got all hot and bothered about it. It was a matter of fact. Then why did she feel warm?

"End of the road," Steve said. Sure enough, they had gone full circle and were back at the parking lot. He walked her to her car. "I enjoyed your company."

"I enjoyed your company, too." She said it to be polite. She was surprised it was the truth. "I'll see you Thursday at class."

That night Karen dreamed of tall men boxing the city idiots.

* * *

Monday morning the vet clinic called him to say Lennox could come home. He said he would be there in two minutes. Lennox was ecstatic to see him.

"C'mon, go ahead let it show. You're just as ecstatic to see him," Jessie whispered with a grin. "I guess dogs are more secure about their manly image than people are."

Dr. Winthrop told him to keep a close watch to make sure Lennox was eating, drinking and wasn't having stomach upsets, the whole healthy dog routine. She said it would probably be fine to take him to the gym for the afternoon.

Jessie walked out with him to his car. "I've been thinking. The world needs to know what great dogs Am Staffs are. I decided you should write a book about them."

"What? Book?" He opened the door and Lennox hopped in.

"Yeah. You know. Famous Am Staffs throughout history. Am Staffs of famous people. And pit bulls. Did you know Bernadette Peters has a pit bull? And Helen Keller? Oh. And Teddy Roosevelt had a pit bull when he was in the White House. Just think. America's First Dog was a pit bull. And James Earl Jones has a pit mix. Darth Vader with a pit bull." She hummed the ominous theme music from *Star Wars*. "There was this pit bull named Stubby who was the most decorated dog in World War One. I think it could be a great book. A guaranteed best-seller."

"You write it." He walked around to the driver's door. Jessie followed.

"I don't own an Am Staff. I have an Irish wolfhound puppy. They don't suffer from the same negative PR. People already know how wonderful *they* are."

He tried to let her down gently. "Jessie, I'm sure it's a wonderful idea, but a wonderful idea would need a wonderful writer. I'm not a writer." He reached for the door handle.

"You could have it ghostwritten."

A niggle of suspicion wormed its way into his mind. He let go of the car door handle. "I suppose you just happen to know someone to do this."

"Yes, I do. Karen Matheson. She could do it. I mean, she never wrote a book, but she wrote a dissertation."

"I don't think a book and a dissertation are the same thing."

"Besides, she knows dogs inside and out. And if we approached her in such a way to make her think we needed her help—I know she'd do it."

"You've known her a long time." He suddenly realized she had maneuvered so she was between him and his car. How had she managed that?

"Most of my life. She always thinks she has to be the one to take care of everybody," Jessie said. "You know, like Atlas holding the world on his shoulders. It must get awfully heavy."

"Why doesn't she let it drop?"

"Because she couldn't face herself if she did and something bad happened. She went straight from carefree teenager to teenage single mother without any intervening life. She had scholarships to all sorts of colleges. Didn't go. Katie was born and her mom baby-sat while Karen went to the community college. Then she drove back and forth to Kent, and went to Indiana for grad school. By then Katie was old enough for daycare. Karen became a bona fide head shrinker and came back to Hartley to shrink the heads of local young people. That's her life. The head thing and rescuing dogs. And Katie, of course, but now Katie's gone." She eyed him. "I think she has a savior complex. I also think someone needs to save her once in a while."

Steve caught her look. "Me? Oh no. I'm no savior."

Jessie nodded. "Better than that. You're a warrior."

"Ex-warrior."

"Marine. Marines don't quit until their mission is complete."

"This is not my mission."

"Yes. It is. You tell me you're gonna stand there and let a woman carry around the world? If your masculine pride doesn't get you, then call it the return of a favor. M'liss and I saved Lennox's life. Course, we'd've saved his life no matter what because that's what vets do. And Karen said she'd evaluate Lennox and write a report to the city if you needed it, and she's teaching the CGC class and that class was filled and I squeezed you into it. This class will help Lennox stay in Hartley. As I see it, you owe some favors here."

"Wait a minute. We started out talking about writing a book, and now we're talking about the favors I owe you?"

"Yeah, well, conversations sometimes evolve."

He chuckled. "You're a trip, Jessie. I like you, but I'll have to decline both your offer to write a book, and your request to save your friend."

She looked downcast, but only for a brief moment. "This is Katie's mom I'm asking you to save."

"I don't go around saving people."

"Not people. Katie's mother. Katie who you helped get into shape so she could go into the Marines and leave her mother all alone. Don't you feel the least little bit responsible to make sure she's okay?" Her expression turned crafty. "You could write to Katie and tell her you'd visited with her mom and her mom was fine, so Katie didn't have to worry. I know that would take a load off Katie's mind. She is worried about her mother, you know. And you told me yourself that Katie has enough to worry about just being at boot camp."

Katie had told him she was worried about her mother. "You do have a point." Jessie also knew how to set up a combination, a couple of jabs followed by an unexpected body shot. And the way she had moved and maneuvered without his knowing . . . "Say, Jessie, did you ever think about taking up boxing?"

"Nah, I don't like to be hit. Besides, I'm more the mouthy-commentator type. You know. The guy who stands ringside and makes snide remarks about what's going on in the ring, and what the boxers could do better, what the ref doesn't see, and then after the fight he gets in the ring and asks the loser, 'When did you know you were beaten?' But, hey, I better get back to work now. I'll talk to you later. Bye, sweet Lennox. I'll miss you." She blew his dog a kiss then trotted back to the clinic where she waved one last time before she entered the door.

That afternoon, when the exercise ladies arrived for their class, they gushed over Lennox. Lennox gushed back. One lady asked Steve, "Have you heard from Katie?"

"Not yet," he said. "The first week is a busy one."

"When you write to her, tell her we all asked about her," the lady said. "She was a great addition to our class. So young. So pretty. Looks just like her mom did when her mom was young."

"Her mom is still pretty," another lady put in. "Do you know Katie's mom, Steve?"

"I've met her." He didn't want to go there.

"Don't you think Katie looks like her?"

He *really* didn't want to go there. "I guess so. I've never thought about it."

The lady nodded. "You take a good look at Karen the next time you see her. She looks exactly like Katie. Just as pretty. She used to baby-sit for my kids when she was in high school. My kids loved her."

Steve glanced at the clock. "It's time for class, ladies. Mary Lou will be there in a second."

"She was so good with the kids," another lady said. "A credit to our town."

No matter how he tried to stow it, that conversation stayed with him for the rest of the day. Was Karen Matheson pretty? No, he thought, not pretty. Katie was pretty. Karen was . . . Karen was . . . he didn't know what Karen was. He didn't want to know.

"C'mon Lennox," he said at last. "Let's go home and call your Auntie May and tell her you're fine and dandy."

That afternoon, Karen saw Candy again.

"I want to have the baby and give her up for adoption." The young girl's expression was earnest. Karen believed her.

"What about the baby's father?"

"He doesn't care. I think he's sort of relieved because he won't have to deal with her. His parents are relieved because he can go to college and won't be stuck paying child support for the rest of his life." She seemed restless, inclined to fidget.

"How does that make you feel, that he's relieved?"

"I guess I figured out he's not as great as I used to think he was." A single tear rolled down her cheek. "I figure if this is the way he feels about it, then he'd be a crummy father. I don't want my baby to have a crummy father. My baby deserves better."

Karen wondered how she'd have dealt with her own pregnancy if Katie's father had lived down the street. She remembered one night when she was home alone, she screamed out loud, "If you don't want me, then I don't want you to have any part of my baby!" If her parents had not been supportive, Karen wondered, would she have been able to give Katie up? "Have you talked to your parents about this?"

"No. But I've talked to my baby. And she is the one who really matters."

Steve unlocked his car door and opened it. Lennox hopped in. "Wait a minute, boy, let me open the windows first." His car was as hot as an outdoor fight at noon in a Las Vegas August. Sometimes those rings, with all the television lights, got up over one hundred and ten degrees. Not good fighting weather.

"Steve!" He looked up to see Jessie across the street. She waved at him. "Hold on!" She looked both ways before crossing at a trot. "I'm glad I caught you before you left for the day. You have to know something about Karen," Jessie said. "She has this antiviolence stance that she takes to a ridiculous level. Or to a level of ridiculousness." Jessie bent down to gush over Lennox.

Steve frowned. "Why?"

Jessie sighed a big one. "The short answer is that she believes any conflict can be resolved by negotiation. The long answer is that—and this is only my opinion and I'm not the brain shrinker, but Sally and M'liss agree—she's trying to be the person she thinks her mother wants her to be. She wants her mother's approval." Jessie shook her head. "Thing is, she's always had her mother's approval. Her mom is the most amazingly *accepting* person I've ever known in my whole life. I swear she was a nun in a former life."

"Some nuns aren't accepting," Steve said with a grin.

"The best ones are." Jessie shot him a mock glare. "So here's Karen who has this dumb idea that the best way she can have her mother's approval is if she's nonviolent, because Susannah and Lloyd were old hippies. Still are. In Karen's mind this means she won't even watch movies she thinks are violent. She hasn't even seen half of Mel's movies!"

"Sacrilege," Steve chuckled.

"I'm serious. We're talking about Mel Gibson. Last January, when we celebrated Mel's birthday, we only watched his peaceful movies." She made a face. "Some of his best work is in *Conspiracy Theory*. And Karen hasn't ever seen it! It's like she's made up her mind about this one thing, and then refused to ever think about it again, like she has psychosclerosis, or something."

"Psycho—what?"

"Psychosclerosis. Hardening of the attitude."

He chuckled. "Lots of people have hardened attitudes."

"But she usually doesn't. In fact, she tends to analyze everything down to the micro level, which can get annoying.

But this peace thing, no. Her mind is made up. It negates the possibility of change in one's attitudes based on one's life experiences. I mean, what's the point of having life experiences if you don't let them affect the way you look at the world? That's how we grow."

"I never knew you were so philosophical."

"Yeah, well, I usually don't talk about these kinds of things. Most people aren't interested. Most people make up their minds and then forget to do reality checks from time to time." She brightened. "Hey, maybe that's my purpose in life. To be the thorn in people's sides to make them check their realities."

He took Lennox into his backyard for an hour-long game of tennis-ball chase. Lennox did the chasing. Finally, when Steve had had enough, he walked down to the street to bring in the mail. He found a letter from Katie.

Dear Steve,

I'm here and it's even more horrible than I thought it would be. And I'm still in what they call the Formation Week. We're being assessed and tested. I have been weighed, I have been measured, and I have not been found wanting. Next week, they say, the fun will really start. You'd be proud of me—I passed the IST with flying colors. A couple of girls were sent to a separate platoon where they'll stay until they can pass. I'd hate that. Thanks for teaching me to box. I know it's helped get me in shape. Thanks for your letters. You don't know what they mean to me. I haven't heard from my mom yet. I hope she's okay. Take care of Lennox.

Katie

What was wrong with Karen Matheson? How could she not write a letter to her daughter? Didn't she realize? Obviously not. Everyone said she was so in tune with her dogs, how could she not have the slightest clue about her daughter? He wrote a short letter to Katie that night, told her he and Lennox were fine, that he'd tape all the important fights for her to see later. He told her what was happening at the gym, and Mary Lou wanted Katie to know she was thinking about her, as did everyone else, including the women in the exercise class. He sent her an article clipped from *The Ring* about the first Ward Gatti fight, and a snapshot of Lennox.

Chapter 13

Dear Mom,

   The weather here sucks. Parris Island has lots of mist early in the morning and when the sun comes up it turns into gross humidity. It's like breathing in a sponge. They wake us up very early in the morning to run. It is not optional. The DI's say it's a motivational run. I don't mind. We ran a mile and a half the other day. I thought of that really old song "One Misty Moisty Morning" from that really old record of Grandma's. (Don't you dare name a dog Moisty! Ferry's name is bad enough—even if I do like the song.) So I hummed it to myself while I ran. At least until one of the DI's started calling cadence. You know how noisy it is at night, with all the dogs snoring? You ought to be here. Our squadbay is this great big room and there are all these bunk beds, called racks, and forty girls breathing at night. But it's not the same. I miss the dogs breathing. We're always in a group. We never have any alone time and I miss that too. You always taught me people need time to process everything. We don't process here, we just yell "Yes ma'am!" and snap to do what we're told almost before they tell us what to do. Hugs and great big sloppy kisses to all the dogs, and a specially big hug to Brian. I miss them and I miss you too.

Love,
Katie

Karen pressed the letter to her heart. "I love you too, Katie," she whispered. She reached to the thin chain around her neck and found Katie's pendant. She rubbed the silver between her fingers and thumb. "I miss you, too."

She sat down at her computer. *Dear Katie*, she began. *We're all fine*. But then she heard the kitchen door slam. Ferry, she thought. She went to check.

Sure enough, Ferry had let herself outside. "Someday," Karen told her, "I'm going to teach you how to read, and then your life will really change."

Karen drove down the bumpy country road to the pole barn that was dog school. She unlocked the door and propped it open. She arranged fifteen chairs in a circle at one end. The ancient file-cabinet drawer screeched in protest as she pulled it open to gather fifteen sets of handouts. One set on each chair. She looked around the large space. She was ready. All she needed was her students.

First to arrive was a young woman with a miniature poodle, followed by a second young woman with some sort of mix. Then Steve Songer and Lennox. Karen had never seen the Am Staff up close. She went to meet them inside the door. "Hello," she said to Steve. Then she turned her attention to the dog. "Lennox, I assume? I'm Katie's mom."

Lennox gave her an enthusiastic greeting. She stroked him under his chin for a moment while she looked him quickly over. She expected a harsh, stiff coat. Instead, it was smooth and soft. There was nothing soft about his muscles, though. This was a powerful dog. He yawned. She looked at his teeth. She thought of Bridgit. She turned away.

"How's he feeling?" she asked.

"Fine. Back to his own self."

"Good. Well, have a seat. Class will begin in a few minutes."

He glanced through the handouts while he waited. Rules for dog school, an introduction to the Canine Good Citizen classes and a description of the test. Out of the corner of his eye he saw a woman with a fluffy dog eyeing Lennox. She looked nervous. She inched her dog further away from him. Lennox didn't bother to look at that fluffy dog. Steve glanced around the group. The chairs on either side of him were empty. Evidently it wasn't just the fluffy-dog lady who was nervous about Lennox. Steve sighed. He was used to this segregation. He reached out to stroke Lennox's silky head. Lennox thwacked his tail on the floor. Then an elderly man with a setter sat down in the seat next to Steve. Lennox and the setter sniffed at each other. Lennox decided the setter wasn't interesting.

"Canine Good Citizen," Karen told the class, "is a test to evaluate your dog's ability to behave in a socially acceptable manner. Whether he's in a crowd of people or other dogs, he must behave appropriately. It is our responsibility, as the human part of the team, to help our dogs learn that behavior. This class is designed to teach you to teach your dog the basic behaviors he needs to be a Canine Good Citizen. So. Tonight we will have a very brief introduction to doggy psych."

Right now, Steve thought, Katie, at boot camp, was probably having an introduction to the M16. For a moment his mind wandered back many years. *This is my rifle*, the litany came rushing to him. Katie would learn this litany, as he had learned it many years ago, and as recruits in the future would learn it. *There are many like it, but this one is mine.*

"There are many, many dogs in the world," Karen said, "and though they may look alike, may have similarities, each dog, like each human, is an individual."

My rifle is my best friend. It is my life. I must master it as I must master my life. My rifle, without me, is useless. Without my rifle, I am useless. I must fire my rifle true. I must shoot straighter than my enemy who is trying to kill me. I must shoot him before he shoots me. I will . . . My rifle and myself know that what counts in this war is not the rounds we fire, the noise of our burst, nor the smoke we make. We know that it is the hits that count. We will hit . . . My rifle is human, even as I, because it is my life.

"Your dog is ready and willing to be your best friend. Your dog is willing to give his life for you. We, as responsible dog owners, have an obligation to learn how our dog's mind works—and each dog has a unique little doggy brain—so we can know how to best teach him, and not confuse him. Many dogs don't do what their people want them to do, not because they are disobedient, or contrary, but because we have confused them. We are also responsible for their health and well-being. Dogs are not little humans in furry coats, they are an entirely different species. One of the many unique things about dogs is their ability to accept us as their brothers. As a matter of fact, dogs think we *are* their brothers. They think we're funny-looking dogs."

Thus, I will learn it as a brother. I will learn its weaknesses, its strength, its parts, its accessories, its sights and its barrel. I will ever guard it against the ravages of weather and damage as I will ever guard my legs, my arms, my eyes and my heart against damage. I will keep my rifle clean and ready. We will become part of each other. We will . . . Before God, I swear this creed. My rifle and myself are the defenders of my country. We are the masters of our enemy. We are the saviors of my life. So be it, until there is no enemy, but peace!

Somehow Steve thought Karen Matheson would not appreciate him comparing dogs to an M16. She didn't seem to have much of a sense of humor when it came to dogs. Or when it came to her daughter. Well, after class, he'd stick around and tell her some things about her daughter, like how her daughter needed letters from her. She probably wouldn't like it, but he didn't much care. He wasn't doing it for her, he was doing it for Katie. He liked Katie. Hell, he respected Katie. She had set out to do a seriously tough thing, and he would not let her be distracted from it because she was worried about how her mother was reacting.

Steve watched Karen move about the large class area. She moved with the same natural grace Katie did; one movement flowed into the next, smooth and serene. He liked watching her move.

After class the pole barn was noisy and bustling with people and dogs. The instructor for the next class was gathering his students. Steve asked Karen if she would talk with him for a moment.

They went outside into the evening. The cool air felt good after the heat of the building. Lennox decided his new mission was to examine every speck of the strip of grass between the barn and the parking lot. His nose was up to the job. Karen leaned against the side of the pole barn. "What can I help you with?"

"Not me," he said, "your daughter. Katie needs you to write to her."

She visibly bristled. She covered it well, though. "Thank you for your concern. I know you helped Katie prepare for boot camp. I know she appreciated it."

"I don't think you understand what letters from home mean to recruits in boot camp."

"Can't she call?"

He laughed shortly. "No. She can't call. We're talking about the Marine Corps, here, not the Army."

"Oh. I didn't know that. I guess . . . I don't know why I'm telling you this. I started writing a letter to her. I guess I wasn't sure what to say."

"Tell her anything. She won't care what you say, as long as you send her letters. Every day. Every single day. Tell her what you had for breakfast, tell her how the flowers are grow-ing, tell her what you watched on television, or what the dogs did. But tell her. Let her know you think of her everyday, you wonder how she's doing, what she's learning. Let her know home is still home. Her letters to you will probably be short. She won't have much time to write, so don't expect long de-scriptions of everything. It's not because she doesn't want to share things with you; she doesn't have the time."

She stared at the parking lot and absently reached for the pendant around her neck to worry. He'd seen Katie do the same thing many times. He followed a sudden impulse and reached out and tipped up her chin. His gaze captured hers and would not let go. "I don't care what you think of the Ma-rine Corps, it doesn't matter. The Corps doesn't need your approval. The Marines who have come before, and will come after, do not care what you think."

There was a time to yell at recruits and a time to build them up. Karen was like a raw recruit, beginning to learn about the Corps. He had yelled at her, metaphorically speaking, now it was time to build her up. He took a breath and lowered the in-tensity of his voice, gentled it. "Katie has set out to do the most difficult thing she will ever do in her whole life. She wants to do this. She needs to do this. She knows you don't approve. As much as she loves you, her desire to do this, to become a Marine, is stronger than her need for your approval. I know you love your daughter. Boot camp is damn hard. Don't make it harder for her."

"I never had any intention of making it harder for her."

"Then write to her. Every day."

For a moment he thought she was going to argue with him, but instead she looked off into the distance and sighed softly. "Thanks," she said in a different tone of voice. "Thanks for telling me."

* * *

That night, Karen sat down at her computer and cleared off the solitaire game. She opened her word processor and stared at the blinking cursor. She stared. The cursor blinked. This letter was too important to be impersonal. She turned off the computer and pulled out pen and paper. Tell her everything and anything, Steve said. So she wrote deep into the night, to the sound of the breathing of all the dogs. She wrote about the weather; how Grandpa was excited about his model-airplane club's upcoming reenactment of World War I; about Dinnie's new mom; how Bridgit's coat was growing back. She wrote about Katie's shawl, and about the plans for the new downtown mall, *which actually seem to be moving along on schedule. A new gallery, called ArtOhio opened last week. They sell only things made by people who live in Ohio. You remember those amazing art dolls we saw at Hartley Days? The other day I met the woman who makes them. Some of her dolls are in that gallery. They're amazing. But they are not nearly as amazing as you. I love you more than you can ever imagine. Mom.*

In the morning, she kept a closer than usual watch out the window until she saw him jogging down the street with his dog. She left the window to Theresa and Vicky. She went outside, to stand on her porch. "Hi!" she called.

He turned, saw her, looked for traffic and he and Lennox loped across the street to stand at the bottom step. "Hi."

"Um. Hi." She bent down to pet Lennox. "I wanted to thank you. For, you know, talking to me last night."

He raised his eyebrows.

"I wanted to tell you, I wrote her a letter last night. Four pages. And I stuck in a picture of the dogs. I mailed it this morning. This afternoon I'm going to stop off at Abernathy's and pick up some Oreos to send."

"Great. I'm glad. But no Oreos."

She frowned. "Why not? She loves Oreos."

"They won't let her have them."

"Oreos are subversive?"

"For recruits in boot camp?" He nodded. "Yeah. They're subversive."

"Does Nabisco know?"

He chuckled. "Oreos are fine, for anywhere but boot camp."

Vicky opened the door to look out. She ogled Steve's legs. "Hello," she said.

"Hello," Steve said with a grin.

"You gonna be long?" she asked Karen, keeping her eyes on Steve's legs. "You have a phone call."

Karen turned to Steve. "I've gotta go. Anyway, thanks."

"Any time." He turned and, followed by his dog, loped back across the street.

"Bye, Lennox," she called after them.

"I didn't mean to run the man off," Vicky said.

"You didn't."

"But I'm glad I did. Look at his buns!"

Chapter 14

Katie's note to him was short and to the point. *As cornermen, drill instructors suck. K.*

He chuckled. Yeah, he thought, they did suck. He found a pen and paper in his desk. *I said they'd be in your corner, not be your cornermen. Besides, at this point, you're supposed to think they suck. Later on you'll figure out they're on your side.* He checked his calendar. Let's see. Katie had finished formation week, and her first week of classes. *How did you like pugil sticks? Boxing should have helped you there, helped you be quick and agile.* He thought for a moment. *Lennox and I are taking a CGC class. Your mom is teaching. We all missed you last night for Friday Night Fights. Everyone says hi and remember to keep your hands up. Steve.*

Sunday morning, after she combed a gargantuan pile of dog hair out of Ferry's thick coat and swept it up into a trash bag, she sat down at her computer to write a letter to her daughter. She reached down and pulled a small clump of dog hair out of the trash. She twisted it into something slightly resembling a short piece of yarn. She stuck it in the letter. *The Marine Corps cooks probably don't serve dog hair as a condiment so I'm sending you some to remind you of home.*

She addressed the envelope and put a stamp on it. She

stuck it in her purse so she'd remember to mail it first thing in the morning.

The phone rang. "It's me," Jessie said. "After all that rain the streets are wet and clean. You and I are taking the dogs for a walk. I'll pick you up in about fifteen minutes. Be ready."

Karen didn't have anything else to do, so why not? Brian couldn't walk very far anymore, and Bridgit . . . She looked into Bridgit's eyes. Bridgit didn't appear to be home. "I don't think you're ready for a good walk yet," she told the dog. "Especially not with Jessie and Sagan. We'll go walk by ourselves. Later this afternoon when there's not a lot of commotion. I promise." Bridgit didn't seem to care one way or another. Karen shut her in her crate. "I wish you'd respond," she said. "You really are safe here. Nothing to be afraid of." Bridgit turned around and settled down with her back to Karen.

With a heavy heart, Karen pulled on her socks and shoes and leashed Ferry and Heck. "Guard the house!" she called to Brian and Bridgit.

Outside, Jessie stood hands on hips, staring up at Karen's Tree. "This tree needs to come down. It's too old to be safe. Look at that branch up there. It's mostly dead and could fall on your house. One of the dogs could get hurt."

"The dog room is in the back of the house."

"It's oak, isn't it? I bet Alex would cut it down for you. I bet he'd do it for free if you let him have the wood to play with."

"I like my Tree."

"Karen, it's a tree, not a dog. You can like it all you want, but it's not safe to leave it there. It's lived its life. I'm sure you gave it a good life. Now it's dangerous. Let it go."

"I know. But I'm not ready to let go of my Tree on top of everything else."

"Speaking of ready," Jessie reached down to give Ferry a hug. "This girl is ready to go see the sights, aren't you? Yes, Heck, you get a hug, too. Watch it, don't step on Sagan. She's an itty-bitty baby, you know."

Karen chuckled. Sagan at five months old was as tall as the Newfs, even though the Irish wolfhound puppy only carried a fraction of their weight. "She'll tower over you guys soon. Hey, Karen, speaking of towering. What do you think of Lennox? Isn't he a cool dog?"

"I guess so."

"And isn't Steve a really cool guy?"

Karen stopped abruptly and faced her friend. "Jessica Virginia Albright. Don't go around here trying to scrape up some sort of relationship between Steve Songer and me. I know the way your mind works. Don't do it. There is no future in it. No possible future."

"What makes you so sure?"

"I have Bridgit. He has Lennox."

"Sometimes twains meet."

"Usually they don't. That's why they're twains."

That night, taking the dogs out one last time, Karen looked up at the full moon sailing across the sky. That same moon was shining on her daughter, far away, where she was turning into a strange thing called a Marine. The same moon was shining on a house across the street where Steve Songer lived. Karen wondered if he lived with someone, other than Lennox. She told herself she didn't care. She told herself she was not interested in anyone who thought boxing was a great thing—especially not after that someone helped her daughter leave to go be a Marine.

How could Katie do this to her? Violence was never a viable option. Karen had taught Katie this. Karen believed this in the very depths of her being. Karen sometimes saw aftershocks of violence. It was not pretty. Violence was never pretty. In fact, it was as ugly as anything on earth. Visions of the Iraqi war, televised as it happened, in living color, flashed through her mind. Katie was going to support that? Maybe be part of that? Karen felt herself grow so angry she wanted to scream. She clenched her fists and the muscles in her face. Ferry and Heck looked at her uncertainly. "It's okay," she told them, forcing herself to relax. "It's okay." How had she sunk so low as to lie to the dogs?

Monday Karen went home for lunch, took the dogs out, then Bridgit separately. She had a zippy bag ready. On her way back to work she stopped at the clinic to drop the sample off. Jessie called that afternoon to tell her the evil round-wormies had been annihilated and Beautiful Bridgit was wormless and germless.

Candy came that afternoon. After she hugged Bridgit, she told Karen about her plans to have the baby and give her up for adoption. She had also told her parents. As usual, she said, they pretended her pregnancy didn't exist. "Finally, I got in their faces and made them look at me. Made them listen to me."

"What happened?"

"My dad got all stone-faced and my mother cried. But in the end, they didn't tell me no. It wouldn't really have mattered if they had, because this is what I'm going to do. But if they'd been impossible about it, I'm not sure where I'd have gone. At least, this way, I know I have a place to live until my baby is born."

"What about after?"

"My baby will go off to spend the rest of her life with a total stranger." Candy sounded as if she'd memorized the words and repeated them over and over like a litany. "I'll never see her again and even though I know it's the best thing for her, I know I'll never forget her. I know I have to find something to do with the rest of my life, other than think about my baby. I don't know what I could do."

Karen was glad to see Candy thought of her baby as an

individual person rather than an object. "Let's talk about how to figure out what you would like to do with your life."

"What I want to figure out," Candy said, "is how to find some way to let my baby know that I loved her. I mean, I know she'll love her mother, the woman who adopts her, but I want her to know that I loved her too. That I didn't give her up because I didn't want her." Candy pressed her face against Bridgit. "Will you help me figure that out, too?"

"Yes."

Candy's request was on Karen's mind all afternoon. Finally, she had an idea. Her last appointment of the day cancelled, so she left work early. "We're going to go visit someone," she told Bridgit.

They walked one block down and two over to the old renovated house that held The Wilde Woman's Wool. She knocked on the door. "Mrs. Wilde? Connie? It's Karen Matheson. I have a dog with me."

"Well come on in," Connie Wilde answered. "Mom's home at the farm today. We had trouble with a lamb so she stayed home to play lamb nurse . . ." Her voice wandered off as she caught sight of Bridgit.

Karen mentally braced herself for the questions and comments always raised by Bridgit's appearance, but now the questions and comments didn't come. The woman and the dog looked into each other's eyes. Bridgit gave a great shuddering sigh and walked forward to lean against Connie Wilde.

"Hello, my beauty." Connie stooped down to look into the dog's eyes. "Hello, my sweet."

"This is Bridgit," Karen said.

Connie's whole being seemed focused on Bridgit. "Your mom mentioned you had a new rescue dog, but she didn't tell us her name. Bridgit is the patron saint of weavers and knitters, you know."

"No, I didn't know. She's named after a song called 'Bridgit O'Malley.'" She hadn't been in the yarn shop for many years, but some things never changed. The Wilde Woman's Wool was one of them. The highly polished hardwood floor reflected the myriad colors of the yarns spilling out of the floor-to-near-ceiling bins. Sweaters and shawls and socks crowded the room, all hand-knit, of every color and size and persuasion and bursting with pattern and texture, begging to be touched, rubbed against a cheek. Comfy chairs arranged around a fireplace invited all comers to sit and knit and bring chaos into order.

"Go ahead," Connie said, "look around. Bridgit is fine with me, aren't you girl?"

Amazingly enough, Bridgit did look fine. Maybe she was coming out of her depression.

Karen wandered around the shop, touching the yarns, drinking in the colors and textures. That wool over there would be perfect for a hat for the Boogaloo, she thought. Baby hats were simple and quick to knit. She reached out to touch it. Yes, it was as soft as it looked, soft as the Boogaloo's baby skin. She picked up a skein and carried it over to the table of patterns. Baby hat, baby hat, baby hat, there. She found a pattern for a baby hat. She scanned the instructions. Yes, she could knit this pattern. She looked through the needle rack.

"Connie Wilde, tell your mom her shop is still dangerous!" she said with a grin as she brought her selections to the front of the store.

"Only to those with a knitter's soul," she answered with a twinkle in her eye. Bridgit still leaned against the woman. The woman still ran her fingers over Bridgit's ears. "How is the shawl for Katie coming along?"

"Fine. Please thank your mom for sending along the pattern. I don't think I'd have been able to remember it."

"You probably would have. It's so simple."

"But it's been so long since I made my last pi shawl."

"Your fingers would have remembered."

"I had forgotten how peaceful knitting is. Connie, I know a young girl who might like to learn how to knit. If I brought her by next Monday afternoon, do you think your mom would be able to start her off?"

"Of course. Mom would love it. You know how she is about teaching people to knit. Make sure you bring Bridgit with you. It's lovely to have a dog in the shop again."

"Mom told me about Rowan. I'm sorry."

"Thank you." Connie's eyes glistened and she gave Bridgit one more gentle ear rub. "We love them dearly, but they don't live forever."

Karen thought of Brian. "No, they don't."

Dear Steve,

We all have rifles. There are many rifles, but this one is mine. It's cool. We haven't learned to shoot them yet, but we clean them. Every single day. I like keeping my rifle clean and free from rust. They say rust is a big problem here because of the humidity. We take our rifles everywhere we go and at night, we hang them on our bunks, pointing down. We don't really sleep with them in our beds—that would be sort of weird. Yesterday one recruit wasn't carrying her rifle correctly, so the drill instructor made us all stand in the sand pits— they look like these great big huge kitty-litter boxes in the yard outside the squadbay—and she made us hold our rifles in front of us and do arm curls. And the sand fleas were nasty. I hate sand fleas. They bite and itch and I have all these spots all over my legs from being bitten. And we couldn't stop doing the curls to scratch or swat the sand fleas or the DI would yell at us and we'd have to do more of them. We have this one drill instructor, Sergeant Kimball, and she's really nasty. She seems to really enjoy making us miserable. But it's strange. When we got our rifles and were learning how to take them apart and clean them and then how to hold them properly and stuff, I began to feel like a real Marine. I know I'm only a wormy recruit, not worthy of being in Sergeant Kimball's Corps, at least that's what she yells at us, but I will be. By the time I'm through with her, I'll be a real Marine. I keep telling myself this all the time she's yelling. Where did she ever find her vocal cords? She can yell at us all day and all night and still be yelling the next morning. I hope she doesn't have kids. I really hope she doesn't have dogs!

Katie

Karen received a letter from Dinnie.

Dear Karen,
My new mom says I'm the best dog in the world. I found the closet where she keeps her winter boots. She said they didn't fit anymore anyway so it was a good thing I found them because it gave her an excuse to buy a new pair. We went to the beach. Lake Erie is big. I liked to play in the waves. I came home wet and full of sand. My mom spent all night brushing the sand out. She bought a new slicker brush just for me. I sleep with Katie's slipper. I sleep on the rug next to my new mom's bed. I miss you and the other dogs, but I am very happy with my new mom. She hugs me a lot and says she's happy with me too. Love Dinnie Burns Jackson. P.S. Here are pictures of me at the beach. I like my sunglasses. I am one cool dude.

Karen put the pictures on her refrigerator. She put the letter in her treasure box.

Chapter 15

"Tonight," Karen said at dog class, "we are going to continue to work on 'sit,' 'down,' 'stand,' and we will introduce the 'stay.' We are also going to begin coming when called. Big rule. Never forget this rule. Every time you call your dog and your dog comes—every time, not every other, but every time—you will tell your dog he's terrific. You will reward your dog—not necessarily with food. You must become like Mr. Pavlov and your dog like his dogs. You call, your dog comes, drooling, knowing he will receive a reward, then you give your dog his reward. Remember that this does not have to be food. In fact, it shouldn't be because your dog will quickly become overweight. Do not ever call your dog to punish him. If you do you will break your dog's trust."

After class, Karen asked Steve if he would wait. She raced through finishing her teacher chores and went to meet him outside. She asked him what else she could and should not send Katie.

"Don't send her food. Or candy. Or books. She's not in a college dorm, and any food you send her will be taken away. Send her pictures."

"Pictures?"

"You know," he said with a grin. For an instant he looked charming. "Pictures, taken with a camera. Pictures of the dogs, of you. Send her newspaper clippings."

She nodded. "I can do that."

He glanced at his watch. "I'm going to take Lennox for a walk in the park. Would you like to join us?"

She decided she would like that.

They strolled around the lake, under the huge trees, walked for a mile along the new bike path.

"But why did she choose the Marines?" Karen asked.

"Is there something wrong with the Marines?"

She shrugged. "No. But she could have chosen the Army, or the Navy or the Air Force, or even the Coast Guard. What made her choose the Marines?"

"We're the best."

"You're not impartial."

"No. I'm not." He grinned. It made him look like an impudent little boy. "I think Katie wanted to challenge herself. Marines are tough. Maybe she wanted to be part of something that is bigger than the sum of its parts. You have to earn the right to be a Marine; it's not given to you. Boot camp is how you prove you're worthy. If you graduate, if you don't wash out, you are part of the Corps. You're a Marine for life. You're part of all the Marines who have gone before you, and all the Marines yet to come."

"You make it sound like a secret society."

"Not secret. But we are a society. Katie will always be one of us."

"Like a religion then."

"The Marines love ceremony. Wait till you go down for her graduation. It's really something. Row after row of brand new Marines in their brand new uniforms, bursting with pride. They arrived a bunch of unruly, undisciplined kids and they have been transformed into members of the United States Marine Corps."

"You sound as if this is all personal to you."

"It is. I was a drill instructor for several years."

"I didn't know that."

"No reason why you should."

Karen tried to imagine Steve Songer yelling as she imagined drill instructors yelled. She couldn't do it. Steve Songer was calm and collected. In complete control. Especially when he talked about the Corps. She wondered if he ever relaxed.

Saturday brought brisk chill air, full of the promise of rain. Karen slipped one of her mom-made wool sweaters on over her cotton turtleneck. She slid her feet into mom-made wool socks and then into her Birkenstock sandals. Ferry needed some one-on-one time.

"Let's go," she told the dog. "Park time, before it rains." Karen loaded the dog into her car and drove to the park. Ferry loved the park. As soon as she realized where they were, she snuffled in Karen's ear. Ferry saw children playing on the playground. Ferry wanted to play with the children, too. "No," Karen told her, "we're going over here, away from the playground." Ferry wanted to stay at the playground and play with all the children. Karen told her she was getting ideas above her station. Ferry hung her head in apology.

"We are going over to the paths," Karen told her. The same path where two weeks ago she'd seen Steve jogging. Of course, she wasn't here to look for Steve. She had no interest in him, except as a student in her dog class.

"Ferry, heel."

Ferry moved smartly along at her side. Karen stopped. Ferry stopped and settled down to sit. That sit was a little slow. Karen looked down at Ferry's eyes. Ferry gave her an expression of total innocence. Karen was not fooled. "You can do better than that," Karen said. "Let's do it again. Ferry, heel." This time, Ferry took a second longer to sit. Karen gave her a slight correction. "Ferry, heel." This time, when she stopped, Ferry sat immediately. "Good girl!" Karen said and gave her a piece of dried cat food. Ferry crunched it quickly.

"Hello!" It was Steve Songer. Today, in view of the chill, he wore sweatpants. Karen missed his shorts.

"Hello, there. How are you? Hi, Lennox. Ferry," she said to her dog, "this is Lennox." Karen held her breath, ready to move instantly at the least sign of aggression. The Newfoundland and the American Staffordshire sniffed each other, then Lennox turned away.

"He sure told her where she stands," Karen said, a nervous chuckle betraying her relaxing tension.

"He won't attack her," Steve said mildly.

"Oh. Of course he won't. I know that. He's a well-socialized dog." She felt herself babble.

"But the reputation of some distant cousins precedes him?"

"I'm sorry. I should know better. It was an emotional reaction, not a logical one."

"We're used to it. We won't take it personally."

She felt the need to explain. "Bridgit—you know, my rescue dog—she . . ." Melissa had promised Frank Schmedlapp. Bridgit was an illegal dog. Karen couldn't explain. Her voice trailed off into oblivion.

"I understand."

Her gaze was caught and held. Like a bird in a net, she thought, but somehow she believed he did understand.

"Look," he said, "it's starting to rain. I don't live far away. Why don't you come home with me for some hot chocolate."

Did she want to go there? Karen wondered. Did she want to take a step forward, a step closer to this man, this man who fascinated her, yet also was a warrior? What did she have to say to such a man? What did he have to say to her? War and peace were two sides of the coin. Two different sides. Different, she reminded herself firmly. They had nothing in common. She would politely decline.

"I'd love to," she said.

* * *

She followed his car the short distance to his neighborhood. His house stood on a corner lot, the yard surrounded by a six-foot tall redwood fence. The man evidently liked his privacy. He pulled into his garage, the big door slowly coming down after him. Karen parked in his driveway. She left Ferry in her car. "Most people do not appreciate a great big wet Newfoundland in their house," she told her dog. "He's a warmonger. We don't want to make him mad. Besides, I'm not staying long."

He stood in his doorway, holding the door open for her. He didn't look like a warmonger. He looked like a regular person. A very attractive regular person. In fact, she could easily imagine this person becoming her friend. She reminded herself they had nothing in common.

"Bring your dog," he called.

"She's wet."

"I have towels."

He didn't know what he was getting into, she thought. "Ferry, you have an official invitation. Let's go."

Ferry was willing. Together she and her dog went into the regular-looking house. Where did you think he would live? she asked herself, in an armed encampment?

Maybe he shouldn't have invited her to his house, he thought. He could have taken her out to the diner for hot chocolate. And even lunch. He'd asked her before he'd thought it through, before he'd considered all the angles. He'd have to be flexible. He would be ready to change his fight plan at a moment's notice. "Use this." He handed her a towel he'd grabbed from the hall linen closet.

"It'll be full of dog hair."

"It'll wash."

"We warned you." He watched her rub the dog's sides, and her back, and her legs and neck. Ferry closed her eyes in bliss. Sure enough, when she was finished, the towel was damp and covered with long, fine, black hairs. He tossed it down the basement stairs. "Laundry," he said.

"Good idea." She grinned at him. Suddenly, he realized the exercise-class ladies were right. Katie did look like her mom. But while Katie was pretty, Karen had developed into beautiful. And Karen had the body of a woman, not a girl. He liked Katie as a boxing student, he respected her for her heart and drive and determination. But Katie's mother . . . that was a left hook he had not seen coming. Katie's mom was something special. He didn't want to box with her, he wanted to touch her in a totally different way.

"Where's Lennox?" she asked.

He blinked. "In the backyard, running off some energy."

"In the rain?"

"He's an Am Staff. Rain is of little consequence to him." He gestured to the large window overlooking his back yard.

"What's he shoving around out there?" She moved closer to the window to peer out.

"An old bowling ball. Even he can't destroy that."

"He destroys things?"

"He's a Marine dog. The Marine Corps," he intoned. "When it absolutely must be destroyed overnight."

She blanched.

"That's a joke," he prompted. "It's from a bumper sticker. You're supposed to laugh."

"I didn't raise Katie to destroy things."

"Katie is her own person with her own ideas about life."

"She's my daughter."

"That doesn't mean she's your clone."

"I taught her to always look for alternatives to violence."

They glared at each other in a strange tableau, like fighters in the ring before the fight, he thought. Each trying to impress the other, out-psych the other, gain an advantage. Jessie had said Karen was a peace monger, but now, Karen Matheson was sure ready to fight for her beliefs. He looked at her more closely, breathing hard, her lips slightly parted. He felt a sudden and unexpected urge to kiss her. In her eyes he saw the instant she felt it too.

. . . maybe she'll be able to have her own life, Katie had told him. *You know. Meet some nice man and fall in love. Roses and chocolates and the whole thing. I don't think she's ever had that.* Jessie told him, *someone needs to save her once in a while.*

He was no savior. He was simply a retired Marine who lived with his dog in this small town and taught boxing. He didn't want complications. He didn't want serious personal relationships with anyone, let alone someone of the female type. A serious personal relationship with Karen Matheson— and it would be serious and personal—would be seriously dangerous. He didn't want . . .

"You said hot chocolate?"

He felt himself flush. "Yes." Hot chocolate. He took cover in the kitchen, while he heated milk and stirred chocolate syrup into two mugs.

"This is excellent!" she exclaimed.

"Thanks."

"Truly wonderful hot chocolate."

"My mother makes chocolate syrup every year."

Her eyes got wide. "My mother only makes socks. And sweaters and things."

He laughed. "Jessie thinks highly of your mother."

She laughed too. "I think highly of my mom as well. Do your folks live around here?"

"Up near Cleveland. Yours?"

"Right here in Hartley, Ohio. I grew up here. Did you grow up in Cleveland?"

He shook his head. "No. We moved around a lot when I was growing up. My folks settled in Cleveland around the time I went into the Corps."

He could see her do the mental math. She had an expressive face. "Was that when they started showing Am Staffs?"

"It was."

"What made them choose that breed?"

He shrugged. "Why did you choose Newfoundlands?"

"Because they're amazing," she said promptly. "And beautiful, and smart, and they were bred to rescue people so they're highly interactive dogs."

"Am Staffs are amazing," he told her. "And beautiful, and smart, and they were bred to work on farms and keep the kids safe while moms and dads worked in the fields. They are highly interactive dogs."

She looked at her big black dog dozing at her feet. Then she looked out the window where Lennox, in the rain, sill pursued his bowling ball. Finally she returned her gaze to his. When she spoke her voice was thoughtful.

"I guess people love the same things in their dogs, don't they?"

"I guess so."

"I don't have much experience with Am Staffs. In fact, I've never known one before. They aren't common around here. At least if they are around here, they don't often show up in dog school." She bit her lower lip. "Do you have pictures of Lennox's parents?"

"In my study. Come on."

He opened the door to his study and turned on the light. He called it his study, but it was rarely used.

She looked around the walls and her gaze stopped on his sword. She eyed it silently for a few minutes. Then she asked, "Is it real?"

"Yes."

"It's yours?"

"Yes. Marine officers are granted the honor of carrying a sword. My father gave it to me when I became a sergeant."

"Why only officers?"

It was a story he knew well. "Katie will learn the whole story in boot camp. It will become one of her stories, too." Then he decided he shouldn't bring up Katie, not now, when they were finally beginning to . . . to . . . he dropped that thought. He kept his gaze on his sword as he spoke. "I will tell you an abbreviated version. In the Marine's Hymn, the words 'to the shores of Tripoli,' refer to a battle that took place in 1805. Lieutenant Presley Neville O'Bannon was assigned to create a fierce fighting force from seven Marines, a few Greek mercenaries, and a handful of cutthroats. His mission was to secure the surrender of Jessup, the Bey of Tripoli. Despite numerous obstacles he did not fail. He lowered the Tripolitian flag and raised the Stars and Stripes. It was the first time the American flag had been raised on foreign soil. When Hamet Karamanli took over as ruler of Tripoli, he presented his own jeweled sword, the sword of the Mameluke tribesmen, to Lieutenant O'Bannon. Marine officers carry this type of sword to honor this piece of our history."

He felt her gaze upon him. He remained focused on his sword.

"Your voice changed," she said. "Were you aware of it? Not just your voice. When you told me that story, your entire way of standing changed. Your whole demeanor changed."

He nodded. "I suppose so." He returned her frank gaze.

"Why?"

"It's an important story. Our stories are part of why we are what we are, who we are. They tell us our history and they inspire us to be more than we think we can be. We give our stories respect." She didn't look away.

"Marines?"

"Yes."

Once more he felt the urge to kiss her. This time kiss her softly, to woo her, to take her hand and lead her. But after a moment she looked away. The expression in her face was confusion.

"So where," she said, "are your pictures of the dogs?" Dogs were a safe topic.

"Here." He pointed to the framed photographs on the other wall.

She went over to study them. "This is your mother?"

"With Piedmont's Barbary Flame."

Karen read the placard. "Lima Kennel Club. It says new champion. She finished her championship that day. And this one? Cleveland Kennel Club," she read.

"Piedmont's Fire Flash. The day he finished his championship."

She leaned closer. "Truly beautiful dogs." She shot him a quick glance. "I'm serious." She turned back to the dogs. "I don't know anything about the Am Staff standard, but these two dogs are wonderfully balanced. You can almost feel their power. Where are they now?"

"Flame lives with my sister, May. Flash lives with my folks."

"Who's this?" She'd caught sight of one more photograph. "Oh. It's you. You must have been in your midtwenties? And who is this with you?"

"I was twenty-four."

"And the other man is . . . ?"

"Gunnery Sergeant Anthony Spriggs."

"A Marine?"

"My boxing coach. And one of the finest Marines—no. One of the finest human beings I've ever known." He didn't want to talk about that photograph right now. She'd ask about the occasion it was taken; he could almost see the questions forming in her mind. He didn't want to tell her that after he'd led the Marine Corps team to the Armed Forces Boxing Championship, that night, when he arrived home, triumphant and cocky, Caroline told him she was leaving. For good. He didn't talk about that with anyone. That subject was closed. Secured.

A clap of distant thunder morphed into a rumble. "I should bring Lennox in," he said. "Rain is fine, but I don't want him outside in lightning." It was a convenient excuse to usher her out of his study and shut the door firmly behind them.

Chapter 16

Saturday morning, Karen's father's model-airplane club was hosting their annual World War I reenactment games. Karen and Roger had accompanied their dad every year when they were little, less so as they grew older. When Katie was born, Karen began coming again, bringing her daughter. Lloyd had drafted Karen once more to help score. So she loaded Ferry in her van and drove out to the field.

"Good airplane-flying weather," she told her dad. She held Ferry's leash in one hand while she helped him with lawn chairs.

"Yes, it is. The weather's not as hot as it was a couple of weeks ago. There's no wind."

There was, however, the slightest hint of a chill in the air. Karen was glad she had a light sweater.

She helped the men set up the obstacles, chatting with them, for she'd known most of them all of her life. They asked about Katie, fully aware she was at boot camp. Karen told them Katie was fine, but because most of the men were veterans, she didn't go into how she really felt. She didn't want to, and besides, she liked them. She didn't want to insult them because she was angry with her daughter.

Then, with Ferry at her side, she took her place at the score table. Soon the air was filled with the whine of radio-controlled airplane engines and the pungent smell of fuel. The men, from the ground, flew their planes, swooped them high and low, did stop-and-go's on top of an apple crate, landed within a foot-wide circle, flew in formation. Karen snapped half a dozen pictures to send to Katie.

After the games, she added scores and announced the winners, and another year's games were over.

She followed her father home. Susannah was at her book club meeting, so Karen fixed a late lunch and they sat in the backyard with Ferry while they ate.

"Dad," Karen said, "can I ask you something?"

"Of course."

"Remember a long time ago, you and Mom went to Washington for the dedication of the Wall. Why wouldn't you let Roger and me come, too?" It wasn't an idle question. She and her father had never discussed the war. As far as she knew, her father didn't discuss Vietnam with anyone at all. She wasn't sure he would answer her question.

Lloyd's eyes shuttered. He didn't say anything for a long while. Then he said, "Too many of my buddies are on the Wall."

Karen was amazed to see his eyes fill. Then she understood how deep his pain was, even to this day. She took a deep breath and let it out slowly. She had to say this. No matter how much it hurt her, she had to say it. "I don't want Katie to be a name on a wall."

Her father reached for her and put his arm around her shoulders and held her like he had when she was a little girl. He patted her back slowly while she cried. "No mother does. Army mom, Navy mom, Marine mom. It's all the same." His voice still soothed her. "None of them want their sons and daughters to be names on the Wall. Fathers don't either. Brothers and sisters don't. Children don't want their mothers and fathers to be names on the Wall."

For the first time, as her dad spoke the soft, soothing words, Karen understood she wasn't alone. Other mothers of other Marines feared for their sons and daughters, too. She was part of something bigger than just herself. She remembered when Katie was born, her mother told her she was now part of the Mothers Club. This was an experience she shared with almost all the women on the earth. It brought women together and gave them a common bond. There will be other bonds, Susannah said, but motherhood was one of the strongest. Now, Karen remembered that. Karen remembered and she was comforted.

Karen waved across the street as Steve and Lennox jogged by. She watched them all the way to the corner. The maple tree on the corner was finally beginning to turn. Every autumn, that tree was the last on the street to turn color. But when it did, oh the colors were glorious. Not content to turn merely plain gold like its neighbors, this maple turned blazingly brazenly scarlet. The year Katie's English class studied mythology, she said that tree was like a phoenix. The year her class read *The Scarlet Letter*, she said that tree was like a painted wanton among church ladies. Now Karen took a brief break and trotted down to the corner. She picked up a bright red leaf and took it back to her office to press between the pages of a thick psychology text. She would send it to Katie.

Karen's last appointment that afternoon was with Candy. When the girl arrived, she went straight over to sit on the floor next to Bridgit. Bridgit didn't protest as Candy hugged her. Bridgit never protested about anything.

"I've been thinking," Karen said, "about what we talked about last week. You told me you wanted to find some way to let your baby know how much you love her."

Candy nodded, her cheek still on top of Bridgit's head.

"Would you like to knit a baby blanket? We could arrange things so the blanket goes with the baby to her new home."

Candy sat up. Thoughts visibly flitted across her face. "That would be good," she said at last. "A blanket is soft and warm and cuddly. But I couldn't make one. I could buy one though." More thoughts flitted. "A store-bought blanket wouldn't be the same, would it?" She looked at Karen. "Only I don't know how to knit."

Karen nodded. "I know someone who would love to teach you, if this is something you would like to do."

"Do you really think I could learn how to knit a baby blanket?"

"I'm sure you could. Mrs. Wilde has had ages of experience teaching people to knit."

"She'd really be willing to teach me?"

"Yes. She really would. We can go see her, if you like."

"What, you mean now?" her face brightened.

"Sure. If you like. We can walk. It's not far."

"Yes, please," she said. "May we take Bridgit?"

"We absolutely must take Bridgit," Karen said.

As soon as they were in sight of The Wilde Woman's Wool, Bridgit actually lifted her head and picked up her pace.

Candy, nestled into one of the comfy chairs by the fireplace, thumbed through pattern books. Elderly Mrs. Wilde sat next to her, discussing them with her, which patterns might be challenging, or tricky, which ones might be easier for a new knitter, always allowing Candy to keep her options open.

Connie Wilde sat in a chair across from them, knitting in her hands, Bridgit's head in her lap.

Karen felt restless. She wandered among the yarns, picking them up, putting them down. Knitting the shawl for Katie brought back the old yarn hunger. Maybe she would knit a shawl for her mother, too, for Christmas. This dark turquoise cotton and silk yarn would be lovely. She fingered a strand of it, considering. The yarn would knit up to drape well, but her mother wasn't a turquoise person. Maybe that deep bronze color. Yes. She scooped up several skeins.

After work, Karen stopped off at Abernathy's with a short list.

"Karen! Hello!" She turned around, looking. Steve waved to her from across the parking lot.

"Hello," she said and they entered the store together.

"Would you like to come to the park with me?" he said. "For an Abernathy's deli supper?"

"That sounds lovely. We won't have many more days warm enough."

"That's like saying life's uncertain so eat dessert first."

"Isn't there a saying about gathering hay and playing while you may?"

"Probably. So is that a yes?"

"Yes."

In the park they enjoyed their deli supper, and the gorgeous autumn day. Most of all, they enjoyed each other's company. After they enjoyed, they walked with Lennox in the park.

"The leaves are turning," she said. "Autumn leaves."

"What's that?"

"When Katie was about nine or ten she had one of those 'Aha!' moments. She had a school assignment to write a haiku. She was looking at that maple tree on the corner by my office and she said, 'Autumn leaves and then we have winter.' Suddenly, she realized words could have two meanings at the same time. She finally figured out puns. She was so pleased with herself."

* * *

Karen hated Ohio's summer humidity. She hated feeling wet and sticky. It made her feel grumpy. At dog school she filled extra dog bowls with cool water and encouraged her students to allow their dogs to drink. Soon, she comforted herself, summer will leave and we'll have autumn. Then autumn will leave and we'll have winter and we won't have humidity. It was a lovely thought.

"Tonight," she told her class, "we will begin learning the down stay. Pay close attention to your dog and you will be able to see your dog think. This is important because I want you to reinforce the stay as soon as you see your dog even begin to *think* about moving. Right now they have the advantage. They are masters at interpreting body language. They read every single one of our expressions, every tightening of our muscles, the narrowing of our eyes. We have to catch up. Remember, all dogs were bred for some purpose," she told her class. "Even if that purpose was to be a lap warmer. Dogs were bred to work with and for man. Some dogs, for instance the Akbash, were bred to guard flocks of sheep. Corgis were used to herd sheep, or cattle, or kids. Afghans were bred to hunt snow leopards."

"What about that dog?" the woman with the poodle pointed to Lennox.

Karen lifted her eyebrow at Steve.

"American Staffordshires," Steve said calmly, "were bred to be all-around family farm dogs. They baby-sat the kids while mom and pop worked in the fields."

Everyone looked down at Lennox. Lennox realized they were all looking at him. He rolled over on his back and wagged his tail more vigorously.

"He doesn't look like he could guard a flea," said the man with Ralphie, the setter.

Everyone chuckled. But after that, the other class members seemed more relaxed around Lennox than they had before.

Chapter 17

After class he and Karen wandered out into the evening air. "There's the first star, the evening star." She pointed. "You ought to be out here late at night. The stars are so close you could almost reach out and touch them. Just you and the stars. It's so peaceful."

"We could use more peace in the world."

"I agree. We have too much violence," Karen said. "We make jokes about aggression—on bumper stickers and coffee mugs. What do we think we're doing?"

"I agree."

Karen looked at him in surprise.

"Katie told me you were a pacifist."

She drew the line in the sand. "I abhor violence."

"I do too."

Karen was confused.

"You and Katie, neither of you like confrontation."

"What do you mean?"

"Right now, I can tell there's something you want me to know, but you won't come out and say it. Katie does the same thing. She wanted you to know she was joining the Marines, but she didn't want to tell you. In boxing terms, she used her jab. She danced around you, throwing hints like little jabs. What she needed to do was use her power punch." He gazed at her easily. "You're doing the same thing. You're throwing hints, like jabs, when what you need to do is show me your power punch. Trust me. I can take it."

She paced for a moment, then finally turned. "You say you don't like violence, but you used to be a professional warmonger. Now you teach boxing. What could possibly be more violent than that?"

He held her gaze steadily. Even when her gaze wavered his still held. At last, when she looked away, he said, "You don't know anything about either of them. How can you, in all fairness, look down your nose at something you know nothing about?"

"I know all I want to know about the sound of a fist hitting a body. In my work I sometimes have to deal with the emotional consequences."

He suddenly felt very tired. He didn't want to fight with this woman. She was Katie's mother. "Katie wanted to protect your feelings. All she protected was your ignorance." He glanced at the dog by his side. "Let's go home, Lennox."

Lennox dashed to the front door, barking. It was his excited bark. Steve opened the door to his sister, May.

"I was passing through town. I know, I know," she said, "it's Friday night and the fights are on. But, not for a couple of hours. Let's take Lennox for a walk."

Lennox loved May.

"I want to know all about Lennox and dog school. How's the class?"

"It's okay, I guess."

" 'It's okay, I guess' is not an answer."

"You know, May, you remind me of a woman I know here. Her name is Jessie. I like her a lot, but she can be a real pain in the butt. The same way you can."

May visibly brightened. "You like her?"

"No. Not that way. She works for my vet, and she reminds me of you. You both have the same irritating traits."

She didn't take his hint. She never did. "I'm glad there's someone down here to keep you in line, then. Anyway, tell me about dog school."

"We go. Lennox has a good time. There are about a dozen dogs. You know how CGC classes are. You've done this."

"Who's teaching?"

"Woman named Karen Matheson. Her daughter was one of my students."

"What does she have?"

Steve knew what she meant. "Newfoundlands. She does rescue."

There was silence. Then his sister said, "And you are attracted to her why?"

"I didn't say I was attracted to her."

"But you are."

He rolled his eyes at Lennox. Lennox wagged his tail. Traitor. "What makes you say that?"

"She rescues Newfoundlands, the peaceful giants. Someone with a mission." She sighed dramatically. "Stevie Steve. Haven't you noticed you're always attracted to the women who are the peace-loving types?"

"Maisie May, that's a load of crap."

"No. It isn't. I think it's because you feel safe with them. You don't have to commit yourself because you know they won't like boxing, so they'll eventually leave you. Like Caroline did."

"Caroline has nothing to do with this."

His sister gave him a pitying look. "She has everything to do with this."

He looked away.

"Stevie Steve," May said in a singsong voice. "Hello. Didn't you ever figure it out? It was partly because Caroline couldn't deal with being a Marine wife. I don't blame her. It can be terrifying. You men don't seem to understand what it means to us to sit at home and wait. I don't know how Mom stood it. First Dad, and then you, and then Rick. I suppose she's used to it by now. But for Caroline it was worse. Not only did she have to wait while you went off to who knew where for who knew how long, when you were here . . . You're a boxer. You came home from boxing all battered and bloodied and then you went out and did it again!"

He stopped her. "May," he said, "I really don't want to discuss this with you."

"Tough tooties. Women don't like seeing the men they love hurt. And they *really* don't like not *seeing* the men they love because that man has to do something the wife doesn't like in the first place." She looked up in his face. "The boxing life doesn't leave much time for relationships."

"I don't want to discuss my personal life with you. You're my sister."

"And I know you better than anyone on the face of this earth and you know it. That's why you have to listen to me. You're always in the gym, or running, or lifting weights, and when you're not, you're watching tapes of fights, or getting ready for a fight, and we all know what *that* means. Women weaken legs. Caroline couldn't bear it. Maybe she could have coped with one or the other, but she got the double whammy." She grabbed his shirtsleeve. "Look at me. Listen, Steve. She had to leave you, because you wouldn't leave boxing. Or the Corps."

Off in the distance a grumble of thunder rumbled itself out.

Jim Tate arrived for *Friday Night Fights* with a new girl du jour. Jim Tate went through girls like a chain saw through butter, Steve thought. Then he remembered what his sister said. *The boxing life doesn't leave much time for relationships.* He wondered if the girls were the ones who left Jim. Like all his

previous girlfriends, this one was pretty and giggled, too. He
wondered what his sister would have to say about Jim Tate.

"This is Lennox," Jim told his new girl. "Hey, Lennox.
Let's do your trick. Pow!" Jim threw a neat right toward the
dog. Lennox immediately threw himself down on the floor.
"Knockout!" Jim crowed. Lennox's tail vibrated.

"Mrs. Matheson, can I come over?" Colleen sounded
upset. "I need to talk to you."

Karen planned to take the dogs for a long walk today. However, the cold steady rain, shot with occasional lightning and
thunder, had changed her mind. It was a good thing Sylvie
and Ray were in New Jersey; Jean-Luc hated thunderstorms.
"Sure," she said, "I'll be here all evening."

Ten minutes later, Colleen knocked on Karen's door.

"Katie sent me a letter. And, um, it's sort of got me really
worried about her so I drove up from school. I thought you
should read it."

Dear Colleen,

Karen read,

> *Boot camp is more horrible than anything I could
> have ever imagined. The drill instructors are beyond
> belief. All they do is yell. I don't think they know how to
> talk in a normal voice. They yell at us and yell at us and
> we have to do whatever they say. The other day a girl
> took too long to make her bed and the drill instructor
> yelled, "Get your face on my deck and start pushing
> up." And the poor girl had to do twenty push-ups just
> because she didn't make her bed quickly enough. And
> if you call it a bed you get yelled at. It's a rack. And we
> have to speak of ourselves in the third person. "This re-*

cruit," we have to say, this recruit doesn't understand. (Of course, if you really did say that you'd get yelled at for not understanding.) Or this recruit doesn't want to do this anymore. Or this recruit thinks the drill instructors are pure evil on a stick! Ma'am! Everything is regimented down to the last speck. We can't just stand in line in the chow hall. No. We have to stand shoulder to shoulder and sidestep down the chow line. And if we even hold our trays incorrectly it's like a major crime and we have to go do push-ups in the sandpits. And our hair. They showed us how to put up our hair in buns. Lots of hair gel and bobby pins. Gross. But then, they show us once and expect us to do it. So we have like, ten seconds to do it, so we have to help each other or we'll take too long and we'll get yelled at. And if we still can't do it we'll have to get our hair cut. And we only have time to wash our hair every other day—if we're lucky—but they won't let us wash it in the showers. We have to hang over these big old steel sinks. I hate it here. What made me think I could ever do this? I'd tell them I quit, only I don't think they'd let me, so I'd have to desert, and that's a crime. Even if I did quit, I couldn't come home because my mom would look at me, like, I told you so. And Steve would think I let him down. What am I going to do?"

Karen read it twice. Then she read it again.

After Colleen left, she rubbed Ferry's ear absently. Who could she talk to about this? Steve would be the logical person, but after Steve had left dog school Thursday night, after she sort of yelled at him, she didn't think he'd ever want to talk to her again. Who then could she talk to? "She's miserable," Karen told Ferry. "She needs to get out of there." Could she talk to her mom? Or her dad? No, probably not her dad. War was probably too close to her dad.

Ferry deserted her to go take a chew toy away from Heck.

Karen reached up to rub Katie's pendant. Who could she talk to? What could she do about this? Katie wasn't given to flights of hyperbole. If she said they yelled at her all the time, they yelled at her all the time. If she said it was more horrible than she could have imagined, it was that horrible. "If she wanted to come home, I wouldn't tell her I told her so," Karen tried to convince the dogs. "I really wouldn't."

If she had imagined it would be horrible, then why did she want to be a Marine in the first place? If only, she thought, if only I hadn't gotten uppity with Steve. So what if he's a war-monger? Or a former warmonger. He's a good person. He would know what to do. He was that kind of guy.

Lightning flashed closely followed by a tremendous clap of thunder. Ferry raised her eyebrows. Brian slept on. Karen held onto Katie's pendant. Why the Marines?

What was it Steve had said? Katie used her jab instead of her power punch. She didn't want to hurt you, he'd said, to worry you. So she danced around you, hinting, jabbing. What she needed to do was use her power punch. That would've gotten your attention. Maybe then you would have listened to her.

Jabs and hints? What was that supposed to mean?

Her hand stilled on the pendant. *Put it up on my dressing table*, Katie had told her. *On my dressing table. Don't forget*.

Karen trotted upstairs and into Katie's room. She shot a baleful glare at the chin-up bar in the doorway. She focused on the dressing table. She saw something small and white, a box, sitting on the linen table scarf. She hadn't seen that box for eighteen years. She would recognize it anywhere.

A blinding streak of lightning flashed with a thunderous clap Karen felt rather than heard. The world tilted on its axis and the earth stopped spinning and split in two and Karen was sucked into the void. Now she knew why Katie wanted to become a Marine.

Inside the box, a Marine emblem, the eagle, globe, and anchor, nestled on a slice of white cotton batting. Tucked beside it were three one-inch pictures from a mall photobooth.

Karen slid down against the doorjamb and cried. She slumped onto the floor and cried like the rain, howled like the thunder. Ferry and Heck thudded upstairs to press against her, to give her comfort, their whiskers and soft snuffles tickling her cheek. Through the torrent of her tears, her wrenching sobs, drowning in despair, she clung to the dogs. The dogs held her up, kept her head out of the water. No matter that she cried an ocean of tears into the night, the dogs were with her. The dogs would never let her go under; they would keep her safe.

Chapter 18

Sunday, Karen woke with swollen and gritty eyes. Rain still poured out of the sky. Rain created a temporary pond outside her back door. The dogs were delighted. Even Brian waded into the middle, but then he got lost, for he stood in the rain and barked, imploring her to come find him.

She wrapped her bathrobe around herself more tightly, stuck her feet into her sandals and went out into the rain to rescue her dog.

After breakfast, she took a mug of hot spiced cider and set it down next to her computer. No, she thought, better not turn the computer on with the storm. That was all she needed, to have her computer blown out by lightning.

Instead, she gathered her knitting and curled up in the living room with the dogs. Besides, she had to think this all through—how to tell Katie, how to word it, how to explain the unexplainable. Was it unforgivable? Karen examined her knitting to figure out where she was in the pattern. She twined the yarn through her fingers and began to knit. *Dear Katie*, she wrote, in her head, *I do not know your father's last name, but his given name was Keith.* She knitted to the end of that round, consulted her pattern, and began the next. The yarn ran through her fingers, chaos becoming order. Her thoughts, though, continued their chaos. All of her professional life, she'd held forth communication as the greatest and most necessary tool for mankind. Yet when it came to her own daughter, where the need for understanding was greatest, she had taken the easy way out. She had chosen silence.

The phone rang. It was Jessie.

"You want to come over for a Mel movie marathon? We can send out for that expensive pizza. Tanner and Micah are in Pittsburgh doing some hockey thing, so Sally's in. Sylvie went to New Jersey, and I'm going to call Melissa next."

It was tempting. Karen pulled aside the curtain to look outside.

"Oh, no!"

"What?"

"My Tree."

"What about your tree?"

"It looks like it got hit by lightning last night. It's all over my driveway."

"Better than all over your house."

"I can't get out. I won't be able to get out until I get it moved . . ." She closed her eyes against the sight. She loved her Tree. The Tree was part of Katie's childhood. Another part of her life had been ripped out. "I'm gonna need a big chain saw."

"Call Steve. He's wonderfully strong. I bet he'd be happy to do it for you."

"I can't. The last time I saw him I sort of yelled at him."

"So. I'm sure you're sorry by now."

"No, Jess. I don't think so. I think this is one of those things I have to do myself."

She pulled on her jeans and a sweater, stuffed her feet into heavy socks and boots. She didn't want to do this. Didn't want to chop up her Tree. Didn't want Katie to be a Marine. Didn't want Brian to be old and feeble. Didn't want Bridgit to be not there. She wanted her life to go back the way it was before.

Ferry stuck her nose in Karen's face.

"I'm tying my boots," Karen told her. Ferry wagged her tail. "I'm not taking you for a walk. I have to chop up my Tree so I can get out of the driveway tomorrow morning so I can go to work to earn money to buy you dog food. I am not in a good mood, so don't push it."

An hour later she was in a worse mood. Her chain saw wasn't big enough to cut through the hunk of tree trunk that blocked her driveway. She'd managed to saw off some of the smaller branches and drag them into the yard, out of the way, but she hadn't made a dent in the ruin of the ruined tree. At this rate, it'd be Christmas before she could get out of her driveway. The sky spit a spurt of wet rain at her. She wanted nothing more than to spit back. Instead she leaned down to wrap her arms around the Tree and press her forehead against the rough bark, as she had done so many times, as she had taught Katie to do so many years ago. The Tree had lost its power. The Tree had no comfort to give her. Her tree was a great big dead stick.

Steve's phone rang. It was Jessie. "Hey, Steve, I was sitting here thinking, and I thought that more than anything you would probably want to go outside on this very nasty day and save a damsel in some very serious distress."

Instantly, he was on guard. "What's up?"

"Do you know how to use a really big chain saw?"

Jessie hadn't exaggerated, he thought as he pulled up in front of Karen's house. That was one big tree. He climbed out of his car and hefted the chain saw. He walked around the tree and then he saw her. She looked like she knew she was defeated. "Hello."

She whirled around. She snagged her sweater on a broken branch. "Why are you here?" Then her tear-streaked face changed. She clumsily tried to unsnag her sweater. "I'm sorry. I didn't mean that the way it sounded."

"I heard you needed a really big chain saw."

Her eyes widened for an instant. Then, "Jessie?"

He nodded. "She said you were in serious distress."

She waved her hand at the tree. It was self-evident. "You have a really big chain saw?"

"No. I don't own one. This belongs to a friend of yours. A guy named Alex Hogan. He has family visiting so he couldn't come himself."

"Alex loaned you his chain saw?"

"No. He loaned Jessie his chain saw. For me to use. To help you. Evidently he thinks very highly of you."

Her eyes filled. "I think highly of him, too. He has one of my rescue dogs."

Steve hated seeing women cry. "I met Burl. Big dog who sort of resembles a small mountain. Nice dog. Anyway, I have this chain saw. So." He had to escape the tears in her eyes or he'd be lost. He stepped back to survey the work ahead of him. "How do you want this done?"

"What?"

"Do you want pieces chopped into firewood size, or great big logs, or what? Alex said, if you don't mind, he'd like a slice of the trunk. I gather he works with wood."

"Sure. I mean, Alex can have as much as he wants. I don't care how it's cut. Whatever's easiest, I guess."

"Then, why don't you go back inside, or sit on your porch or someplace out of this wet, and let me get to it."

"Okay." Her voice was small and miserable-sounding. She hung her head as she made her way through the dead-tree debris toward her house. Then she stopped. "Say, Steve. Thanks."

"You're welcome."

Karen rocked her front porch swing with one foot. She huddled deeper in her mom-made sweater and watched Steve chop apart the tree. Steve had it, too, she realized. Why hadn't she seen it before now? Steve had that same quality she'd found so devastatingly attractive in Keith. That air of competence, of confidence. It didn't occur to either of them that there was anything in the world they could not do if they set their minds to it. Not that they bragged about it, or swaggered, or got all macho. It was simply who they were. Whatever life threw at them, they would throw back. Period.

Where did that supreme confidence come from? Why did she find it so attractive? And why did she fall so hard for it in Keith and not in Steve? Was it because she had been so much younger then? She was older than that now. Now she had a grown child. She was too old to fall in love. Wasn't she? *Wasn't she?* Sure, she liked Steve Songer; he was a nice guy and all that. He was very polite and he was in terrific shape. He liked dogs. He didn't behave like someone who beat people up for a living. In fact, if she didn't know better, she'd think he was a normal everyday peaceful kind of guy. Who happened to have an Am Staff named after a guy who beats people up for a living, but lots of nice people had Am Staffs; that didn't mean they were violent. Sure, her heart rate had seemed to speed up a little when she'd seen him just now. Sure, she looked forward to seeing him on Thursday nights at dog school. But that didn't mean she was falling for him. That would be really dumb. To fall for someone who taught kids to hit really, really hard. The fact that she was very aware of him whenever they were in the same room, and the fact that last weekend, she thought he was going to kiss her, in fact, she was sure he was thinking about it, and she found herself getting all warm, but then he didn't and she wasn't sure if she'd been disappointed or relieved. Certainly that didn't mean she was falling for him. She pulled out her box of emotions and looked through them carefully, one by one. She even unfolded a couple of them, shook out their wrinkles, examined them closely for moth holes and even tried them on, to see if they fit. And she didn't let herself cheat. Not even when—oh, no!

She fell back against the porch swing and blinked. It couldn't be. No. Yup. It had snuck up on her without her even being aware of it, without her even suspecting it. She had to face it. She had fallen for Steve Songer. Fallen hard. Hard as a grown woman falls on her first fall. Fallen across her life like her tree had fallen across her driveway. She didn't know if she should be happy or not. She did know she was terrified.

"Did you see a ghost?"

Her thoughts snapped back. "What?"

"You look shocked." He stood at the bottom of her porch steps, the chain saw resting on the step. The man she had fallen for. Was falling for. Would fall again for, and again.

"No. I, um, I was just thinking about things."

He nodded. He didn't believe her. "Well, I've done what I could for today. It's getting dark. I'm not finished, but at least you'll be able to get out of your driveway tomorrow morning. I can do the rest of it next weekend. Next Saturday afternoon if you like."

She realized she was staring at him dumbly. "Sure. Okay. Thanks."

"You want to come tell me where you want this wood stacked?"

She followed him across her lawn to the tree. Rather, what was left of her tree. Her tree fallen as completely as she had fallen. She agreed the side of the garage would be a good place for him to stack the wood. Yes, next winter it would burn well. Of course, Alex could have that big round slice of trunk. Of course the slice could stay here till Alex could come help lift it onto the truck.

"Then let me get to it."

But she had to ask him. "Steve. Katie sent a letter to her friend Colleen and Colleen showed it to me. Katie's miserable. She says it's even more horrible than she ever could have imagined. Is she safe?"

"Karen, I promise you, she is fine. What she feels—anger, confusion, rebellion—it's normal. Most recruits do. I promise you, she is not in danger."

She searched his face but could find only sincerity. She nodded.

"Would you like to come in?" she asked quickly, before she lost her nerve. "I mean, when you're finished, can I make you supper? To thank you?"

He gazed at her for a long moment. What did he see? Did he suspect she was as fallen as a woman could fall? "Yes."

"Okay, then."

"Okay."

She escaped his steady gaze and found her way into her house and leaned against the door. How had this happened? She was supposed to be a professional. She helped people figure out their own lives. Why had she not seen this? Ferry sat in front of her, looking at her curiously. She looked down at the dog. "Ferry, I'm in trouble here." She had to pull herself together and process all this before he finished stacking the wood and knocked at her door. Then he was at her door. And in her house. In her kitchen. Before her emotions were processed.

"I hope you like faux Mexican."

"I eat everything. Except okra."

She wrinkled her nose. "Don't worry. My house has been declared an official okra-free zone."

He held his hands out to her. "Um. Where can I wash up?"

"Down the hall, second door on the left." Then she remembered she'd left her bedroom door open. He'd go past it. Would he look in? What would he think?

She pulled out a skillet to heat on the stove. Best way to deal with men was to treat them like they were your little brothers. It had worked for her for lots of years. She'd had lots of practice. No reason it wouldn't work this time, too.

"Do you trust me?" She tossed him an over-the-shoulder grin when he returned. "This is really good, and really quick, but it isn't pretty."

"I trust you."

She used the spatula to point him to the table. "Sit."

He sat at her table and watched her at the stove. Something had changed, he thought. She was acting differently. She was putting on a show. Sometimes, in the ring, an opponent put on a show because he was scared. One of the dogs came up and set a great big head on his knee. He looked. "This is Heck, right?"

She turned around. "Yes. Sometimes people can't tell Ferry and Heck apart."

"This guy has a bit of white under his chin. Ferry doesn't. She has a different expression, almost as if she's playing a joke on you. This guy here, he's up front. What you see is what you get. No hidden agenda."

"You're very observant."

"Over the years I've learned to watch people closely. Especially faces. It carries over to dogs." He decided to try out his jab. "In the ring, you watch your opponent closely, see how they do things, then, when they do something different, sometimes you can tell what they're thinking."

She dropped the spatula. Score, he told himself. Before he could jab again, she turned around. A plate was in each hand. She showed heart. He liked heart. He respected heart.

"Dinner," she said with a brave smile.

She didn't know she'd been saved by the bell.

She thought he liked it. At least, he ate it all. When asked, he said yes to seconds, so she made more. He ate that, too.

Annie Smith

And salad, he ate lots of salad. He liked the dressing, that new recipe of her mother's.

She kept the conversation light, impersonal, and superficial. She felt she was doing quite well. She was careful not to allow herself to gaze too deeply into his eyes, not to study his face, not to show him more than the big-sister type of interest. She should go on the stage, she thought.

She was a good cook, he thought, if this was any example. "You're right," he told her, "it isn't pretty, but it's excellent." He watched her during this break, between rounds. He watched her carefully, without seeming to do so. Boxing had taught him to read people, but so had his years as a drill instructor. Taught him how to read people and use that knowledge to exploit their weaknesses. In the ring this was wholly justified. He was in the ring to win. During boot camp this exploitation was also justified. He was responsible for turning raw, nasty recruits into Marines. But now he was toe-to-toe up against a totally different situation. He didn't know how to handle this.

Yes, she thought, she could do this. She could be his big sister. All she had to do was to keep herself on a training collar and a short leash. A very short leash. A shorter leash than any she'd ever had. She didn't even know if anyone made leashes that short.

She wasn't his opponent, to defeat. She wasn't a recruit, to train. She was, she was . . . very much a woman. What did he want from her? What did he want for her? *Chocolate and flowers*, he heard Katie say. *She's never had that*. He didn't like that idea. Boxing was easier. He knew how to box. Chocolate and flowers? He didn't know how to do that.

And he even, she thought in wonder, helped with the dishes! He told her that in boot camp all the recruits did a rotation in the mess hall. She realized she stood too close to him, at the sink, handing him the soapy plates to rinse, their fingers touching briefly as he took them from her. She liked standing this close to him. She gave herself a jerk on her leash. She needed a still shorter leash.

The break, he told himself, was almost over. When the last dish was washed, it would be time to come out of the corner. Back into the ring. One way to wear out your opponent was to go to the body. He liked the idea of her body. She had a nice body. He could go for it.

This was the skillet, she thought. The last dish to be washed. Then she would drain the water, rinse out the sink, and the scrubber. She'd dry her hands and turn to him with a big-sister smile. At least, that's what she meant to do.

He held her, without touching her, very gently, on the ropes. Her back was to the sink. She faced him with a bright smile that seemed to falter for a moment, then, almost on its own, that impersonal smile became something else, something sensual, even slightly sexy. Suddenly, this new smile caused him to catch his breath. That smile made for one hell of a body punch!

She had slipped her leash and run free! She didn't come back when called! Her body, without her permission, was beginning to respond to him. She didn't know how to stop it. Didn't know if she wanted to stop it. Wrong! She knew she didn't want to stop it. She knew she wanted it to go on forever and ever.

A good Marine, like a good boxer, was always aware of his opponent, able to adjust, to refine his fight plan. Steve was highly aware of Karen. As soon as she changed her tactics, he prepared to change his, to counter hers—but he discovered he didn't know what to do. This was not a simple case of ring-rust. The rules of engagement were gone and no boxing commission covered this. This was unfamiliar territory. He was on his own. He was in the dark. He had to feel his way.

Never touch your dog in anger; she'd taught her students

this for years. Your dog must always, *always,* see your touch as a good thing, a safe thing, something he likes, something he wants. Now Steve's touch on her cheek, on her hair, his touch on her body, was a good thing, a safe thing. She liked it very much. And oh, how she wanted it.

His arms found their way around her while her arms slipped around him. They held each other tenderly, held each other close. Savoring. Delighting. Memorizing. He'd fallen onto the canvas a time or two in his years in the ring. But he'd never, ever, fallen as hard, or as completely, as he fell now. He fell and was down for the count. The referee waved his arms. For Steve, the fight was over.

After what seemed, to her, like that forever she'd wished for, he began to softly hum. And without loosening his arms, he began to move, slightly, to the rhythm of his humming. She went with him into a slow waltz around her kitchen. She was dizzy, not with the easy turning, but with him. This is why people in the Regency didn't allow unmarried girls to waltz, she thought. It was too easy to fall.

"When can I bring Lennox over to your house?" he whispered against the sweet scent of her hair. "He needs to meet the rest of your dogs. When people have a relationship they tend to spend a lot of time with each other. It's difficult to always make the dogs stay home."

"Is that want we're going to have? A relationship?"

"No." He stopped the waltz, opened his eyes, and pulled away from her, just enough so he could look at her, so she could see how serious he was. "A relationship, lady, is what we are having." He watched the expression in her eyes. Then he kissed her.

Chapter 19

The next morning, at work, Karen rearranged some of the furniture in her office. She told herself it was so Bridgit had more room to stretch out. Now, though, she conveniently discovered she could see out her window more easily. So she could see him as he and Lennox jogged by. Karen told herself when their relationship—it still sounded foreign, even to her—cooled, when she was more used to him, oh, yes, and when Bridgit was more comfortable, she would move her furniture back the way it was. If Theresa noticed, she didn't comment.

That morning, he called to ask when she was going to have lunch, to ask if she was free, to ask if he could take her to Lola's.

Noon, yes, and—she almost said yes. But she looked down at her feet, where Bridgit slept. She had Bridgit. Steve had Lennox. Lola did not allow dogs into her restaurant.

"Is there a problem?" Steve asked.

"No. It's . . . well, I have Bridgit with me. I'm not sure how she'd react if I left her shut in my office. I don't know if she'd bark, or whine, or try to claw her way out." Dogs were coming between them? She was stunned. This had never happened to her before. Of course, she'd never had a relationship, this kind of relationship, before.

"I'll leave Lennox here with Mary Lou, and you and Bridgit and I can have a picnic lunch."

He made it sound so easy, as if he'd thought it out ahead. As if he'd expected her to—she didn't want to go there. "It looks sort of chilly outside," she said, "and breezy. Can we have a picnic here? We can eat in the kitchen."

"Sure I'll stay with Lennox," Mary Lou said. "Oh, and by the way, bring a dozen of Lola's chocolate cookies for her to share with her coworkers. It'll impress her, and besides, you want her coworkers on your side."

He hadn't said anything about meeting a woman for lunch.

Mary Lou grinned at him. "I eavesdropped." She shrugged. "So fire me." She shot that wicked grin at him again. "But you're gonna need some help with this one. Boxing you know. Women you have no clue about."

So Steve picked up soup and sandwiches, and also a dozen of Lola's chocolate cookies. To share with her coworkers, he said.

Theresa was visibly delighted. "He shares well with others," she told Karen.

Steve said, "I'm trying to impress Karen with my generosity."

Karen nodded. "You have," she said. "I'm impressed." It was true. He even brought one of Lola's dog cookies for Bridgit. He held it out for Bridgit to sniff at. She took her time and sniffed it carefully before she took a small nibble. Finally she accepted the whole thing. Steve gently stroked the dog's head. "Good girl," he said in a quiet, soothing voice. Yes, Karen was very impressed.

Dear Katie, she wrote that night, *Jessie's predictions finally came true. We had a big storm here on Saturday, and our Tree came down. No one was hurt, except the Tree and that injury was fatal. I'm sending you a leaf from the tree, so you can look at it and remember how much I love you and miss you. Steve came over yesterday and chopped enough of it so I could get out of my driveway today.* She thought about dancing with Steve in her kitchen. She realized she was smiling. *Anyway, he's going to chop the rest of it up over the weekend. He says it'll make excellent firewood after it's had time to dry. Your shawl is coming along nicely. Of course, with pi shawls you begin in the middle and work your way out so the first rounds go much more quickly than the later rounds.* Much like life, she thought. Katie's childhood had gone much too quickly. *Other than that, there's not much news.* There weren't many things she couldn't share with her daughter, but her budding relationship with Steve Songer was one of them. This relationship, if it lasted, would definitely affect Katie, but no need to tell her now, not until . . . until . . . *The dogs are all fine. We all love you. Mom*

"I suppose," Theresa said, peering over Karen's shoulder, "it's too cold this morning for those shorts of his." She sighed.

"I know," Vicky said mournfully. "Sweatpants don't do his legs justice."

Karen's stomach went for a ride and she felt all soft and gushy.

Vicky glanced at her and chuckled. "It looks like you'll be spending some lovely winter nights with those gorgeous legs of his."

"Maybe. We'll see." She didn't want to commit herself.

"Yeah, right," put in Theresa.

"Say, don't you have some social-worker type of work to do, or something?"

"I'm being social."

"And I'm assisting," said Vicky.

That night, after Steve finished at his gym, he and Lennox drove to Karen's. Karen and Brian waited for them outside.

Again, it was a neutral place. Not that Brian would ever get it into his head to start any kind of argument; he'd have to stay awake too long. Indeed, he wasn't much interested in Lennox. He settled down on the sidewalk and closed his eyes. For his part, Lennox ignored Brian.

Tomorrow, at dog school, they agreed they would introduce Heck and Lennox. That left only Bridgit. And Bridgit might be difficult.

Karen and Steve arrived early to class that evening. She brought Heck. Steve brought Lennox. They introduced the two dogs outside, on the lawn, on neutral ground. The two dogs sniffed each other's most fragrant places. Then they both looked bored.

"Tonight," Karen told the class, "we're going to change directions. While we're walking with our dogs who are on a loose leash, we're going to turn left, and turn right, and do what we call an about-face."

After class they took Lennox and Heck to the park for a brisk walk. In the shadows of large trees they stopped, very close together, so their dogs could sniff around, and so they could kiss. Karen had never realized there were so many large trees in the park.

Friday was clear and bright. At noon he brought over a picnic lunch. They ate on the porch of the old Victorian. "The kids from the gym have a standing invitation to my house every Friday night to watch the fights," he said. "Would you like to come over, too?"

Karen looked up at the clear blue sky. She could deal with him, she could deal with Lennox, who she had discovered was a very friendly and well-socialized dog, but she couldn't deal with boxing. She didn't know if she could ever deal with boxing. Didn't know if she wanted to even try. Didn't like that stream of thought. "Not tonight," she said with regret, regret for her thoughts. "I have lots of chores to do. I've put them off for too long."

"Maybe another time, then," he said in a tone of voice that told her he knew her refusal was not as simple as she'd made it out to be.

"Maybe," she agreed.

While she brushed Ferry that evening, the coordinator of Newfoundland rescue called Karen. She told Karen she had an application from a family with lots of kids and absolutely no experience with dogs. They'd checked into different dog breeds and had heard Newfoundlands were wonderful with kids. They wanted a girl, thinking a girl might be easier to handle. "What about Ferry?" the coordinator asked.

"Oh, my." Karen looked at the dog on the floor next to her. Ferry returned her look. "I'm not sure," Karen said. She propped the phone between her cheek and shoulder and continued to brush. "Ferry is so smart, I think she'd be best with someone who had lots of dog experience. She needs things to do, things to learn so she doesn't get bored. When she's bored she gets into trouble. Well, it's not really trouble, but she finds little ways to amuse herself, and those ways are not always the things people would like her to do. And she's sneaky about it, she puts on this really good act of total innocence. She's absolutely believable—unless you know her. Then you don't fall for it."

"Sounds like you know her pretty well."

"Well, she's the kind of dog you have to figure out. She's not at all trying to be disobedient, really. She just wants to have fun. She's the alpha dog here, and sometimes she tries to climb on top of me, not because she's so dominant, but just to see if she can get away with it. I tell her she can't and she sort of shrugs and says that's okay. And it *is* okay."

There was a pause. Then the coordinator said, "Maybe you

should keep her yourself. Maybe I should take her off the list of adoptable dogs. At least for a while."

Karen looked at Ferry.

Ferry looked back at her.

Karen had a feeling Ferry knew exactly what this conversation was about. She reached up to worry Katie's pendant.

She glanced at the clock. It was way past time to talk to her mother. She loaded up her knitting and Bridgit and drove to her parents' house.

"They don't match," Karen pointed at the offending socks on the kitchen table. "Look. This sock starts with green, then blue, then red-and-yellow checks. That one starts with blue and then the red-and-yellow checks."

"They match. I used the same colors for both socks."

"But . . ."

Her mother smiled that old Mona Lisa smile. This was one of those times when that smile was irritating. "You don't like them because they're not the same. But I made those socks for Sylvie."

"She'll love them."

Susannah nodded. "I know. Sylvie will enjoy the serendipity of them."

Serendipity? Karen thought.

"You, however," her mother continued. "You don't like the unexpected. You're not comfortable with change. You like things precisely and completely spelled out in advance."

What's wrong with that, she thought. Then she remembered. "I finally learned why Katie joined the Marines," she told her mother. "She found out something I should have told her long ago. Something I should have told you."

Without a pause in her knitting, her mother nodded. Her mother did not look surprised.

"And I will tell you. But I have to tell Katie first."

"That's okay, dear. I always knew you'd tell us when you were ready."

Karen felt a great lump grow in her throat. Felt tears well up in her eyes. She concentrated on her knitting.

"Tell me how war changed Daddy."

"Back then," her mother said, "I read in a magazine that a group of writers and illustrators got together to make a statement against the war. I don't remember the exact quote, but it was something like every day war pulls us further and further away from what we truly are and can be. When your dad came home, he'd been pulled so far away from himself I thought he might never return. I had to help him find his way back home."

"*How* did you work through it?"

"I was living on the Wildes' farm, with Connie and her husband when you were born. Actually, I lived on the farm for my whole pregnancy. After your dad returned, we decided to stay here in Hartley." She paused and her face tightened, but just for an instant. "Our folks pitched in to help us raise the down payment for this house. I planted a garden, we watched things grow. Flowers, vegetables, you. Reentering and participating in the rhythm of the seasons is the great healer, you know. It isn't Father Time, it's Mother Earth."

"Maybe Jessie is wrong. Maybe you weren't a nun in a former life, maybe you were a Druid."

"Maybe I've been both. Not in the same life, of course."

How could Mother Earth heal Bridgit? Karen wondered.

Saturday morning Steve called her from the gym. "I'll be there about one-thirty," he said. "I'm finished here around one. I told Alex Hogan I'd pick up his chain saw shortly after. Then I'll be over."

"Would you like me to make lunch for you?"

* * *

It was lovely to have someone to cook for, Karen thought as she chopped a carrot into four pieces and tossed a piece to Ferry and one to Heck. She handed a piece to Brian who was awake for the event, and held a piece out to Bridgit and waited until she took it. She finished chopping carrots and added them to the Crock-Pot. She and Steve would have wonderful homemade chicken soup for supper. And bread. One of the benefits of having an old hippie for a mother was knowing how to make bread. Karen hadn't made bread for a couple of years, but it was just like riding a bike, something you never really forgot. But she *had* forgotten where she put her bread bowl.

An hour later the bread was rising, the soup was crocking, and Karen sang as she swept up dog hair. She lugged in a load of last year's logs and laid her first fire of the fall. She sat back on her heels and dusted her hands on the seat of her jeans. "Sorry, Brian," she told her most geezerly dog. "You can't sleep in the fireplace again until—" she stopped. Brian probably wouldn't make it until spring. The old guy leaned against her and snuffled in the general direction of the fireplace. "You smell something unusual, don't you?" Karen said. "That's wood. It's been outside all summer drying in the sun, soaking up summer smells. Now the weather is turning cold. We're going to have a fire in the fireplace tonight." He leaned a little too far forward. She put out her arm to steady him. "It will be cozy and warm."

His big brown eyes, milky now with age, gazed at her with complete trust.

"Don't worry, if the fire is too hot for you, I'll help you find my room and you can take a nap there." Her room was always too cold. A legacy of elderly houses built before efficient heating systems. Great cool rooms for cuddling up with great big dogs to keep warm. Thoughts of cuddling with Steve made her suddenly warm. Oh my. Last weekend they had kissed and held and did the standing cuddle in the

To start your membership, simply complete and return the Free Book Certificate. You'll receive your Introductory Shipment of 3 FREE Zebra Contemporary Romances, you only pay $1.99 for shipping and handling. Then, each month you will receive the 3 newest Zebra Contemporary Romances. Each shipment will be yours to examine FREE for 10 days. If you decide to keep the books, you'll pay the preferred subscriber price (a savings of up to 20% off the cover price), plus shipping and handling. If you want us to stop sending books, just say the word… it's that simple.

FREE BOOK CERTIFICATE

Yes! Please send me 3 FREE Zebra Contemporary romance novels. I only pay $1.99 for shipping and handling. I understand that each month thereafter I will be able to preview 3 brand-new Contemporary Romances FREE for 10 days. Then, if I should decide to keep them, I will pay the money-saving preferred subscriber's price (that's a savings of up to 20% off the retail price), plus shipping and handling. I understand I am under no obligation to purchase any books, as explained on this card.

Name _____

Address _____ Apt. _____

City _____ State _____ Zip _____

Telephone (____) _____

Signature _____

(If under 18, parent or guardian must sign)

Offer limited to one per household and not to current subscribers. Terms, offer and prices subject to change. Orders subject to acceptance by Zebra Contemporary Book Club. Offer Valid in the U.S. only.

CN113A

Thank You!

lll..l..l..llll.....lll..ll.l..ll.l..l.l..llll.l.l...lll.l..lll..ll

Zebra Contemporary Romance Book Club
Zebra Home Subscription Service, Inc.
P.O. Box 5214
Clifton , NJ 07015-5214

PLACE
STAMP
HERE

kitchen. They both had work the next day and Steve had to return the chain saw, so he couldn't stay late. But now, this was
Saturday. She was cooking supper. He didn't open his gym on
Sundays. She didn't go to work on Sundays. He was going
to bring Lennox with him when he came over. He might
spend the night. They would cuddle all night and keep warm
in her too cold room. "Oh, my!"

Karen scrambled up and down the hall to change the sheets
on her bed.

The only thing left to worry about—and it was a big
worry—was how to introduce Bridgit to Lennox.

Chapter 20

The doorbell rang. He's early, she thought, but —

"What're you doing this morning?" her mother asked. "I was out at the farm picking apples and I picked many more than your father and I can eat by ourselves. So on my way home I thought I'd drop by for a visit and share my bounty." She held her arms tightly around a big basket of apples. "Hello, dear dogs," she said to them, over Karen's shoulder.

Karen loved apples. Fresh-off-the-tree apples, apples that had never even dreamed of the inside of a grocery store. Her mother knew she loved apples. Her mother currently wore the same kind of innocent-me expression that Ferry had when she'd been thinking up something clever. Her mother had her ubiquitous knitting bag slung over her shoulder. Karen narrowed her eyes. This was no casual spur-of-the-moment visit.

"You're up to something."

"Me?" Her mother was the picture of pure innocence. "Karen, dear, please step aside. These apples are quite heavy. I'm not as young as I used to be, you know." Her mother pushed past her and down the hall to the kitchen. "I smell chicken soup. Smells luscious. I see you have bread rising. Where would you like the apples?" Without waiting for an answer she set the basket on the table. "Don't these apples look divine?" She whirled over to the counter and opened a drawer. "Here's that old granny knife of yours. Let's have an apple, shall we?"

Her mother's knitting bag, dropped on a kitchen chair, looked rather more lumpy and full than usual. Her knitting bag looked as if her mother had been on a Stash Enrichment Expedition and had found the mother lode. "Did you also stop at the yarn shop this morning?" Karen asked.

"Why, yes. I did." Her mother scrubbed a pair of apples at the sink. "Check my bag. I found some heavenly silk and rayon stuff. Of course I had to bring it home." She whacked an apple into twain, as she called it, and carved out the core. "Just wait till you try this apple. I told Mrs. Wilde these were the best apples I'd ever picked off their trees." She whacked the second apple. "I also found some wool for a sweater for your father for Christmas."

Karen reached for her mother's bag. She had a sudden suspicion. "Did you see anyone at the yarn shop?"

"Connie, of course. And Laura, you remember her, the woman who quilts like a dream and has convinced herself she can't learn to knit? We've kept at her and kept at her until she's finally decided to go ahead and try one of those Einstein coats."

"Anyone else?" Karen said around a mouthful of apple. "You're right, these are wonderful!"

Her mother took a big bite of apple. "Your friends Sally and Jessie," she said.

Karen nodded to herself. She scrubbed another apple and cut it up for the dogs. "The dogs think these are wonderful apples, too."

"Of course. They have impeccable taste."

The doorbell rang. "Are you expecting someone, dear?" Her mother was the epitome of innocence.

Karen put Bridgit in her crate, closed the door to the dog room and went to greet Steve with a quick kiss. Karen glanced over her shoulder to make sure her mother wasn't watching. Then she kissed him again, and this time she was more thorough. "My mom's in the kitchen," she whispered.

"She found out you were going to be here and she arrived a little bit ago."

The other dogs were thrilled to see Steve. They did the sniffy thing with Lennox again, then ignored him. Susannah, of course, was delighted to meet Steve and Lennox. Her mother showed no sign of leaving. Finally, Karen said, "Mom, I'm fixing a sandwich for Steve before he works on my tree. Do you want one too?"

Her mother bestowed upon her a beatific smile. "That would be lovely, dear."

So the three of them ate sandwiches and apples. The dogs watched them from across the kitchen, where they waited on down stays. Karen's stomach was full of fluttering butterflies. She couldn't finish her sandwich.

After the quick lunch, Steve took Lennox outside with him. Soon the whine of the chain saw pierced through the gray gloom of the day.

Susannah washed the few dishes while Karen dried. When Susannah settled back in her chair, set her mug of tea on the table, and pulled out her knitting bag, Karen knew her mother wanted something more.

Karen watched a squirrel scamper up the big tree in her backyard. She watched a sparrow flutter down to one of the feeders. Her father made those feeders. Working with wood was for her father what knitting was for her mother. She thought about her mother and father.

"After Daddy came home from Vietnam, how long did he have nightmares?" she asked.

"At first, quite often. Then they came less frequently. Why? Do you remember his nightmares?"

Karen nodded. "I remember once. When I was six or seven." She'd jolted awake to hear her father's scream. For a moment she was frightened. Then she heard her mother's voice calming and soothing. And she heard that old Joni Mitchell album her mother played. Finally, she heard the springs on her parents' bed creaking rhythmically. It'd sounded like they were jumping on their bed. They must be happy, she'd thought, to jump on their bed. It'd made her feel better and she'd fallen back asleep. Her mother set down her knitting to pet Brian, who'd wandered over to see her. Susannah crooned softly to the old dog. Karen thought of the sound of those old bedsprings. She thanked God her father had had her mother.

"So," said her mother in a deliberately calm tone of voice, "tell me about this man who is chopping down your tree. Are you happy?"

Was happy the right word? How about delirious with joy? Or ecstatic? Or thrilled? Or was what she was feeling merely the burgeoning, heady, rush of excitement over something new? Yes, she felt these things, but she was also scared to bits. The new was terrifying. The new meant change. Sometimes new things were exciting in the beginning and then fizzled out into nothing. The risk was frightening. Was she ready for this change? Only time would tell. In the meantime, "Yes," she told her mother. "Yes. I am very happy."

Her mother, satisfied, nodded. "Good. Yes, Brian, you're a good boy, too. You're a very good boy. For such an old man you're truly something very special." Then she looked up at Karen. "Would you let Bridgit spend the night with your dad and me? He'd never come out and say so, but I think he misses having a dog. If I could borrow Bridgit I think she'd help me convince him." Her eyes twinkled. Karen knew her father didn't stand a chance.

Karen packed up a dog bowl and small bag of food, which her mother insisted on cramming into her knitting bag, which made it even lumpier than it was before. Susannah tried to convince Bridgit that "a sleepover with your Grandma Susannah and your Grandpa Lloyd" would be loads of fun.

Bridgit adopted a wait-and-see expression, but she followed her "Grandma Susannah" out the front door. Karen pulled on her boots and a thick sweater and followed them down the steps. She helped Bridgit clamber into the old VW bus and waved to them as they drove off down the road. She didn't know whether to be relieved or not. On the way back to the house, she stopped to watch Lennox chew on a small log. Lennox dropped his loglet and pranced over to the fence for a short visit. She reached over to pet the Am Staff.

Steve had the wheelbarrow half loaded with wrist-width logs

"Mom took Bridgit for a sleepover," she told him.

She read the question in his eyes.

"She's the Original Earth Mother. She's the High Priestess of Saint Rochus, Patron Saint of Dogs." And, Karen was too shy to admit to Steve, I think she wanted to take some of the pressure off of us today. Tonight. Karen stubbed the toe of her boot in the lawn.

Steve reached out to touch her cheek.

She wanted to close her eyes and lean into his touch. Instead she said, "What can I do to help you?"

Steve said she could stay inside where it was warm. "Let me do this for you," he said. "Please." *Let me do this for you*. No one had ever said that to her before. She had always been the one to do things for others. *Let me do this for you. Please*. So she returned to her house to punch the bread down, shape it into the pan, and let it rise again. She sat at her computer and opened up her word processor. *Dear Katie . . .* She stopped. What could she tell her daughter right now? Steve, your friend, is chopping up the last of our Tree, then he'll come in and eat dinner with me, and then we'll sit in front of a fire in the fireplace, and then . . . and then . . . I am not ready for this, Karen thought wildly. She closed out her word processor and opened solitaire. She started a game, but closed it before she finished it. *Let me do this for you*. She hurried down the hallway to her room, where she scooped up the stack of books on her bedside table and took them into the dining room and set them on her desk. Then she picked through them but couldn't make up her mind so she chose one at random and took it back to her room to her bedside table—in case he decided not to . . . Well, she always liked to have something to read before she turned out the light.

She quickly scanned her bedroom. No clothes on the floor, or hanging over the back of her rocking chair. She picked up an old dog bone and what used to be a fleece toy football, but was now gummed almost past redemption and gray with very aged dog slobber. Every night Brian slept with that thing stuffed between his big front feet. Tonight Lennox would sleep in the bedroom with them, and Brian would have to sleep in his crate—if Steve . . . She would be optimistic. She carried the old bone and the former fleece football into the dog room and dumped them in Brian's crate.

She checked the bread. It was ready for the oven. She popped it in and set the dinger. What am I doing? she asked herself. I'm not ready for this. She felt like a deer frozen in the headlights; unable to move forward or retreat. So she did neither. Instead, she settled down next to Brian and brushed him while he slumbered on.

The back door banged shut. "Hello!"

Let me do this for you. How could she ever have doubted? Suddenly, she was sure. At least for now. She went to him in her kitchen. They stood very close, her head on his shoulder. He smelled of cold weather and newly cut wood and fresh sweat. She kissed him lightly on that place where his cheek became his jaw. "Thank you," she said. "I don't know what I'd've done without you."

"You're most welcome." His lips met hers. They were gentle. They were giving, undemanding. "I'm not finished," he said against her lips. "But most of the light is gone. Alex said I could return the chain saw tomorrow." He kissed her again, and held her close. "Lady," he murmured, "you grow big trees at your house."

She smiled. "I can tell."

He held her close and carried her with him again into that silent waltz. She closed her eyes and let herself follow. Let herself feel. Let herself move as one with him.

"Something smells wonderful," he whispered.

"Bread baking," she said.

"No. It's you," he said. "Your hair. Wonderful. Speaking of smells, may I use your shower?" He nodded to the neatly folded clothes on the kitchen table. "I came prepared."

The bathroom off the hall didn't have a shower, but the bathroom upstairs did. So did the bathroom off her cold bedroom. Karen was glad she'd changed the sheets and made her bed.

Her bathroom was as straightforward as she was, with clean pure lines, and not a lot of fluff. Steve didn't have much use for fluff. Her towels were fluffy though. They felt good. And her soap smelled like she did. He liked the smell.

Lennox curled up on the bath mat while Steve showered. It felt good to stand under the hot water and scrub away the sweat from a morning at the gym and an afternoon working out with a tree and a chain saw. Karen's shower pounded onto his muscles . . . almost as soothing and relaxing as Karen's arms. Karen's shower felt so good that singing was a reflex rather than a conscious decision. *I'm singing in the rain . . .* he even did a highly abbreviated soft-shoe.

In the kitchen, setting the table, Karen stopped with the silverware in her hand. She'd heard . . . no. She felt her face break into a huge smile. The man sang in the shower. And he had a good voice. Instinctively, she knew this wasn't something she could share with her friends. First of all, if she told them he'd showered at her house they'd get all sorts of ideas, especially Jessie, and Jessie didn't know when to let things go. But it was more than that. Somehow, Karen knew Steve didn't sing in front of people. Somehow, she knew he wouldn't want her to share this. Somehow she knew he trusted her to keep this a secret. She would keep it safe. She would keep it well. She wouldn't even let him know she knew. "He is special," she whispered to Brian. "I've never known anyone as special as he is." She brought out her great-grandmother's silver candlesticks.

The dogs went out one last time for the night. Their black coats made them all but invisible in the backyard. Karen waited for them on the porch and shivered until Steve came outside too, and then she was warm in his arms. Karen put the three Newfoundlands in their crates, gave them all kisses, and wished them pleasant dreams and good night. Lennox followed Steve back into the living room to settle down at their feet.

They watched the fire burn down low, casting soft dancing shadows. Her head was on his chest. She listened to his heartbeat and to the snapping and crackling and little bursts of flame.

"You make a great fire." His voice was hushed. She loved the sound of his voice. His voice was soft around the edges. His voice was like the worn flannel of his shirt against her cheek. His voice was soft, but his body was hard and strong.

"I grew up in the country in a drafty old farmhouse. The electricity had a habit of going out. Firemaking skills were not optional."

"Near here?"

"Then it was about a mile and a half out of town, but the town has been closing in for years. My folks still live there. The house is still old and drafty."

"You and Katie and your mom, you all look alike."

Karen frowned. "We do?"

"Not so much physically, but you all move the same way, graceful, but unconscious of it. Trust me on this. I watch people move. Grace, agility, they're very important qualities in boxing."

She didn't want to talk about boxing. Not now. "My mom and dad used to do ballroom dancing a lot. When they were younger. I think Dad put up with it because Mom wanted to do it. She loved it."

"Your mom is special, isn't she?" Steve said.

Emotion welled up within Karen's whole being. "Yes. I think she is. Thank you for recognizing that."

"I'd think it would be obvious." His hand stroked her hair.

"Not always."

Evidently he heard something in her voice. "Tell me." It was an invitation, not a command.

"I didn't appreciate her, at least, not in high school. Not until later." Later she would tell him all of it. But not now. Not until later. After she told Katie.

He said, "We're not supposed to appreciate our parents when we're in high school. You work with teenagers. You should know that."

"I know. I do know that."

"You expect more from yourself?"

"Maybe."

"I think you're wonderful just the way you are." With one finger he tipped her face up and she saw the flickering of the firelight reflected in his eyes. "Let me show you how wonderful you are."

This was it, Karen thought. What her mom called one of life's stitch markers. A moment after which nothing would ever be the same. A moment you remembered for the rest of your life.

"Please," he said.

"Yes," she said. "Yes. Please, yes."

He held his hand out to her to help her up. He led her down the darkened hallway to her room. In the moonlight he undressed her. In the moonlight he caressed her. He held breathlessly still while she undressed him, while she caressed him. They caressed, kissed, nibbled, stroked, gloried in each other. "Now?" his lips pressed his question against her breast. "Yes." Her lips pressed her answer against his shoulder and he showed her how wonderful she could be. And when she'd seen what he could do for her, what she could do for him, when they were past exhilaration and gasping, they melded together, arms and legs twined around each other, a perfect fit in afterglow they lay. "Thank you," she whispered, still slightly breathless, and, sounding almost asleep, he answered, "My pleasure."

As Karen drifted off to sleep she caught sight of something small and crimson out of the corner of her eye. She turned her head slightly to see a single red rose in a bud vase next to the book on her bedside table.

Chapter 21

She opened her eyes to see him close to her, his calm gaze fixed on her face. "It's a new day," she said.

"You are the new day. Let me show you the ways." When he'd shown her to her satisfaction, when he'd taken her again and again to the top of the world, when it was almost more than he could bear, with a cry, he leapt into the light and spiraled from the great heights down, down until he collapsed onto her, into her. He was thoroughly and utterly knocked out.

"Your shower is even better when you're in it with me."

"Yes," she said. "My shower has never been this good." She licked his clean shoulder. "Do you like French toast?"

"Almost as much as I like what you're doing right now."

Wrapped in her terry cloth bathrobe, she made French toast. Steve took all the dogs out and brought the Newfoundlands in. They swarmed around him, nosing him, catching his scent, leaning against him. He followed her directions to scoop dog food into their bowls and put the big dogs in the dog room in their crates to eat. Only then did he let Lennox in and showed him he was to eat his breakfast in an out-of-the-way spot in the kitchen.

"Your dogs are not used to men here in the morning." He

stood behind her and wrapped his arms around her, nuzzling her neck.

"No," she said. She wasn't either. But she liked it. She liked it a lot. "They're not. They're used to only Katie and me. Now only me." But she smiled at him over her shoulder. "They're smart. They'll learn."

"Good." He released her. "That smells wonderful."

She carried the two heaping plates to the table. He followed her like a puppy. He was sparing with the butter and syrup, but the rapture on his face told her he liked her French toast very much.

All through breakfast, Karen chewed on thoughts about her daughter. When her French toast was finished, she pushed her plate away and leaned her elbows on the table. "What is Katie doing right now? Do you know?"

Steve leaned back in his chair. "She finished pugil sticks last week." He mentally counted. "She'll be at the swimming pool all this week. Huge indoor pool. Biggest swimming pool east of the Mississippi."

"She'll do well, then. She's an excellent swimmer."

"Different kind of skills. It's not about swimming. It's about water survival."

She asked Steve. "What did your mother say when you told her you wanted to be a Marine?"

"It was expected. I'm a fourth generation Marine on my father's side, and second generation on my mother's."

Karen took this in. "But surely you had a choice."

"I had a choice. I chose to make the decision I was expected to make."

She frowned. "Oh. Then I guess not all Marines are rebelling."

He leaned forward. "The Corps isn't made up of society's misfits and castaways."

"Of course not. I didn't mean . . ."

"Did you ever think maybe Katie wasn't going away from you, but toward something else?"

No. She hadn't. Then she thought of that little white box. "Maybe I should."

He reached out to tuck a lock of her hair behind her ear. "Maybe." He drew his finger down her cheek, lingering at the end. "I'd love nothing more than to spend the entire morning with you, getting to know you better and better. But I have a tree to finish." He pushed his chair away from the table and called to his dog.

Soon the whine of the chain saw broke the morning peace. Karen let her dogs out of their crates and put the dog bowls and dishes in the sink for later. She quickly dressed, then stopped and fell onto her thoroughly rumpled bed. She buried her face in his pillow. She breathed deeply of the faint scent of him.

"Karen!"

She started awake.

"Where are you?" It was Jessie. "Hi there, you great big big dogs. Ferry, don't step on Sagan. You'll give her a complex."

Karen struggled to her feet. She swiped the sleep out of her eyes and made her way down the hall. "Hi, Jess." She sort of shuffled into the kitchen. "You want a cup of tea?" she yawned.

Jessie and the dogs followed her. "You're lazing away all day while Steve toils to chop your tree?" Her voice was crammed with impudence. "What, not enough beauty sleep last night?"

Karen felt her face redden.

"Hmm," Jessie said. "I count three dogs inside and one dog outside. I count four dog dishes in the sink and I know one of them is not Bridgit's because I happen to know Bridgit spent the night with your folks. I called you a little while ago. You didn't answer the phone, so I called your mom. Oh. She said to tell you she was taking Bridgit out to the Wildes' farm and she'd bring her home after supper. Speaking of supper, let's see what else is in your sink. Hmm. Two plates and the stuff you use when you make French toast. Which I happen to know you do not make for just yourself."

Karen waved her hand at her friend. "Knock it off," she said without rancor. She pulled two mugs from the cupboard. "Did you say you wanted tea?" At her friend's nod she pulled out another mug.

She should have known, Jessie never knocked things off. "When I saw Steve outside just now, he had this sort of *energy* aura around him. And you, now, assuming one ignores the fact your face has a pillow-wrinkle crease, you have that same kind of soft, glowy aura."

"And you, you look like the Cheshire Cat."

"Yup. I'm pleased as punch."

"Good. Now drink your tea and go home."

The Newfoundlands were romping in the backyard when Susannah brought Bridgit back after supper, as promised. "We went out to the farm and she stuck to Connie Wilde like a burr in a shorn fleece. I think she likes farm life. She was quite curious about the sheep. We introduced her to that little ram lamb, the one who was orphaned. Bridgit decided he was quite cute. She was very gentle with him." She reached down to hug Bridgit. "I had a wonderful time, beautiful Bridgit. Thank you for going with me." Bridgit actually wagged her tail. Not a great wag, but a definite swish. Maybe a little bit of farm life had given Bridgit a little bit of healing.

Karen let the other dogs in. In a rush to greet Susannah, Ferry shoved Bridgit aside. Heck shoved her too. "How rude, you two," Karen told them. Only Brian waited politely for Susannah's attention.

Karen gestured at Brian. "I like to think," she told her mom, "he is being courteous. But I know he's too old to do any shoving. And Ferry and Heck aren't really being rude to Bridgit. They think so little of her they not only don't see her as a threat, they almost don't see her at all."

Suddenly she couldn't bear it anymore. She sank down on the floor, her arms around her two poor dogs, gathering Brian and Bridgit to her. She loved them all the more fiercely for their frailty. "I don't know what to do about Lennox."

Susannah dropped a kiss on her head. "I love you, Karen."

"I love you too, Mom."

"Don't worry. It will all work out."

"How?"

"I don't know. As the man said, 'It's a mystery.'"

She called Steve to invite him to meet her for lunch. Leftover chicken soup.

"Is there more of your bread?"

"No. We finished that off yesterday. After you finished off my Tree. And then me." She remembered their second shower, and what had followed, in her bed, ending with the bread. "It was marvelous," she whispered, more to herself than to him. But he heard.

"Your marvelous bread." Even over the phone, his voice was intimate. "With marvelous you."

"I'll make more for you."

"It will be marvelous, too."

He arrived with a fresh-out-of-the-oven loaf from Lola's, and a bag of oatmeal raisin cookies for the others in Karen's office.

That afternoon, Candy talked about knitting the blanket for her baby. "My dad ignores it. I think my mom is surprised I wanted to learn how to knit. I told her why I learned. I told her I wanted my baby to have something from me, something really special, so she'd know I didn't throw her away, so she'd know I loved her."

"How did your mother react?"

"She turned around and walked out. But I think she was crying."

"Why do you think that?"

"I heard her go into her bedroom and shut the door. A little while later she came out and I could tell she'd put on more makeup than usual. But her nose was still a little red."

Jessie called. "Can you give me Katie's address? I found an article I think she'd like."

Karen gave Jessie the address. She hung up and heard the kitchen door thump against the wall. She went to investigate. Ferry had nosed the door open and stood staring outside while the cold air rushed into the house. Karen moved her to close the door. "It's cold outside. We don't want all the cold air to come into the house," Karen explained. Then she had an idea. "I should teach you to shut the door."

The guys at the gym were working hard that day. Steve was proud of them. When Mary Lou called, "Steve, phone's for you," he assumed it would be Karen. "Hello, there," he said with a hint of seduction.

There was silence. Then, "Hello there, yourself Stevie." It was May. "I hope you're planning to come to the Birthday Ball. They expect to see you this year. No excuses. And that's not a good way to answer your phone. Lots of people might get the wrong impression."

Steve felt foolish. "You think Dad is going to disown me?"

"No. He'd never do that. Once a Marine, always a Marine."

She clucked. "You aren't very smart about him sometimes. For him, being a Marine means all of it. That means the Birthday Ball. Why don't you bring that woman who teaches your CGC class? Karen, isn't it?"

May said Karen's name so casually, Steve knew she knew perfectly well. "Bring Karen to the Birthday Ball? In the middle of all those dress blues and ball gowns? The Marine Corps at the right hand of God?" That would turn her off instantly.

"Yes. Dress blues, swords, the birthday cake, all of it."

"I don't know."

"Yes. You do know. They expect you. It's the closest thing to an order from Dad. Besides, I want to meet her. I like peace types."

Chapter 22

Dear Mom,

Parris Island has lots of cats hanging around. I think they're feral—don't tell Jessie, she'd have a fit and start some sort of movement to have them all spayed. The only dogs I've seen so far are police dogs. I don't know what breed they are. They sort of look like brindle Belgians. But Belgians aren't brindle, are they? If I thought I'd get a reasonable answer, I'd ask Staff Sergeant McNamara what they are. She's the highest ranking of our three DI's and I think she's the most human. Besides, she's the one who does the classroom teaching and stuff, so she doesn't yell as much as the others. Anyway, I only saw those two dogs once.

He watched her move as she taught the class. He imagined moving with her. He liked moving with her. He tried to imagine her in a fancy gown on his arm at the Birthday Ball. Maybe.

"Girls' Night tonight," Jessie told her, "to welcome the summer opening of the South Pole."

"You must have been a polar explorer in a former life," Karen teased.

"Yeah," Jessie agreed cheerfully. "Either I froze to death with Scott's men or I ate penguins and endured with Shackleton. Pun! Hah! I endured! His ship was named the *Endurance*. Get it?"

"I got it," Karen said dryly.

"Anyway, it's all arranged. You're coming. It's not optional because Melissa is leaving early to pick up the pizza, so you have to give me a ride. Be here at six. We're going to Sally's. Micah is spending the night at Jeremy Martini's and we told Tanner to go test some puppies or something. Actually, he's going out to Jake's. They've decided to work their dogs in team obedience. What a hoot! We all know Wing is perfect, and Balzac is great, but can you just see the two of them? This uber-intense Border collie and this big galooby Lab? Anyway, pick me up at six. Pizza and girl talk and a movie. Sally got that new Heath Ledger one. Yum!"

So they ate that expensive pizza, talked about Karen and Steve, and Sylvie swore that more than anything, men loved their women in silk. Nothing but silk. Karen thought about silk and forgot to pay attention to Heath Ledger. Poor Heath. He was cute, but there was no way he could ever compete with Steve Songer.

Dear Mom,

Today was picture day. Sort of like the assembly-line pictures in elementary school. Only here they tell you not to smile. I guess they want us to look serious and sober. I think we all felt that way, at least, I did. Being a Marine is really important to me. I hope you'll come down for my graduation. At least, if I pass everything. If not, I'll be put back a week. So I can't tell you the exact date yet. Please come down. They're sending you some pamphlets and stuff about where to get hotel rooms in Beaufort—that's the town closest to Parris Is-

*land. That's where most of the families stay when they
come for graduation. Please. I want you to be here.*

*Love,
Katie*

"What does she mean? If she passes everything?" Karen
couldn't relax until she had the answer.

"Requirements for graduation." He kissed the inside of her
elbow.

"What if she doesn't pass?"

He kissed her neck. "They will put her back a week with
whatever platoon is working on that requirement. But don't
worry. She'll pass."

"Why are you always so sure?"

"Because I know Katie. I have seen her work hard to
achieve a goal. She has what it takes, both physically and
mentally. She has heart. Besides, this is important to her. She
will succeed. She wouldn't accept less." He kissed her neck
again. "It's something she inherited from you."

He didn't know. He only saw her from the outside. He
didn't see her cringing in fear on the inside. She didn't want
him to see her fear. "What will she be doing this week?"

He paused mid-kiss to think. "She'll be in the field-training
battalion for two weeks. They'll live out there."

"What's that?"

"Marksmanship. One of the requirements for graduation."

"Why Katie? She's a girl—a woman. She won't be in combat."

"She'll be a Marine. All Marines, *all* of them—even female Marines—are required to pass marksmanship."

"But—"

He put his finger to her lips. "This is the way the Marines
do things."

* * *

She didn't know how they ended up talking about high school and proms, but somehow he said something, and then she said she'd never been to a prom, and then he said, "November tenth is the Marine Corps' birthday. Every year we hold a Birthday Ball. It's pretty fancy. Dress uniforms, and those swords you like. Would you go with me this year?"

She was stunned. Lunch at Lola's was one thing, but a formal ball was something totally different. A formal ball was a big thing. She wasn't prepared for a big thing. She had never done a big thing. She didn't know how to do big things. She didn't even know how to find out how to do big things. "What do women wear?" She wasn't sure she wanted to know the answer.

"Long fancy dresses. Ball gowns."

"Oh." She didn't own a ball gown. She never had. She didn't know anyone who did. Jessie and Melissa wouldn't be caught dead in dresses, ball or any other kind. Sally didn't own any clothes she couldn't teach kindergarten in. Sylvie might conceivably own such a thing—but Sylvie's idea of a ball gown would surely include hand-painted fairies and dragons and lots of glitter, and it would certainly have gauzy wings attached to the back. Sylvie could pull something like that off and make it look stunning. Karen couldn't.

"You're frowning." He kissed the wrinkle in her forehead. "So what are you thinking?"

"I guess I'll need a really great dress." Though how she would manage to perform that major miracle was beyond her.

He kissed her. "I'll have my sister call you. She'll help you figure out all the female stuff. You'll like her. She's dog people."

"Your sister who raises Am Staffs?"

"Yes. My sister May."

* * *

Steve always completed his missions. The next day, he called May to ask her to call Karen to help with the ball gown stuff.

"You must like her a lot," May teased, "to inflict the Birthday Ball *and* Mom and Dad on her all at once. Or are you bringing her up beforehand so we can all meet her?"

"Uh . . ."

"I guess not. Okay, I'll tell everyone to be on best behavior. And of course I'll call her and answer any questions she has. Any and all. Even if she wants to know about the time when we were at the beach and Mom was pregnant with Rick and—"

"On the other hand," Steve interrupted her, "I can always call Mom and ask her to help."

"And deprive me of meeting her first? You better not!"

"Then don't threaten me with blackmail."

"But, Stevie, you were so cute!"

"May or Mom? And don't call me Stevie."

"Oh, all right."

"Karen? This is May, Steve's sister. I have Am Staffs."

Karen knew anyone who identified themselves by their breed was dog people. Everything was going to be okay. She relaxed. "Hi, May. I'm glad you called."

They talked for almost an hour. They talked about dogs, and Steve, and Ohio, and May said to be sure to ask anything she wanted to know. "I've been doing this Marine thing all my life. Oh, when you say Birthday Ball, it's pronounced with capital letters."

But the main question Karen had, the thing she most needed to know, was, "Do you know where I can get a really great dress?"

"Do I ever. I know exactly where to go. Come up on Saturday. We'll spend the whole day shopping."

* * *

Steve stayed at the gym till nine on Wednesday nights. So after work, Karen stopped at the Hartley mall. Sylvie told her to go to that new department store. The second floor, she said. Karen went to the second floor and bought a deep red silk robe. She felt wanton. She felt daring. She felt sexy. It was a new feeling for her. She liked it.

Then it was Friday again.

"Would you like to come over for *Friday Night Fights*?" he asked. Just as Karen knew he would ask. She was dreading the question. She didn't want to say no. She didn't want to disappoint him. But he asked, and even though she wished she didn't have to, she said, "no."

"I promised Mom I'd bring Bridgit over for the weekend. They really like having Bridgit around. Besides, I have to get up early to take care of the dogs and drive to Cleveland. I'm going shopping with May, remember."

Steve said, of course, he understood. She didn't know if he did or not.

She drove Bridgit out to her parents' house where her mother and father welcomed Bridgit with open arms. Bridgit felt at home in their house. Karen watched her carefully. "She seems more like a whole dog, not a shadow."

"Bridgit's not a shadow," her father said. "She's a great dog, aren't you, girl?"

Bridgit wagged her tail. She actually wagged her tail. Bridgit wasn't autistic, Karen realized, she was protecting herself. "What are you afraid of?" she asked the dog.

"Karen," Susannah said. "Come see your father's Christmas present." Every year, her mother knit a sweater for her dad. By now it wasn't a surprise, it was a tradition, and as a tradition it did not have to be hidden from the recipient.

Karen admired the sweater-in-progress. "You do amazing work," she said.

"I've been knitting so long I could do it in my sleep," her mother said.

"Why do you need to knit?" Karen asked. "What keeps you knitting one more sweater, one more pair of socks?"

Susannah thought. "I think," she said at last, "it's more than the feel of the wool, or the rhythm of creating a pattern. Knitting a sweater, or socks, or a shawl, or afghan, it's an act of faith."

"In what?"

"In the permanence of the relationship. Don't you think so? Some knitters believe it is bad luck to knit a sweater for a man you're not engaged or married to. I'd rather think it's an act of faith that the relationship will grow."

Karen fingered the yarn. Maybe she would knit a sweater for Steve for Christmas. Christmas seemed like a long way away.

"You said you're going to Cleveland tomorrow?" Susannah asked.

"Yes. I'm going shopping with Steve's sister May. Which reminds me, I have to get home. Thanks for keeping Bridgit for me."

"It's our pleasure, dear. We love having her."

Chapter 23

Karen drove up to Cleveland in the early morning rain. Steve's directions were clear and she found May's street easily. She counted the houses on the right side of the street. One, two, three. There it was, the redbrick split-level with a tall privacy fence on the side. She was here. She pulled in the driveway and turned off her engine. She was about to meet Steve's sister. Meeting family was important. Still, she'd rather meet them one at a time then all in a group at the ball.

May's front door opened before Karen was out of the car.

"Karen!" May held her hands out in welcome. "I'm so very glad to meet you. Come in, come in."

Karen liked May immediately. May was comfortable. May was a dog person. "Is this Flame?" The dog looked like an older, more feminine version of Lennox. "Hello, there," Karen said.

Flame was as cheerfully outgoing as Lennox. Karen liked her immediately, too. Flame crawled up on the couch and appropriated her lap so Karen could pet her. "Lennox is the first Am Staff I've ever met," she told May. On the way up, she'd decided she had to be honest with Steve's sister. "Before I met him, I didn't think I'd like him. In fact, I was sure I wouldn't. My friend Jessie told me I was a racist. I guess I was. Then I met Lennox. I like him a lot."

May nodded. "People often feel that way about Am Staffs. Jason, my husband, who is doing guy things today by the way, was that way. When I met him he'd never heard of Am Staffs. He'd heard about pit bulls, of course. You can't live in Ohio without hearing about pit bulls. I was living with Mom and Dad then. They had Flame's great-grandmother, Synge. Jason was really nervous around her for a while. But she won him over."

May drove them to the new mall and they spent the morning trying on dress after dress after dress.

"I'm glad you're coming to the Birthday Ball. We will have so much fun!" May said as she zipped Karen into yet another possibility. "I bet you've never seen Steve in his dress blues. He's really a hunk."

Karen thought Steve was a hunk without his dress blues. She thought he was a hunk without anything at all. She blushed. May laughed in delight. Then they turned their attention to the possible dress. They thought not.

They stopped for lunch in a little bistro in the middle of the mall.

After they ordered, May told Karen how she felt when her husband was first sent to Iraq. "I used to have these dreams. They were always so real. The phone rings, and it's him. He starts to tell me he's okay—and then all of a sudden, I wake up. And I desperately want to be back asleep so I can hear him talking to me again. "

"Did you talk to him? When he was over there?"

"Once. He was in Baghdad. He was talking to some guy from CNN—not an interview, just talking. The guy pulls out his phone, hands it to him and says, here, call your wife. Tell her you're okay." May's eyes filled. "That guy from CNN will never know he gave me the best present in the world."

"I bet he knows," Karen said.

May wiped the corner of her eye. "Steve tells me your daughter is at Parris Island."

"Katie. Yes."

"You must be very proud of her."

Karen searched May's eyes. May was absolutely serious. Karen didn't know what to say. Karen didn't know what she felt. She was sure it wasn't pride.

"Well," May said, "if you aren't now, you will be. Trust me. When you go down for her graduation, you'll feel so proud you'll want to burst."

"I'm not so sure," Karen admitted.

May reached across the linen tablecloth to press her hand. "I am."

After lunch, they went to one more store. There they found The Perfect Dress. As soon as she slid it over her head and May zipped her up, she knew. May knew. There was no doubt. This was The Dress.

"Of course," May said, "you'll need a strapless bra."

"I've never had a strapless bra."

"Then it's way past time." She snapped her fingers. "I know. Let's go over to the lingerie department and find you one. It'll be my present." She grinned wickedly. "Sort of kinky. Buying underwear for my brother's date."

An hour later, at the mall entrance, Karen stood guard over their purchases while May ran through the rain to get her car. They didn't want The Dress to get wet.

Back in Hartley, Karen pulled into her garage so she could carry The Dress into the house without going outside, so it wouldn't get wet. She draped the huge garment bag over the kitchen table while she let the dogs out. They came in all wet. She toweled them, but Newfoundland coat held more water than a towel could deal with. They were very interested in this big thing on the table. They sniffed all over it. They sniffed all over her. Ferry's ears were on alert as she sniffed.

"You smell May's dogs?"

Ferry sniffed.

Karen looked at the garment bag that dwarfed her kitchen

table. She thought of the small closet in her bedroom. Nope. She hauled The Dress, in its cocoon, upstairs and hung it in the extra bedroom so it wouldn't get crushed. And so it wouldn't get long, silky, black dog hairs all over it. Or worse, dog slobber.

She called Steve. "I'm home."

"Did you have a nice day?"

"Yes. I found a dress and I like your sister very much." She decided not to tell him about the strapless bra.

"She's okay," he said in a tone of voice that told her he thought May was more than just okay.

"I always wanted a sister. I guess that's why my friends mean so much to me. They're as close to sisters as I'll ever get."

"Speaking of close to you," he said.

"You want to get close to me?" she asked.

"If I show up on your porch, will you let me in?"

"You want to come in?"

"Yes I do."

Where did this come from? she wondered. Where did she learn how to do this? To speak in double entendres; use innocent words in suggestive ways? This was one of those times she really needed a sister. Did other people talk like this when they fell in love? Other people, such as her friends. Sally. Oh my! No! Sally and Tanner would never say those kinds of things to each other. Of course not. Would they? She had to call Sally to find out.

"Hello. Karen, are you still there?"

"Yes. I'm here. I just had a thought. I'll see you soon. Please hurry."

"If that thought has anything to do with whipped cream, you bet I'll hurry."

"Whipped cream? What does whipped cream have to do with anything?"

"You haven't seen that commercial?"

"What commer—oh." Karen felt the warm melt all the way down to her toes.

"I'll stop at Abernathy's for whipped cream. We'll act it out."

She dialed Sally's number and drummed her fingers while Sally's phone rang. "Sally," she said when her friend finally answered. "Can you talk?"

"Of course I can talk. I learned to talk when I—"

"No. Not that. I mean, can you talk freely. Without any men-types listening."

"Oh. Sure. My men-types are at the Croton show. Just me and Maxie and the cats. And the fishies. And they know how to keep secrets. What secrets are we keeping?"

"Um. When you and Tanner . . . I guess this is sort of personal, but I really need to know. When you started . . . when your relationship started getting . . . um . . . personal, did you say things to each other in private ways?"

"What are you talking about?"

"I need to know I'm normal."

"Normal how? You're confusing me. I have absolutely no clue what you're talking about."

So Karen told her about the conversation she'd just had with Steve. "It's like I have a secret life. On the one hand, I'm me, professional shrink, but then when I talk to Steve, especially on the phone, on second thought, no, it's not only when we're talking on the phone . . . I . . . um . . . turn into some private secret femme fatale. Is that normal? I mean, do you and Tanner talk like that? I've known Tanner for years and years and I can't imagine he even knows what some of that *means*."

Sally laughed. Sally howled. Sally dropped the phone. It sounded like Sally fell off her chair. "Oh Karen," she said, her words coming in gasps between the gales of her hilarity. "If you only knew! Believe it or not, Tanner is . . . I'm getting hot just thinking about it!"

She was normal then. Good.

Karen met Steve at the door. She had on her new silk robe. Nothing but her new silk robe.

They finally crawled out of bed around noon. Earlier they'd taken the dogs out, fed them, then Steve held something out to Karen. It was the extra container of whipped cream. "Buy one, get one free," Steve said, a gleam in his eyes. They'd taken each other back to Karen's bedroom. They stayed until the whipped cream was all gone.

In the shower, Steve said, "Let's take the dogs for a walk."

So they took Ferry and Heck and Lennox to the park. Karen looked at the big trees. She and Steve had kissed in the shadows of those trees. She smiled to herself. Even though there were no shadows today, they continued the under-the-trees tradition.

Back home Steve picked up the brochure on her counter. Where to stay in Beaufort. The Marines had sent it.

"Have you made hotel reservations yet?" he asked.

"Hotel reservations?"

"For Beaufort. For Katie's graduation."

"Oh. It's so far off." She didn't want to admit she'd all but forgotten about it.

Steve said, "You don't understand how many people come to Parris Island to see their Marines graduate. Hundreds of new Marines graduate every week. Their families come to see them. Most of them stay in Beaufort, South Carolina. Trust me. If you don't have a room by now, you won't find one. It's too late."

"I will." Karen was sure he exaggerated. Besides, it was so far off, and Katie didn't even know for sure that she was going to graduate. But she couldn't say that to Steve.

* * *

Monday was gloomy and gray. "Not a ray of sunshine in the sky," she told Theresa that morning.

"Until your guy jogs by. He's sure a day with sunshine."

"The other night I overheard my parents argue," Candy told her. "They were yelling at each other. I think they were fighting about me."

"What happened?"

"They were up in their bedroom with the door closed. But they were yelling awfully loud. Then Dad went out and slammed the front door. My mom really hates that; the whole house sort of shakes. Mom stayed in her room all evening. I didn't see her again. Dad came home really late. I guess he bumped into something and made a noise. Anyway, I woke up and had to go to the bathroom. I ran into him in the hallway. He smelled like he'd been drinking."

"Does he drink a lot?"

"No. Hardly ever."

May called her the next evening. "I have an idea," she said. "Why don't you come up here next Saturday morning. We can spend the day doing girly things together. You know. Getting our hair done, manicure, pedicure even; the whole before-the-ball thing. I won two free passes to this new beauty spa. Besides, you'll need help getting into that gorgeous dress. And I could sure use help getting into mine."

Maybe, Karen thought as she hung up the phone, she could ask May why in the world a young girl, with her whole life ahead of her, would want to be a Marine.

* * *

"She reminds me of Jessie," Karen told Steve when he arrived for supper.

"Who? May?"

Karen nodded.

Steve grinned. "You're right. She does. They both like to stick their noses into other peoples' business."

"It's a good thing they've never met. Can you imagine what would happen if the two of them got their heads together? The rest of the world wouldn't stand a chance."

Chapter 24

In spite of the raw breeze Wednesday morning, Steve and Lennox jogged past Karen's window and waved. He actually blew her a small kiss.

"Neither rain nor sleet, blah, blah, blah," said Theresa.

"That's the post office."

"That's your man and his dog," said Vicky.

"And you always seem to know when he's jogging by," Karen teased.

"I always appreciate beauty. Even in sweats, that man is a sight to behold."

Out of sweats, Karen thought, he was even more of a sight to behold. But she didn't share that with the two women crowding to look out the window with her.

Theresa said, "We should get over to that gym for an exercise class. Watching him for an hour would be such an inspiration."

"I think some woman teaches the exercise classes."

Theresa's face fell. "He ought to teach them. The women of Hartley would never dread bathing-suit weather again."

Speaking of inspirations, if Steve and Lennox could brave the weather, so could she. One of her clients had cancelled their morning appointment. So Karen snapped a leash on Bridgit and they set out for the yarn shop. They did not jog. They walked at a sedate pace until they were within sight of Wilde's. Then Bridgit picked up the pace and even began to pull on the leash. Karen told herself it was because Bridgit was cold.

"Beautiful Bridgit!" Mrs. Wilde exclaimed. "Hello, Karen, how lovely to see you. Connie," she called, "Karen and Bridgit are here."

Bridgit pawed the shining floor. She wanted to find Connie. Karen sighed and unsnapped her leash. Bridgit found Connie. Connie reached down to hug the big dog. "Hello, Beautiful Bridgit. Would you like to help us choose a pattern for a baby hat?"

The woman with Connie looked slightly familiar to Karen.

"Karen Matheson," one of the knitters in the chairs called out to her. It was Laura, the woman who could quilt like a dream. "I haven't seen you in ages. How are you doing?"

So Karen left Bridgit with Connie and went to chat with Laura for a few moments. She looked at Laura's knitting. "That's lovely!"

"Thanks. I blame it on the Wildes and your mother. They bullied me into this. I told them I couldn't knit to save my life and they refused to listen. I think when it comes to knitting they're selectively deaf."

Karen chuckled. "You've got that right."

"What can we help you find today, dear?" Mrs. Wilde said.

"I want to knit a sweater. It's a Christmas present for a man."

Mrs. Wilde's faded blue eyes twinkled merrily. "Sounds lovely. What did you have in mind?"

Karen chose yarn and a pattern she thought would fit Steve. She set her finds on the counter and moved over to the side to look for needles. The woman making the baby hat pulled out her checkbook. She asked Connie about knitting classes. "I haven't knitted since I was a girl," she said. "I've never done anything on double-pointed needles before."

Laura, the woman who quilted like a dream, spoke up from

one of the cozy chairs. "You can do it. If I can learn to knit, anyone can learn to knit!"

After work, Karen stopped off at that store at the mall. She bought another silk robe. This one was very dark blue. This one was from the men's department.

That night, after a quick supper of leftovers, Karen settled down on the couch, pulled out her new yarn, looked over the pattern and cast on.

"Tonight," Karen told her class, "we're going to talk about supervised isolation. That's the official test language. In real words, it means you can leave your dog alone and he won't howl or bark or whine excessively; he won't become worried and turn into an emotional wreck. Your dog is not really alone. The evaluator is there, and other dogs doing their supervised isolation. You are behind a door, or behind a screen, but your dog cannot see you. Your dog trusts you to return to him. This trust gives him the confidence to wait calmly for you to come back."

After class, she and Steve took Lennox and Ferry for a walk in the park. Steve slipped a white envelope from his pocket. "Letter from Katie. I thought you would want to read it."

Dear Steve,

   During grass week, we wore our desert cammies and moved to the rifle range. It's noisy. I guess I never realized how loud a gazillion rifles are when they're all fired at the same time. Only, yesterday it rained all afternoon, so we stayed under cover and cleaned our rifles over and over again. At first here, I didn't know if I could do it. But now I know I will make it to the end.

*You know why? Because I refuse to give up. Every time
I think I can't do it anymore, I think of the first Ward
Gatti fight and I get up and do whatever it is I thought
I couldn't do. Give Lennox a kiss for me.*

Katie

Karen finished the letter and folded it up. "She sounds happier."

"She is."

Halloween came on Friday this year. In the afternoon, the
schoolkids all came downtown to trick-or-treat along the
main streets of town. Ghosts, witches, princesses, mummies,
and several Darth Mauls. "Why do grown-ups encourage the
kids to want to play the bad guys?" Theresa asked as she
handed out candy. "When I was a kid, no one wanted to be the
bad guys. We all wanted to be the Lone Ranger."

"You're saying Darth Maul isn't an appropriate role model
for today's children?" Karen teased. She recognized Theresa's
soapbox.

"I most certainly am. The manufacturers are at fault here
for putting his face on kids' shoes and bikes and underwear
and now Halloween costumes. As if he were a hero or something."

Vicky wrested the candy basket from Theresa's hands. "We
always tell kids it's so important to be themselves. Now they
can be. Here, let me take over the candy detail."

"Trick or treat!"

Heroes, Karen thought as she went back to her office.
What heroes do we need for this new world of ours? Melissa's
hero was James Herriott of course. Jessie's heroes were
mostly scientists like Carl Sagan, or polar explorers like
Ernest Shackleton. Mel Gibson didn't count as a hero, even
though Jessie would have argued this point. Liz at the library

worshipped Julia Child. Sylvie made up her own heroes, valiant characters who dispatched dragons before breakfast. What about me? Karen thought. Who are my heroes? She stuck her elbows on her desk, chin on her folded hands and stared out the window at the trick-or-treaters dressed in all manner of costumes dancing down the street. Who? Karen thought.

The answer came to her as a gentle breeze rather than a stroke of lightning. Her mother. Susannah the Serene. She always wanted to be like her mother, always wanted her mother to be proud of her. Well, that was normal, Karen defended herself. Mothers are role models for their daughters. What decisions did you make based on how your mother might feel about them? she asked herself. "No," Karen said. Not going there. She pushed away from her desk and went to the front door.

"Yo, Victoria!" she said in the kind of voice she thought a gangster would use. "Hand over the candy and no one gets hurt. It's my turn to pass it out to the little guys."

"You're real tough," Vicky played along. "You want me to run away in fear?"

No, Karen thought. I'm the one running away. "The parents of Hartley should be the ones running," she said. "With all this sugar we're giving their kids, the little goobers'll be bouncing off the walls tonight."

Her mother called. "I'd like to pick up Bridgit tonight," she said. "We've been invited to the farm for the day tomorrow. We told them we'd help pick the last apples. They want to get a truly early start and I didn't want to come over and get Bridgit that early and have to wake you up."

"Okay. Hey, Mom, I know what you're doing. I appreciate it. I know it's a temporary fix, but—"

"I'm doing nothing at all. You're doing me a favor by allowing me to borrow your foster dog so I don't feel left out at the farm tomorrow. Connie has all her sheep, and all those other various critters, now I have a critter, too."

"Yeah, well, thanks."

"You're welcome, sweetie. I'll see you after dinner."

Sylvie showed up on her front porch.

"What's up?" Karen asked.

"The Buckeyes." Sylvie made a face as she gushed over Ferry and Heck. "They're playing the Fighting Illini. Ray and Jean-Luc and the Boogaloo are all glued to the TV, and the place was filling up with so much testosterone that I had to escape! Ray is doing his darndest to turn the Boogaloo into a Buckeye!"

Karen patted her friend's shoulder. "There, there," she said with a grin.

"I couldn't even go upstairs and work. Ray believes watching OSU football is a participant sport. If he doesn't like one of the ref's calls, he incites Jean-Luc to riot, and Jean-Luc runs around barking. Boy! The things we don't know about men before we marry them! I was ready for the toilet-seat thing. But football? I want sanctuary."

Ferry and Heck wandered off, leaving Brian, who tottered over to Sylvie. Sylvie put her arms around Brian and hugged him, carefully, so he didn't lose his balance. "Hi there, old guy. Gee, I really like the slow-motion wag of the tail thing. Newest craze among geezer dogs, is it?"

"Watch out," Karen teased. "You're hugging some testosterone."

"Nah," Sylvie said, her affection for the old dog apparent. "He's too old. I think any testosterone is way past the sell-by date. Besides, he was fixed a long time ago, so he probably hasn't had any testosterone for ages and ages. But I don't see Bridgit."

"Mom borrowed her. Third weekend in a row Mom found some excuse to borrow her. I think it's fishy."

"Nah. I think she wants a dog."

"Then why doesn't she just tell my dad they're getting a dog?"

Sylvie smiled. "Sometimes it's best if you help your husband think it's his idea. Of course, if he really took the time to sit down and think it through he'd probably come to the same decision himself, so really, you're just saving everyone a bunch of time." She looked pleased with this bit of logic. "Speaking of manipulating men, I heard through the grapevine you got this really great dress."

"Which has nothing to do with manipulation."

"Of course it does. Clothes are designed around manipulation of the opposite sex. Women have known that since the days of the caves. So, are you going to let me see it, or what?"

"Sure. Unhand my dog and follow me. The Dress is upstairs."

Sylvie made her put it on. Including the strapless bra. She made Karen stand still while she studied it critically from all angles. Finally she nodded her approval. "It's gorgeous," she pronounced. "Stunning. It's a total knockout. That décolletage screams pure and unadulterated manipulation. Steve, poor unsuspecting man, doesn't have a chance."

The doorbell rang. Downstairs, the dogs rushed toward the door, barking happily. "I'll get it," Sylvie said. "Turn around. I'll unzip you. Quick." And she was on her way down the stairs. "You put that dress away," she called back. "Don't let him see it until you're ready for the ball." Karen heard the front door open. "You must be Steve," she heard Sylvie say. "I've heard a lot about you."

She gave him a flat box.

"What's this?"

"You like me in silk so much I decided I wanted to have the same thrill. I thought I would like you in silk, too. Nothing but silk." She was right.

Drowsing in bed the next morning with Steve, also drowsing, Karen caught sight of the two silk robes tangled together over the back of her rocking chair. She smiled to herself. Sylvie was right about silk. Suddenly, she hoped Sylvie was right about The Dress. Was this manipulation? And how did Sylvie ever learn about manipulating men? If this was one of those things women shared, why hadn't Karen heard it before? Because, she could imagine Sally, always the teacher, answering, if you weren't ready for this piece of women's wisdom, you'd never have heard it, even if we'd screamed in your ear.

"What're you thinking?" Steve asked. His voice was sensual and lazy all at the same time.

"About silk." And she showed him.

Chapter 25

Monday afternoon, Candy said, "I felt the baby move," and then she burst into tears.

Karen nodded. She understood only too well. She offered a tissue.

"Thanks," Candy said. She wiped her nose. "She's real now. The baby. Before she was . . . I don't know . . ."

"Abstract?"

"Yeah. I mean, she was always real to herself, but to me she was abstract. I didn't feel much different, so it was easy to pretend she wasn't there, or to wonder if the doctor was wrong. But now, now I can feel her move sometimes."

"So you realize the baby is really real."

"Yes." She started to cry again, this time her tears welling up from the deepest depths. "I don't know what to do."

"You must be feeling overwhelmed right now."

"I am."

"What do you not know about? Maybe I can help you figure it out."

"I don't know about her. About giving her to someone else. Before, when she was abstract, I could think about it. But now, now that she's real, can I do it? Mom says it's the best thing for me. Before, I used to think it was the best thing for her. But now, is it?" She turned an anguished face to Karen. "How do I know that I'm making this decision because it's the best thing for *her,* and not because it's easiest for me?"

"Is it the easiest thing for you?"

"I don't know. I don't expect giving her away will be easy. I think that part of it will be really hard; I feel really connected to her now. I took the responsibility for her when I didn't have an abortion, like my parents wanted, when I didn't kill her. But that was still before she was really real."

"And now?"

"Now she's real and I'm connected to her. She's part of me. Giving her up would be like cutting off my arm. Well, not really my arm. But it *would* be like cutting off part of me."

"Cutting off part of you would be difficult."

"But would it be the best thing for her?"

"What do you think?"

"I think it would. But do I think this because it's the easiest thing for me?"

"In other words, you feel it's important to make this decision based on the baby's needs rather than your own."

"Yeah."

"You know what I think?" Karen asked. "If you were only considering your own needs, you wouldn't even ask the question."

Candy worked on that. "Really?" she said at last.

"Really."

The girl's face relaxed in visible relief.

"You're also right that it's going to be difficult to give the baby to someone else to raise."

Candy placed her hand on her still-flat belly in that protective way mothers do. "I guess it'll be easier because I know it's the right decision for the right reasons. Even if it's really hard."

Karen watched Candy walk down the sidewalk, the ends of her scarf flying in the chill wind. She liked Candy. Candy was one great kid, a very special young woman.

* * *

She stopped at Abernathy's on the way home. She was almost out of yeast and bread flour. She pushed her cart up and down the aisles, not seeing the crowded shelves at all, but thinking about Candy. She wondered if Candy's parents saw their daughter's maturity, and understood how rare it was, and hard-won.

"Oh, I'm sorry! I wasn't looking where I was going." She found herself surrounded by shelves of aspirin and throat lozenges and apologizing to a mother with a flush-faced and fussy child.

"Then at least," Steve said that night when he called, "tell me what color it is so I can order your corsage."

"Corsage?"

"Yes. You know. That flower the man brings so she can pin it on her dress."

"I know what a corsage is. I've never . . . It's deep turquoise. Not dark as much as deep." A corsage. This was going to be a really big date. Bigger than either of the two dates she'd had in high school.

Karen's throat felt scratchy when she woke up the next morning. She fed the dogs and made herself a soothing cup of hot tea with honey and lemon. It helped, but by lunchtime she upped the stakes from scratchy to sore. She filled her antique teapot with hot, sweet tea and set it on her desk where she could refill her cup over and over. It didn't help.

The next day, along with her sore throat, she felt generally lousy.

"You okay?" Theresa asked.

"Sure, why?"

"I wondered why that sweater was on the back of your chair instead of on the back of you. I'm chilly." She shivered.

"The heating system in this old house is having a tantrum about something."

"I'm fine. I think I caught a little bit of a cold, that's all. Here, you borrow my sweater. My mom made it. It's really warm."

She woke up in the middle of the night and knew it wasn't a little bit of a cold after all. It wasn't a little bit of anything. It was a great big chunk of sore throat. She listened to the rain stomp on the roof for a while. Then she got up and dug out her thermometer. She had a fever. This was not good. She pulled the quilt from her bed and got another from the closet, and spent the rest of the night huddled on the couch wrapped in two quilts and a woolen scarf. The cup of hot tea with lemon and honey didn't help.

In the morning, she called Vicky to say she wouldn't be in. She called her doctor to say she needed to come in. Then she called Jessie. "I think I'm sick. Can you please teach dog school for me tonight? Please?" It even hurt to talk.

"Sure. What's going on?"

"Sore throat and fever."

"Yuck. You *should* stay away from dog school then, even though dogs usually don't pick up things from humans."

The doctor said her throat was certainly a bit red. Yes, she did seem to have a fever. Karen tried valiantly not to gag when the doc swabbed her throat for a culture. She swept the swab away and returned a few minutes later. "The quick test was negative for strep. However, your throat does look sore. Do you want some antibiotics?"

Karen shook her head. "No, thanks. I don't want to contribute to the creation of superbugs."

"Then stay home, take aspirin, drink plenty of fluids. The usual. Chicken soup. Call me if you don't get better." And she whisked out of the room, on to the next patient. Karen climbed off the exam table. She was glad she wasn't a medical doctor. Imagine having to take care of patients and at the same time kowtow to HMO's and insurance companies. God and mammon.

She wound her scarf around her neck, buttoned her coat all the way up to her chin, and headed out into the gloomy gray drizzle.

At home she put on her flannel nightgown and an Enya CD. She wrapped herself in a quilt and picked up Katie's shawl. After only three rounds she was too tired to knit.

The phone woke her. It was Jessie.

"What did the doc say?"

"I have a cold. Strep test was negative."

"That's good, because strep is just plain nasty in a basket and Sally says it's going around her school. Say, I have half an hour for lunch. Is there anything you need from Abernathy's?"

She started to say no, but then she changed her mind. "Some of Lola's chicken soup would be heaven."

"You got it," Jessie said.

Jessie arrived bearing Lola's chicken soup. She took one look at Karen and ordered her back to bed. If her room was too cold, then back to the couch. She loaded Karen's CD player with Celtic music. She filled the water bowl, took all the dogs out, let them back in, and dried them off. She even put a load of dog towels in the washing machine. Then she made Karen a cup of hot tea with lemon and honey. "I'm going to put it over here on the table," she announced cheerfully. "Next to the tissues. And I'm not going to give you a hug and tuck you in, either. Those germs of yours look perfectly loathsome. Oh," she added, one hand on the doorknob, "you're almost out of honey. I'll bring more over later. Bye."

Karen ate the chicken soup, drank the tea, blew her nose, and huddled under her quilts. If she stayed warm and took care of herself she'd be fine by Saturday. She'd wear The

Dress and knock Steve out and her very first ball would be a night she'd remember for the rest of her life. She fell asleep and dreamed Candy came over and took Bridgit and Brian away and sent them to live with her baby. She said the dogs would keep her baby company, and her baby wouldn't be sad anymore.

Popsicles and honey, Steve muttered to himself as he pulled into Abernathy's parking lot on the way home after dog school. That's what Jessie told him to take to her. He grabbed a basket and headed to the frozen foods. He made up his mind quickly. He pulled the frosty doors open and tossed into his basket a box of pure 100% fruit pops, and a box of those red, white, and blue ones, and a box of tropical pops, even though they were only 10% juice. And a box of those vanilla ice cream and orange sherbet things. Then he thought she might like lime sherbet so he added a pint of that as well. Then he went in search of honey. His final stop was on the way to the cash registers—one dozen red roses in a glass vase. They may only be grocery-store roses, but he figured they'd convey his meaning.

She didn't answer his knock, but he could hear the dogs on the other side of the door, so he let himself in. He held food and flowers high as he waded through the dogs. In the kitchen he shoved the frozen things in the freezer. Then, carrying the roses, he went to find her.

She was asleep on the couch underneath piles of blankets. Her face was flushed and locks of hair clumped around her forehead, stuck together with perspiration. If anything, Jessie had underestimated how sick Karen was.

He glanced at his watch. Under the circumstances, he didn't think it was too late to call. He found the phone and looked for the phone book.

"Hello, Susannah?" he said. "This is Steve Songer."

Chapter 26

From a drowsy distance, she thought she heard her mother's voice, but that couldn't be right, so she decided she must be dreaming and went back to sleep.

He pulled his chair next to the couch where he could keep a close eye on her while she slept. Brian was asleep in the bedroom. He hadn't woken up even when Susannah arrived and, a few minutes later, left. Heck snored softly stretched out under the window. Ferry and Lennox sat next to him, one on each side. "I guess you two have decided to keep fire watch with me tonight." he said. "Thank you. I'm glad for your company."

At midnight, he left Ferry to watch over Karen while he and Lennox took a brief walk around. The house was secure. In the kitchen he discovered a loaf of bread. Karen made the best bread. He sliced a thick slab and put it in the toaster. He found the butter and opened the refrigerator for that cherry jam. Karen told him her mother made it. Last weekend she brought him warm toast with butter and cherry jam and he was careful not to let it drip on the sheets. Or her. He told her it tasted like summer. She tasted like summer.

Now he leaned up against the counter and ate warm toast with butter and cherry jam. It tasted like summer.

Her eyes fluttered open. "Hello," he said softly.
"Hello," she said. She winced.

"Throat sore?"

She nodded.

"Don't talk. I'll be right back." He brought her a 10% real juice frozen pop.

"Thanks," she whispered.

When she handed him the stick he gently wiped her face and neck with a cool washcloth. "Don't talk," he said.

She suddenly seemed to realize he was here. She saw Lennox sprawled out in front of the fireplace and her eyes widened. She quickly glanced around.

"She's not here," he told her.

"Where?" Her voice was a croak. It sounded painful.

"Your mom is taking care of her. I called your mom. I told her you were sick and I was going to take care of you. She came over immediately and took Bridgit home with her. Remarkable woman, your mom. I assume your father is remarkable as well."

She nodded.

"I'd like to meet him sometime. Now. You wait here. I'll be back." He brought her a dry nightgown and her pillow. "Your room is like a refrigerator, so they'll feel cold." He helped her off with the old and on with the new.

"Feels good," she whispered. She pressed her hot cheek against the cool pillow.

He shook out her quilts and tucked them around her. "Go back to sleep," he told her. "I'm here if you need anything."

She closed her eyes. "Thank you," she whispered.

"You're welcome," he whispered. He dropped a kiss on her hot cheek.

In the morning he washed her in the shower. His touch was one of comfort and care rather than seduction. He gently tipped her head back and washed her hair. His fingers on her scalp felt marvelous. She closed her eyes to better concentrate on the feeling. Shampoo never felt this good when she washed her own hair. He dried her, taking care not to tangle her hair. He slipped her last clean nightgown over her head, tied her bathrobe around her and led her back to the couch. "Sit," he said. She sat. He wrapped a quilt around her. "Wait here."

"Where are you going?"

"I'm going to bring you something cold. I'm going to feed the dogs. And I am going to make myself summer on toast," he said. "Too bad you have a sore throat. I make terrific toast."

He called her office and told them she was sick.

He disappeared and she heard the washing machine start filling.

He called the gym and told them he wouldn't be in.

"You don't have to baby-sit me," she croaked. She'd finished two more frozen pops so her throat was cold and numb.

"I know. But I'm going to stay here anyway."

"I'll be fine," she promised. "I'll take aspirin and by tonight I'll be terrific."

He tenderly cradled her face in his hands. Her cheeks felt hot and his hands felt cool. "Let me do this for you," he said. "Please."

He called Susannah and told her how Karen was doing.

"Promise you'll call me if you need anything, if Karen needs anything."

"I will."

"Steve, thank you. Thank you for taking care of my daughter."

"You're welcome." When he hung up the phone he realized Karen was crying. Tears streamed silently down her face. He hurried to her side. "What's wrong?"

She couldn't speak. She gestured to the table next to her, to the dozen roses in the glass vase.

* * *

She slept most of the day on the couch. He made Jell-O and took care of the dogs. He sat in a chair next to the couch and read. When she was awake, he brought her Popsicles, and aspirin, and tissues. He wiped her face and neck with a cool washcloth. She slept.

In the late afternoon, Steve heard a quiet knock on the front door. Quiet or not, the dogs heard it—all but Brian, who slumbered on in Karen's bedroom—and leaped to their feet in a rush to be the first to help Steve open the door. It was Susannah. "I brought you dinner," she said. "Nothing special. Lasagna and salad and rolls. Heat it in the microwave."

For dinner, Karen ate a bowl of Jell-O. Then Steve brought her a fresh nightgown still warm from the dryer.

"I forgot to call your sister," Karen said. Her face was full of worry.

"I called her."

"When?"

"Yesterday. While you were sleeping."

"Yesterday? What day is it?"

"Saturday."

"Saturday! Tonight is the Birthday Ball." She tried to struggle to her feet. "What did you tell her?"

"I told her you were too sick to go. I also called my folks."

Karen sank back on the couch. She looked perfectly miserable. "I'm so sorry."

"Don't be."

"But the Birthday Ball. May told me how important it is to Marines. You could go without me."

"I could. But I won't."

"May said it was important to your father."

"You're important to me."

Let me do this for you, he'd said. *Please.*

* * *

Before noon, the doctor called. "How are you feeling?" she asked.

"Miserable. Even my eyeballs feel hot."

"You have strep."

"You said I didn't."

"The quick test was negative. The long test was positive. What pharmacy do you use? I'll call in a prescription. I don't want you driving around town. Is there someone who can pick it up for you?"

Susannah came over to sit with her while Steve went to the pharmacy. She brought Karen a stack of books from the library. "I called Liz and asked her to gather some books for you. She put sticky notes on them for you. Bridgit stayed home, to keep your father company." She fluffed up Karen's pillow and smoothed the quilts. She gushed over the dogs and settled down to knit. Brian went to sleep with his head on her foot. He snored.

"I like your young man. He's something special."

Karen nodded. It still hurt to talk.

"We'd already heard about him from Katie, of course. She thinks he's terrific, you know. I'm very happy to know she was not exaggerating." She knitted several stitches. She nodded to the table by the couch. "Lovely roses, by the way."

"Don't you catch it, now," Susannah said to Steve when he saw her to the door.

"I'm never sick."

"That's what they all say."

"I have a very healthy lifestyle."

She reached up to touch him on his cheek. "Bless you."

* * *

A letter from Katie arrived in the mail.

Dear Mom,

I passed marksmanship. Now I have the rest to get through. I feel certain I will succeed. I will be a Marine. I can't wait to see you. You are coming for my graduation, aren't you? I really want you to be here. I asked Steve to come down too. Maybe you could drive down together. Big sloppy kisses for the dogs.

Love,
Katie

"I stopped off at my place and picked up my mail. I have a letter from Katie too. Do you want to read it?"

Dear Steve,

I want you to come to my graduation. I want you to be here to see me graduate. After all, you're part of the reason I have gotten this far. I know I will graduate. You helped me get into shape, but you also taught me how to go on when I thought I couldn't. You and Mickey Ward and Arturo Gatti. I can't thank you enough. So please come down. I'd really like that. Maybe you and my mom can drive down together.

Katie

They watched an old movie on television and when they went to bed, Steve held Karen to him, her head on his shoulder, giving her comfort, caring, asking nothing in return but that she feel treasured.

"I am so glad you're here," Karen whispered. "I don't know what I'd have done without you."

They spent Sunday on the couch snuggled together reading. Karen looked through the stack of books her mom brought. She tried a Terry Pratchett. Jessie practically swore on his books, but it was too complex for her to deal with then. She gave Steve the Pratchett. She picked up the book Liz said was her comfort book. It was about nuns. "I wonder if my mom has read this," she said. "Jessie says Mom was a nun in a former life."

Steve thought. "I can see that. She looks like a nun."

"She does not."

"Yes. She does. She looks calm. I think nuns probably look calm."

"Jessie calls her—even to her face sometimes, to tease her—Sister Susannah the Serene."

"Sometimes Jessie's right about things."

Karen wasn't in the mood to read about nuns. Not with Steve's arms around her. She picked up another book. *Some Brief Folly* by Patricia Veryan. The sticky note from Liz said it took place during a snowstorm in Regency England. With her fever, the idea of a snowstorm was appealing.

By evening, her eyeballs didn't feel hot anymore, and she could swallow without wincing. "But I still feel wiped out." It was an excellent excuse to stay curled up on the couch with her excellent book.

Monday morning, Steve and Theresa convinced Karen to stay home for at least one more day. She thought it was an extravagance. She was hungry. She realized she hadn't eaten anything but Jell-O and Popsicles for three days. Hardly a nutritious or balanced diet. She sliced a loaf of bread. She wanted summer on toast.

She would bake bread. She set the dough to rise. She thought of May. What had she said about the Birthday Ball? They had a birthday cake.

Karen stuck her chin on her fist and thought. Steve did something for her. She'd do something for him. She pulled out her cookbooks and looked up recipes for cake.

Well, she thought at last, it wasn't a professional job, but it was definitely recognizable as a birthday cake.

"Watch your mouth, TJ," one of the guys said, "there's a lady here."

Steve stopped wrapping a guy's hands to look up. His heart skipped. In the doorway stood Karen Matheson. His woman, in his gym. "Be right back," Steve said to the guy. He walked toward his woman. She stayed still. She waited. She waited with a smile on her face.

"What are you doing here?" he asked when he was close enough so the guys wouldn't hear.

"I brought you something," she said. But her smile slipped. "I hope it's okay. Maybe I should have called first."

"What is it?" he asked.

"It's a birthday cake."

He raised his eyebrows and waited.

"Today is the Marine Corp's birthday. May told me there's always a cake." Her voice faltered. "She said the first piece goes to the oldest Marine there, and the second piece goes to the youngest. You missed the Birthday Ball because of me, so I thought at least you could have a cake."

Steve was aware the guys in the gym were watching him. He knew they were curious. He knew he was about to surprise them. He didn't care. He tipped up Karen's chin with his finger and in the middle of his gym, with a dozen men dripping sweat and no doubt watching, he kissed her. He kissed his woman. For all that she held a cake between them, it was a long kiss. Not nearly long enough for him, though. But that would have to wait. He could wait. He put his arm around her, turned to the guys in his gym and said, "Everyone, this is Karen. Karen, these are the guys in my gym. Guys, we're all going to take a break now. We are going to have a birthday party."

They did. They even sang "Happy Birthday" to the Marine Corps.

Chapter 27

"You did what?" Jessie screeched. "You actually took a cake to his gym?" Karen held her ear away from the phone for a moment.

"Yes. What's wrong with his gym?"

"Well, nothing. I'm surprised, that's all. I mean, you've never been to his gym before, have you? What was it like?"

"A regular gym, I guess."

"How many gyms have you ever been to."

"None. But I assume they all smell like sweat. Steve introduced me to the guys in his gym. It was amazing. They were all very polite."

"You expected them to be a bunch of thugs?"

She thought. "Maybe. I don't know. I never thought of people actually going in his gym to box. I never thought about it much at all. I mean, I knew he owned a gym, but—" she realized she sounded like Candy. "It was an abstraction, not a reality. I had never been there before, so it wasn't part of my reality. It's as if it didn't exist. But now I've been there and everything's different. Why, Jess?"

"You're smart. You'll figure it out. Pretend you're someone who has come to you for counseling. Pretend your name is, oh, Perdita X. Nitt. Sorry. I'm reading Terry Pratchett. Anyway, Karen, you're good at helping people figure things out, so pretend you're someone you have to help."

* * *

May called Steve. "How is Karen?"

"She had strep."

"That's bad."

"She's better now. Antibiotics knocked it out."

"I'm glad she's better. I wanted to call her. I'm so sorry she missed the Birthday Ball. And after she'd gotten that dress, too. It was great. I wish you could've been there. It's every young girl's dream—the dresses, the music, and all the men looking so princely. Straight out of a fairy tale. Oh well. We took lots of pictures. I'll bring them down sometime soon. Besides," she added in a more cheerful voice, "Karen can always wear her dress next year. Oh. And she can wear it when you marry her."

When they were in elementary school, Steve learned that when May stuck an idea in her head, there was no earthly use trying to argue it out of her. Even if the idea was unrealistic, impractical, or just plain wrong, May held onto it as tenaciously as any Am Staff with a stick.

But this idea, to ask Karen to marry him, stuck in his head. He chased after it, pinned it down, worried it, held on and shook it. Finally he ignored it and hoped it would go away, but the thought still stuck.

Friday was Micah's birthday. Karen stopped at the bookstore to pick up a copy of *Dogzilla* for him. When she arrived, she gushed up the dogs thoroughly. Jessie handed her a cup of punch. "Sally's in the kitchen," she said. "Micah and a clump of his friends are in the dining room in the middle of a belching contest."

"Hi, Karen," Micah called to her.

"They're belching breeds of cars," Jessie explained.

"Yeah," belched Jeremy Martini. "Hey, listen to this." He

concentrated for a moment, then slowly belched out, "Lincoln Continental."

Micah and his friends cheered loudly.

"You are aware, of course," Jessie said oh so casually, "that you're contributing to global warming."

"No way!" Micah said.

"Yes way. A couple of years ago Americans drank almost twenty-one and a half *billion* gallons of carbonated beverages, which sent eight hundred thousand *tons* of carbon dioxide into the atmosphere. Carbon dioxide is a greenhouse gas. I read about it in *Popular Science*."

"Why do you always know so much about everything?" Micah asked.

Jessie wagged her eyebrows. "I have a library card, and I'm not afraid to use it!"

"Ozone," belched Jeremy Martini.

Jessie shrugged. "Pearls before swine," she said.

Sally came over to stand with them. "He's fifteen. They all are. In some cultures they'd be considered old enough to get married. Scary, isn't it."

Micah, Karen thought, was only three years younger than Katie. I was eighteen when Katie was born. My mother was not much older when I was born. My mother was my age when she became a grandmother. But grandmothers are old. My grandmother, she thought, has always been an old woman.

"Karen!" Jessie's voice startled her.

"What?"

"I said I am going over to Steve's to watch boxing. Do you want to come with me?"

Karen couldn't stop thinking about being a grandmother at her age. "No," she said. Steve told her he'd come over to her house after the fights. "I need to go talk to my mom for a while. Besides, I'm dropping Bridgit off with her."

"She's spending the weekend at Camp Susannah again, eh?"

* * *

Susannah set out two mugs. Karen pulled Katie's shawl from her knitting bag. "I've caught it from you," she chuckled, "taking my knitting bag wherever I go."

Susannah poured their tea. "If it brings you comfort, I'm glad."

"I guess I usually think of you as my mom and dad, not as people separate from myself. I mean, I know you're a separate person from me. That's one of those early childhood developmental things. But your role in my life is still my mom and dad. So, it's sort of odd thinking of you outside that role. Thinking of you as young—Katie's age—and in love, getting married and then him going off to war."

Her mother picked up her knitting. Her smile was very Mona Lisa. "But we weren't married when he left for Vietnam. We didn't marry until he came home for good."

Karen almost dropped her mug. Tea sloshed over the side onto her knee. It was hot.

"You and Roger were conceived when he was home on leave. You were about six months old when he came home."

Karen felt her eyes popping open wide. "Did he know about us?"

"Of course. As soon as I knew I was pregnant, I wrote him. As soon as you were born, I sent him pictures. I think knowing about you kept him alive, kept him from giving up over there."

"What kept you from giving up?"

"I knitted socks. Outrageous, ridiculously colored socks. More colors than Kaffe Fasset, and you know what he always says. 'When in doubt, add twenty more colors.'" She smiled. "It's impossible to feel down in the dumps with all those screaming colors raging around on your feet."

Karen kicked off her sandals and held out her feet. She considered the socks her mother had given her last spring.

The plethora of colors strolled rather sedately. "My socks do not rage," she pointed out.

"I tone down your socks, dear." Her mother kicked off her own sandal and presented her foot. Sure enough, her sock was a riot of reds and rampaging blues and screaming yellows with an occasional bit of purple calm. "After you started middle school, you decided you didn't want to wear bright colors anymore. Don't you remember?" She held her knitting at arm's length and squinted at it. "Halfway up. What do you think? Will Katie like it?"

Katie loved to wear bright colors, Karen thought. She looked at the half-finished sweater in her mother's hands. Bright many-colored stars danced through a dark sky. "She'll love it. It's beautiful." But her mind was still on her mother's thunderbolt.

"What did your mom say? When you told her you were pregnant?"

Susannah's knitting slowed. Stopped. Then started briskly. "She was not happy about it, but there was little she could do. When you and Roger were born, of course she fell in love with you instantly. Who could not?" She smiled up at Karen. "Two beautiful babies, her own grandchildren."

Sometimes people tell you more by what they leave out than by what they say. "They weren't supportive of you, were they?" she asked.

Susannah didn't answer at once.

Karen continued. "That's why you were so supportive of me. Because you knew what it felt like."

"Maybe that was part of it," Susannah admitted. "But mostly it was because we loved you."

"But it must have embarrassed you."

Susannah put down her knitting. She reached out to take Karen's hand. "Listen to me. Don't you ever, ever think we were embarrassed by you. You were a terrific person then, and you're a terrific person now, and we are proud of you. Do you hear me? Your father and I are bursting proud of you. And we were then, too. You took responsibility for your actions. I can't call it a mistake, because it turned out to be Katie, and Katie is most certainly not a mistake."

"That's why I couldn't tell—she's not a mistake."

"How could we possibly be embarrassed by this perfect baby of yours? Besides, when you love someone, you love all of them, not just the parts that are convenient."

"I wonder," Karen said, "if I would have been as accepting as you were."

"Of course you would. You would understand immediately."

Karen wanted, more than anything, to believe her. "When Daddy was in Vietnam, when you wrote to him—did he write you letters? What did he say about us? Can I read them?"

Her mother stared down closely at her knitting, knitting she could do in the dark, and her cheeks turned pink. Her mother was blushing! "They are quite personal. Maybe someday." Karen thought of her parents jumping on their bed. They had learned to love even the inconvenient parts of each other and their love had become stronger for it.

Late that night, when Steve came over, after *Friday Night Fights,* she said, "Next week, may I come over to watch boxing with you? Please?"

"Yes." He pressed the word on her lips, and again on her cheeks, and on her brow, on her neck, on her eyelids. "Yes." And again. "Yes."

"My mom made a hat for my baby," Candy said. "She gave it to me last night at dinner; in front of my dad. I think that part was really hard for her. I mean, she could've given it to me after dinner, up in my room, or when he was at work or something. But she didn't. She gave it to me in front of him. She said, 'Candy, I have something for you. I knitted a hat for your baby.' "

"Why do you think she did it that way?"

Candy frowned in thought. "I think it was her way of telling me she loves me. Even if I got pregnant, she still loves me. And she wanted my dad to know she loves me, even if I got pregnant."

"How does that make you feel?"

Candy thought some more. "It makes me very glad to know she loves me enough to do something that's really hard for her to do. Because maybe someday my baby will understand I loved her enough to do something for her that was really hard for me to do."

"I'm sure she will."

You don't only love the parts that are convenient, her mother had said. The words swirled around and around in Karen's mind. Boxing was not convenient. Boxing was not comfortable. But boxing was a part of Steve.

Late that afternoon he called. "Do you like Mexican?"

"I love Mexican."

He took her to the new Mexican restaurant in town.

"What made you want to box?" she asked him that evening.

"It wasn't what, it was who. Gunnery Sergeant Anthony Spriggs."

The name was familiar to her.

"The photograph in my study," he said.

She remembered now.

"I was a little kid. I was the shortest boy in my class. I got picked on a lot. My father took me to Gunny Spriggs. He lived on base, too. He taught me to box."

"Why did you like it? Something that's about violence."

"This is where you're wrong. Boxing is a violent sport, but it is not about violence. It's about challenging yourself. It's about being the best. It's about never giving up. It's about sheer will winning over physical weakness."

"That sounds like Katie becoming a Marine."

"They're related."

"And your Gunny Spriggs. How did he teach you about sheer will?"

"He inspired me to be more than I thought I could be. He's the best. You'd like him."

"That letter from her. The one she wrote you. She mentioned a fight that helped her get through things."

He nodded. "The first Ward Gatti fight."

"Can you tell me about it?"

"No. It's something you have to see for yourself. Boxing isn't about two guys in a ring slugging it out. Boxing has rules. It requires skill. You try to hit the other guy and at the same time, keep the other guy from hitting you."

"Why do people like to watch boxing?"

"You'd have to ask them. I watch because I learn from watching other boxers. Also because a perfect combination is a thing of beauty. Seeing a guy give everything he has and then, going on pure grit and guts, finding somewhere deep within him a little bit more. That's beautiful too."

"That fight. The one Katie wrote about. Was it beautiful?"

"Breathtaking."

Karen shook her head. "I'm sorry," she said. "I don't get it."

He reached out and took her hand. "You've opened your mind to the possibility that there's something to get. That's a start."

Karen paced up and down her hallway. She paced and thought and thought and paced. The dogs watched her for a while, then decided she wasn't going to do anything more interesting than pace and wandered off to find something to do.

At least Ferry and Heck did. Brian rolled over on his side and went to sleep. Karen paced.

"Confucius allegedly said," Karen told her sleeping dog, "if we see what is right and do not do it, our lack of action is due to cowardice." She paced. "Of course, Confucius said lots of things. That doesn't make him right, merely verbose. But even if he didn't say it, there's still truth in it." She paced. "If we see what is right and do it, even though we are afraid, does that mean we have courage?" She thought of Jessie. "If someone came to me for counseling and asked me that, I'd say yes." She paced. "I guess I have to decide if I'm courageous or a coward."

She wanted to have courage. She was afraid she was a coward. She called the gym. "Hello, Steve, can you come over and spend the night with me? Bridgit's with Mom."

Chapter 28

Dear Katie, Of course I'll be down for your graduation.
She was sure Steve would drive down with her, even though they hadn't discussed it. He'd tried to bring it up, but she always turned the conversation to something else. Steve. Oh, my. She had to tell Katie about Steve. How could she possibly tell Katie about Steve? *By the way, dear, your friend Steve and I are lovers?* No. That would not be good. She couldn't think of any good way to tell Katie about Steve, so she finally gave up and wrote about the dogs and the weather, and how wonderful the apples from the Wildes' farm were, and that she was sick, but she's fine now. *Love, Mom.*

She folded the letter and slipped it into an envelope addressed to Katie. She stuck it in her purse so she'd remember to mail it the next day. Then she pulled out Katie's shawl. She knitted while she waited for Steve. She kept telling herself she was bringing order to chaos, reminding herself that knitting always made her feel calm. She took a deep breath and let it out slowly. She thought about lions and mice.

"You told me once Katie would learn the Marine stories in boot camp, they would become her stories, part of who she is. This means they're also part of who you are." She chewed on her lip. "I figure that makes them my stories, too, once removed. They might help me understand my daughter better, when I see her at her graduation. So, would you tell me a Marine story?"

"You want to hear Marine stories?"

"Yes. Please."

Steve pondered this. "I will tell you the story of Corporal Germaine Catherine Laville. She was only twenty-two years old when she gave her life to save her fellow Marines."

That night, sleeping safely in Steve's arms, Karen dreamed of burning buildings.

"Tonight," Karen said, "is our last class. As you know, the Canine Good Citizen test will be held down in Columbus on Saturday morning. Be there no later than eight. I have driving directions for all of you. Also, on the same paper is a list of things you must bring. Proof of up-to-date shots; your dog's comb or brush. Your dog must wear a flat collar during the test. Remember, during the test you may talk to your dog, you may praise your dog as much as you normally do, but you may not bring squeaky toys or food."

A student raised his hand. "Why won't it be here?"

"The test is sponsored by a Columbus dog club. People from all over the state will be there with their dogs. I will be there, too, but I won't be testing. I will be there as an observer only. I want to see how wonderfully well you and your dogs do. Don't worry," she added with a grin. "I am sure you'll all do fine. Remember, this is not competition obedience. This is a great thing to do with your dog. So relax and have fun."

She had a free hour during the afternoon. She pulled her cell phone out of her purse, along with the pamphlet from the Marines. She called every hotel on the list. Not a single room was to be had in Beaufort for the week of Katie's graduation. One desk clerk told her people made graduation reservations three months in advance. "You might try over in Hilton Head," he said, obviously trying to be helpful. "They might still have some rooms." Why hadn't she listened to Steve and called earlier? What would she do now? She had to be there. Even if she had to sleep in her van! But she couldn't ask Steve to sleep in her van.

She took a quick walk to the library and asked Liz to show her the travel books on South Carolina. One of them had a list of hotels in Hilton Head. Karen reserved the very last room of the very last hotel on the list. She wouldn't have to sleep in her van after all.

Walking back to work she called Steve. "What time should I come over for boxing tonight?"

"I called the guys and told them I wasn't having boxing tonight."

"Why not?"

"Canine Good Citizen test. Early wake-up. That means early to bed. Your bed, I hope."

She felt a warm rush. "Absolutely."

"I have a video I want to show you."

For the first time in her life, she watched boxing. She witnessed the pure grit and guts of two battered and bloody boxers who both refused to give up when even she could see they staggered in exhaustion. She didn't see how they could possibly go on, but they did. They went on and on and on until she wanted to weep for them. When the final bell rang they held onto each other and hugged.

"I don't understand," she said. "They don't hate each other. Look! Did you hear that? He just called the other guy a great warrior! How can he say that?"

"Because it's true. Because they each acknowledge their respect for the other."

Karen sat back. "It's not personal. They don't hate each other."

"Some boxers do really hate the guys they fight. But Ward and Gatti? No. They respect each other."

"How do their wives stand it?"

"Some of them don't."

She realized she'd knocked on a door she hadn't known was there. The door did not open.

That night, after they made sweet love, she asked for another story. He told her the story of Private First Class Fernando L. Garcia. In Korea, during an intense hail of enemy fire, a live enemy grenade landed near another Marine. Private First Class Garcia, himself wounded, threw himself, without hesitation, on the grenade. He took the full force of the explosion. At the cost of his own life, he saved the life of his fellow Marine. Steve held her in his arms, in his heart, as she shook with tears.

"Are you sure you want to hear these stories? They always make you cry."

"They're Katie's stories. Mine once removed. I need to know them."

The Canine Good Citizen test was held at the Ohio Fairgrounds, right off I-71. Steve stopped at the gate for the parking ticket and they wound their way around and around until they found the building. Steve pulled into a parking space and turned off the engine.

"Are you nervous?" Karen asked.

"No." He reached over the back of the seat for the bag that held the required brush and papers. "I think we'll have fun."

"I hope so. I hope the others do, too."

"They will." He peered at her face. "Are you worried that if some of the dogs from our class don't pass it will be a reflection on your abilities as a teacher?"

"I don't think so."

"Good; because you're a fine teacher. You know dogs, and

you know how to inspire other people to learn about them. You know how to convey the important things."

She blinked. "I do? I inspire people?"

"Yes. You do. Didn't you know that?"

She shook her head. "Thank you for telling me."

He kissed her quickly and sweetly. "You're welcome. Now. It's almost eight. We gotta get in there before they shut us out."

Quickly she pulled him back. "One last kiss. For luck."

"Lennox is terrific. We don't need luck."

"I do. Kiss me." He did.

"You realize what this means, don't you?" she asked as he opened the car for her.

"No. What does this mean?"

"Nonverbal clues. By arriving together we are announcing our relationship. We can't pretend it's not happening."

"I don't want to pretend it's not happening."

"I don't either."

"Well, that's okay, then." He opened the back door and told Lennox to wait. Lennox waited while Steve clipped on his leash. "Let's go. We have a test to pass."

Pass they did. Lennox passed with flying colors and he knew very well he had done something wonderful. The evaluators told Steve the AKC would send him his official certificate, but in the meantime, they would sign a statement for him to take to the city council stating Lennox had completed the requirements for his Canine Good Citizen title.

"Look at your dog," Karen said. "He is actually strutting. I have never seen a dog strut before."

"He's like Ferry," Steve said. "He has a diva personality."

She stooped down. "Come here, Lennox."

Lennox came when he was called. Karen rewarded him for coming. Karen told him what an excellent dog he was. Oh, he was such a great guy dog.

"Watch out," Steve cautioned. "He has a habit of jumping up and sticking his tongue in your mouth."

"Gross." She would gush carefully.

"It is."

Karen was thrilled to see all her students passed the test. The man with Ralphie the setter was as proud as Lennox. He strutted, too. He strutted over to Karen and gave her a great big friendly hug.

"Thanks, Karen, from Ralphie and me. We couldn't have done it without you."

She was embarrassed. "Sure you could have. Ralphie is such a smart dog you wouldn't have had any trouble teaching him. Have you ever thought about working with him in competition obedience?"

The man shook his head. Ralphie leaned against him and the man gently fondled the dog's long feathered ears. "No, this is the first thing like this we've ever done." Ralphie sighed.

Karen smiled at the dog. "You had a great time. Ralphie had a great time. You made a wonderful start. Now you should keep that great thing going."

"I might," the man said. "I just might. It would sure get us out of the house." He looked down at his dog. "What do you think, Ralphie? You think another class would be fun?" Ralphie wagged his tail. Personally, Karen was pretty sure Ralphie would wag his tail any time anyone spoke his name. "You see that, Karen? Ralphie would like that."

Karen nodded. "Good. Whenever you're ready, call the dog school and we'll sign you right up."

On the way home, the windshield wipers swiping and swishing the scattered snow, Steve said, "You were an inspiration to that man."

"He didn't need much inspiring."

"What do you know about him?"

"Why, nothing much. Only what he wrote on the registration form."

"Ralphie was his wife's dog. She was from Colorado and named Ralphie after the University of Colorado mascot. She died last year. Since then, he's had nothing to do but sit in his empty house with her dog and know she's gone."

Karen was amazed. "How do you know that?"

"I talked to him."

"When?"

"Before class, between exercises, after classes while I waited for you. He told you the literal truth. Your class was the first thing he ever did with that dog." He glanced over at her. "You inspired him. Now he'll have something to look forward to each week."

Karen felt small. She felt humbled. She felt lucky to be in the right place at the right time.

They spent the rest of the trip in companionable quiet.

Steve stopped off at his house to check for mail. "Katie's graduation is so close, we don't want to miss any last-minute letter from her," he explained. Sure enough, one white envelope from Parris Island waited in his mailbox. Steve handed it to Karen. "You want to read it to me while I drive?

Dear Steve,

Next week is the Crucible. I think I'm looking forward to it. Everyone says it will be grueling and a test of endurance and so far, the things everyone says have been true, so this is probably true, too. I've decided I can gruel and endure for two days. I've decided I can do whatever needs to be done. I'm really glad you and Mom are driving down for my graduation. I'll see you then. Because I will graduate.

Katie

P.S. I realized I don't need cornermen anymore. They're nice, but nonessential.

"I guess this is it," Karen said. "She's really going to do it. What's the Crucible? Like the Salem Witch Trials?"

"What?" Then he got it. "No. The Crucible is . . . What do you know about alchemy?"

"Middle Ages, alchemists tried to turn base metal into gold. Not much more than that."

"The alchemists were interested in transformation. Of base metal into gold, but also in the transformation of the spirit. They put their dross metal into a crucible, a kind of vessel, and subjected it to extremely high heat and great pressure. This was supposed to turn dross into gold. That's what's going to happen to your daughter. The Crucible is a fifty-four hour endurance test. The recruits are subjected to intense pressure, physically and mentally. They are allowed very little sleep, hike for forty miles carrying full packs, and they're only allowed two and a half meals for the duration. The challenges they face, the obstacles they must overcome, are physical and mental. The only way they can survive it is to work together."

"You have that formal Marine tone of voice again," she said. "Like when you tell me your stories."

"The Crucible is important. It's the process of that final transformation."

Another letter waited for Karen.

Dear Mom,

I am so happy to know you'll be coming down for my graduation. It's a big deal to Marines. Wear comfortable shoes and don't forget your coat. It's cold. Autumn has most certainly leafed and left the southern shore of South Carolina. The other day, I asked Staff Sergeant McNamara about the dogs. The ones I told you about, they looked like brindle Belgians but they had a heavier head. I told her you were a serious dog person and when you came down for my graduation you would

want to know. I told her I'd never seen a brindle Bel-
gian at any dog show I ever went to. She was really nice
about it. She said she didn't know but she'd find out.
And she did! The next day she yelled, "Matheson get
over here and hit my deck." While I did push-ups she
bent down and whispered, so the other recruits
wouldn't hear and think I had some special privilege,
they're Dutch Shepherds. I've never heard of Dutch
Shepherds before but Liz at the library could probably
track down a picture of one. I love you, and I love the
dogs. I can't wait to see you!

                                        Love,
                                        Katie

Karen stared at the letter. "Who wrote this, and what did
they do to my daughter? She actually sounds happy. Steve,
she sounds like herself." She looked at him. "You certainly
look smug."

"When you see her you will see how much of herself she
has become."

Chapter 29

After they took care of the dogs, Steve took Karen by the hand and sat her down at the kitchen table. He sat across from her. "We have to talk."

She felt suddenly chilled. "Let me make tea first." Things went better with tea—a legacy from her mother. She busied herself with cups and tea balls and tea leaves. Finally the tea was poured.

"We must decide what to do about Bridgit. It isn't fair to your mother to shuttle her off everytime I spend the night with you. Not spending the night with you is not an option. It is not fair to Bridgit to be shuttled from one place to another like an inconvenient package. You told me you wanted to keep her because she needed a stable home. We are not giving her a stable home."

Karen stared miserably into her tea.

"You're right. I know you're right, but I don't know what to do."

"When I told you about the Crucible I told you the only way they can succeed is if they work together. This goes for you, too, even if it's only once removed." He waited for her to smile before he went on. "We can survive this, but only if you and I work as a team. It doesn't matter that you don't know what to do. What matters is that you and I, we, work it out together."

"I . . . I never considered asking you to help me. I assumed it was my responsibility."

"It *was* your responsibility. It *is* our responsibility." He shook his head. "Lady, you need to start listening to those Marine stories. They're all about working together, not about personal glory. Those Marines are honored not because they were individuals, but because they exemplify the value of a team."

"Oh," she said in a small voice. "I guess I'm not used to . . ."

"You're used to playing Atlas and holding the world on your shoulders."

"I guess so."

"Get used to you and me working together."

"Okay."

"Then let's work on a solution for Bridgit. Together."

"Okay."

"Here we go. You are afraid to introduce her to Lennox. Lennox will not hurt her."

"I know." She glanced at Lennox who was on a mission to destroy a large leg bone. She called him. He dropped the bone and came to her at once. She stroked his head. "I know you wouldn't hurt her," she told the dog, "but I'm afraid she doesn't know that." Lennox was quite agreeable. Then he went back to the destruction of his leg bone. "I'm afraid her past, what she endured before I got her, did some permanent emotional damage. I believe dogs recognize different breeds. My dogs recognize standard poodles because they know Jean-Luc. They see standard poodles at a dog show and they look really closely to see if it's him. I think Bridgit would see Lennox and in her doggy mind she'd think, 'bad dog.'"

"You can say pit bull. I have a fairly good idea where Bridgit came from."

"You do?"

"Not the actual place, but the situation. I've been around

Am Staffs for many years. I know about dog fighting. I recognize the signs."

"Please don't tell anyone. I promised . . . Melissa and Jessie promised. According to all official records, she's supposed to be dead."

"I won't. I want what's best for Bridgit, too."

She drank her tea, mostly to give herself time to think. "Do you have any ideas?"

"Let's go out to your parents' house. Lennox and I will stand outside, in the driveway. You bring Bridgit outside. You don't have to introduce her to Lennox, not yet, just let her see him, from a safe distance. Maybe she can become used to him gradually."

So they called Susannah and Lloyd. They drove over and Steve waited in the driveway with Lennox on a sit stay at his side. Karen went inside and snapped a leash on Bridgit's collar and led Bridgit onto the porch. Bridgit followed her without protest, but as soon as the dog caught sight of Lennox she cringed. She tried to hide behind Karen. She whipped around to frantically scrabble at the door, scratching at it in her panic to get away, to get back inside where she felt safe.

Karen rushed her back inside and hugged her. "I'm sorry, Bridgit. I'm so sorry. Please forgive me. I won't ever do that to you again. I promise."

Bridgit pulled out of her arms and fled into the kitchen to Susannah. The big dog crouched behind Susannah and shook. Susannah sank down on the floor next to her. "That's a good girl, Bridgit," she said in a calm, rather than comforting, voice. "I'll take care of her, dear," she told Karen. "She'll be fine in a bit. She's had a scare. We have to help her calm down and realize there's nothing to be afraid of. Why don't you bring me my knitting bag; I feel like knitting."

Karen wept slow silent tears all the way home. They did

not speak of Bridgit again. Karen knew Steve was giving her space to process. But how could she process this?

That night Steve told her the story of Private First Class Robert H. Jenkins Jr. who, during the Vietnam War, sacrificed himself to save his men. Sometimes we have to think of the good of others instead of our own.

Sunday morning, Karen made French toast. Steve heaped his high with Susannah's cherry jam. French toast with summer, he called it.

"You're trying to cheer me up."

"Am I succeeding?"

She gave him a wry smile. "Maybe. It makes me feel better because you're trying. But I still feel like I've been emotionally run over by a truck." She felt like Candy.

"We will solve this together. I promise we will." *Let me help you. Please.*

"Can you listen while I think out loud?"

"Yes."

She knew he would listen well. He always listened very well; even when she did not speak. She stared down at her fingers and started. "If I was someone else, and I came to me and said I have a problem with this dog, I'd tell the other me to tell me all the things I think Bridgit needs. And then I'd tell the other me to tell me all the things the other me needs. And I would. And then we would go over these two lists and see where they were compatible. But Steve, I've already done that, and they aren't."

"What is the most important issue?"

"I've always told myself Bridgit is best with me; I am the best home for her."

"What do you think now?"

"Depends on if I'm honest or not," Karen said. "If I was honest, I'd recognize that I needed Bridgit to need me. *I* needed that. But for some reason, she *doesn't* need me. I guess if your Marine stories are mine too, even once removed, I have to learn from them and I have to put Bridgit first, because I am responsible for her. She has decided she needs Connie Wilde. Whenever I take her to the yarn shop, it's clear as crystal."

"What does Connie Wilde think?"

"I know Connie Wilde feels a strong connection to Bridgit. Even Mom has seen it."

Steve was silent.

"Mom believes—I know this might sound crazy, but remember, she's an old hippie and probably the reincarnation of a nun and a Druid and who knows what other earthy types—when we're really, really close to a dog, and they die, they come back to be our dog again. And sometimes they remember us. Jessie believes this, too. Sometimes even I believe it. Maybe Bridgit was Connie's dog once before, in another life. That's why they want to be together now."

Steve searched her face. He thumbed away a tear.

"Now," she said, "right now, before I lose my courage, will you go with me to take Bridgit to the Wildes' farm?"

"Yes."

Steve drove her van. Karen sat in the back with her arms around Bridgit. Her tears made the side of Bridgit's neck wet. Bridgit didn't mind, any more than she had minded when Candy cried. Bridgit showed little emotion—until Steve turned down the country road. Then Bridgit began to pace. Then Bridgit pawed at the door.

"She knows where we're going," Steve said.

Karen nodded silently. "It's that house, up there, on the other side of that sheep pasture. The house with the big blue barn."

Bridgit clambered out of the van and strained against the end of her leash.

Karen let her lead the way up the steps. Bridgit pawed at the door. Karen knocked. And the door was opened.

"Karen!" Mrs. Wilde exclaimed. "How lovely to see you, and Beautiful Bridgit!" She held her hand out to Steve. "You must be Karen's friend, Steve. Susannah has told me so much about you. Come in, come in. Connie," she called, "come see who is here."

Bridgit joyously threw herself at Connie and Connie caught her up in a great loving hug. Bridgit was home.

On Monday, when he came to Karen's office for lunch, Steve brought soup from Lola's, along with lunch loaves. She knew he brought them specially to cheer her up. He also had one dozen sugar cookies for Karen to share with her office.

"Today is an excellent day for soup," she told him. She wrapped her sweater more snugly around her. "Our heating system is in dire straits. It's so old most repair guys don't know how to fix it; they've never seen anything like it. I only hope it lasts through the winter. One of the joys of working out of an old house instead of a brand new office complex."

"You wouldn't like working in a new office complex."

"I know. Even with all its geriatric creaks and groans, I love this old house."

"Cookies!" Vicky exclaimed as she came into the kitchen. "How wonderful! Steve, you are an absolute gem! I keep telling Karen she better keep you around." She picked out a cookie and took a bite. "Look at those big snowflakes. It's too bad they don't stick."

"The ground's too warm," Steve said. "Wait a couple of weeks."

"I hope snow doesn't keep you from coming to lunch," she

said with a grin as she flourished her cookie and went out the back door.

"Connie Wilde called this morning," Karen said as she brought out spoons and poured drinks.

"Is everything okay?" Steve asked, pouring the soup into nice crockery bowls instead of leaving it in Styrofoam containers.

"She wanted to tell me everything was fine. She knew I'd be worrying."

"Were you? Worrying?"

"Of course. It's what moms do when their kids go off into the world."

"You're thinking of Katie."

"Is it that obvious?"

"To me."

"She starts the Crucible tomorrow."

"She'll be fine."

"You keep telling me that."

"I have to keep telling you; you keep worrying about her."

"I'm her mother. I'm supposed to worry." She absently reached up to rub Katie's pendant. Then she remembered something. "You're driving down to Parris Island with me, aren't you? We've never discussed it; I've assumed . . ."

"Is that an invitation?"

She blushed, but she could see he was teasing her. "Yes."

"I accept. But we will take my car. The trip might be too much for your old van."

When he left Karen's office, Steve walked over to the city office. Once more he wound his way through the same maze of hallways until he found the administrative office. He opened the same frosted glass door and stepped inside to see the same woman looking over her rhinestone glasses and down her long nose at him with the same distrust. Steve adopted the most professional demeanor in his arsenal. Once more he explained he had received a letter from the city, that

his dog was not a pit bull but an American Staffordshire. He
explained that Lennox had passed the CGC test and the AKC
would send him the official paper. Until then, Steve had a
statement signed by all the evaluators.

The woman studied it suspiciously. She turned it over, and
held it up to the light. Perhaps it would turn into a bird and fly
away. Perhaps it would turn into a bomb and explode. Perhaps
it would sprout teeth and bite. Most people would say these
things were impossible—but they *might* happen. The woman
took no chances. Finally, she handed the signed statement
back to him.

"This is not the official certificate."

"I know. The AKC will send me the official certificate."

"Before the council can discuss your case, they need the
official certificate."

"As soon as I receive it I will bring it over to you."

"The council cannot discuss your case without it."

"I understand. However, this statement proves Lennox
has passed the requirements for the CGC, while we are
waiting for the certificate. He has earned his CGC. Why
won't the council members accept this statement from the
evaluators?"

"Because it is not the official certificate."

"I know." Steve was patient. He perversely wondered how
long she would continue to go around and around in circles
with him. He decided it would not be noble to try to find out.
"I'll tell you what," he said cheerfully. "As soon as the AKC
sends me the official certificate I will bring it by. How's
that?"

She studied him as if he were a bug under a magnifying
glass. She obviously did not trust him; she obviously thought
he was trying to pull a fast one on her. She obviously had trust
issues. "The official certificate. We need the official certificate."

"I will bring it. As soon as I receive it."

"We cannot proceed without the official certificate."

"I'll be back when I've received it. Have a lovely holiday." He could feel her stare stab him in the back as he left the office and closed the door behind him. Whew! Where did she come from? He bet Susannah would know, or Mrs. Wilde.

Chapter 30

Thanksgiving dawned clear and bright. A warm breeze from the southwest washed over Ohio. Karen and Steve loaded up the dogs, all of them, and drove out to Susannah and Lloyd's. When they arrived, Crosby, Stills and Nash were singing about Woodstock. Lloyd, singing enthusiastically along, held the door open for them. "Come in, come in, come in, you lovely people bearing dogs. *We are stardust, we are golden.*"

Karen made sure Brian kept his balance when the others shoved him aside in their eagerness to greet Susannah. Even Lennox remembered Susannah was a good person to know; she usually had tiny bites for dogs in her pockets.

Lloyd gave Brian some special gushing and led him away from the door, away from the hot fire in the fireplace to where it was quiet. He brought Brian a pillow. "For his old head," he told them. Karen realized it was one of her mother's good guest pillowcases hemmed with knitted lace. Her father said Brian was most certainly a guest and an honored one at that. The honored guest settled his great gray head onto the pillow and twitched his tail. Then he went to sleep.

Lloyd invited Steve down to the basement to show him his woodworking. A few minutes later, Karen stood at the top of the stairs. She had intended to go downstairs to be with them, but now stood still and listened. Steve and her dad were not talking about tools or wood. They were talking about Vietnam. She tiptoed away.

She ended up in the kitchen with her mother. Susannah drew her into a warm hug. "Thank you for giving Bridgit to Connie. You have given her the gift of life. I cannot begin to tell you how much this means to her."

"I guess I figured out that I needed Bridgit more than she needed me. I needed her to be a substitute for Katie. She isn't. She's her own individual self. She needed something I couldn't give her."

"But you did. You gave her Connie."

Karen stared at the stack of plates on the table in front of her for a long minute. "I guess so."

Brian slept through the dinner, through the football game, through all the conversations. Susannah divided leftovers between the dogs, but Brian was sleeping so peacefully she didn't want to wake him. "I'm wrapping up some Thanksgiving dinner for Gracie and Bob," Susannah told Karen. "They're with Camille's family this year. I'll wrap some for Brian, too."

"Not too much, Mom. I don't want to give him a tummy upset."

Susannah looked surprised. "Is he having tummy upsets these days?"

"Once in a while. He doesn't eat much."

"What does Melissa say?"

"She says he's a very geriatric dog. He's slowing down. Everything seems to be working, though."

"I have her phone number right here, next to the phone," Susannah said. "In case I need her next week. I'm glad we'll have the dogs with us. Lloyd has a wonderful time with them. Are you sure we can't keep Lennox, too? It's not too much trouble."

"Steve's taking him up to Cleveland to stay with May."

Ferry bounced into the kitchen and shoved herself between Susannah and the counter.

"You're asking Grandma for something else to eat?" Susannah asked her.

Ferry wiggled.

Susannah sliced an apple. "Ferry, sit," she said.

Ferry sat. The apple slice was gone in an instant. Ferry was up and dancing around Susannah. "Karen, your dog has a diva personality."

Steve helped Brian up the steps when they got home to Karen's house. "That's it, old man," he said. "You can do it. Just like Mt. Everest. One step at a time. There you go. That's it."

Karen, arms full of Thanksgiving leftovers, held the door open for her dog as Steve helped him up the last low step into the house. "I'll call Melissa on Monday and ask her if we need to up his arthritis meds."

Steve spent the evening at the dining room table, sketching something on a piece of paper. Karen sat on the floor brushing her geezer dog. Brian slept.

"You know," Steve said, coming over to sit beside her, "I bet your dad would help me make a ramp for Brian. It would make it easier for him to get in and out."

"He hasn't had a problem with the steps until now." She bent down to hug her dog. He had lost weight.

"Now he has a problem." He showed her his rough sketches of a ramp for Brian. "We can do one in the front and in the back."

"A ramp would be wonderful."

The next morning, Brian Boru did not wake up.
Steve called Lloyd and Susannah who came right over,

bringing shovels. Susannah stayed in the house with Karen and Brian while Lloyd led Steve outside to the back of the yard, the stretch of trees and bushes that grew just inside the fence. Lloyd handed Steve one of the shovels. "Here," he said, "is where we will dig."

Jessie arrived, and Melissa with Peter and Angie, Sally with Tanner and Micah, Sylvie and Ray with the Boogaloo and Alex and Liz. Roger arrived with his wife Camille, and Camille's brother Jake. They all helped dig the grave for Brian Boru. They all hugged Karen and didn't tell her everything was going to be okay, because they knew all the words in the world wouldn't help. Connie Wilde brought a baby apple tree, a Pink Lady which was Karen's favorite kind of apple.

"I know it's late in the season," she told Steve, "but I think the ground is still warm enough for it. I hope the ground is warm enough."

Karen and her mother wrapped Brian Boru in one of Karen's favorite quilts to keep him warm. They wrapped him along with his favorite bone and his old, gummed, once-fleece, football. Steve carried him, all wrapped in the quilt and Karen's love, out of the house. Alex jogged back to him.

"Do you need help? Newfs are not exactly flyweights."

"Thanks, but no. Brian doesn't weigh much at all. He's lost—he had lost a lot of weight recently." He was glad to have company as he carried Brian to the spot where everyone was gathered. They buried Karen's dog, and planted the apple tree over him, so he could help the tree grow. "That's a pretty good job for a dog," Steve heard Jessie whisper to Angie.

"I know," he heard Angie whisper back. "It's from *The Tenth Good Thing About Barney*. But Barney was a cat."

Steve looked at the long row of trees and the few bushes. He whispered to Lloyd, "Are all of these trees planted over Karen's dogs?"

Lloyd looked down the row of trees too. "No," he said, "not

all of them are Karen's. Let's see. Jessie's old dog Hubble is there, under that Russian Olive. And one of Melissa's dogs, I forget her name, is under the lilac. It's a good thing Karen has a big yard."

"It's not as big as her heart," Steve said.

Lloyd looked at him. Evidently he liked what he saw, for he patted Steve on the shoulder. "I'm glad you're here."

The friends stayed near the little tree. They talked about Brian, they told their favorite stories about him. They told lots of stories. They told stories until the snow started to fall. It fell quickly enough to cover the ground, to cover Brian up, to keep him warm, while he helped the baby apple tree. Jessie was right, Steve thought. It *was* a pretty good job for a dog. He put his arm around Karen's shoulders and held her close as they walked, side by side, with all of her friends, back to the house.

Karen's house and heart were crowded to overflowing. She had to escape for a little while. She slipped on a heavy sweater and went out the back door and there he was.

"I'm glad you're here," she said.

"I will always be here when you need me. Like you will always be there when I need you. We can't help it."

"Well, I'm still glad. Thanks for coming over. I assume Jessie called you?"

"Right after Mom called her, right after Steve called Mom."

Karen slipped her arm in Roger's and they walked together to the back of the yard, to Brian's newly planted tree.

"He was a great dog," he said. "We'll all miss him."

She nodded.

"Your Steve," Roger said. "He's a great guy."

"I know."

"I watched the way he took care of you, and Brian. Dad

thinks he's great, too. In fact, the other day when Camille and I had them over for dinner, Dad made a highly deliberate point of telling me how much he likes Steve."

Karen chuckled tearfully. "Thanksgiving we went over to their house. Dad and Steve went downstairs, and guess what? I heard them down there talking about Vietnam."

"No! Dad never talks about Vietnam."

"He talked to Steve about it." Karen reached out with her foot to nudge a bit of soil in place. "And there's something else. A couple of weeks ago, I finally asked Dad. I asked him why he didn't want us to go to the dedication of the Wall."

"He didn't ignore you and walk away?"

"No. He didn't say anything for a while, and then he said he had too many buddies on that wall. His voice was sort of blurry. I think it's because he wanted to protect us from how much he still must have hurt. People say it's not easy for kids to see their parents in the middle of such heavy grief. I don't mean people should keep it from their kids, only that it's not easy for the kids."

"Karen," Roger said, "that might be true, but you still shouldn't have flown into such a snit and run off to Columbus by yourself. That was really stupid. I was worried about you. Then there was that blizzard."

She smiled up at the sky. "It *was* stupid. But if I hadn't, if I hadn't gotten in a snit and run off, I wouldn't have Katie."

"Camille says life's a funny creature."

Karen smiled at her brother. "She's right."

"Your Steve, keep him around. I'd like to get to know him better."

Chapter 31

Steve and Karen spent Saturday taking down Bridgit's crate and Brian's crate. They propped the pans up against the side of the garage to scrub them and hose them down. They left them in the winter breeze and when they were no longer wet they took them into the garage and leaned them up against the back wall, along with all the other extra crates.

"How many Newf crates do you have?" Steve asked.

Karen counted. "About four others out here. And Ferry's, and Heck's. I've always made sure I had extras for emergencies. I never know when I'll get a call in the middle of the night and find I've acquired another foster dog."

"Have all of your dogs been foster dogs?"

"Most of them."

He knew from her voice. "Brian?"

"Yes. Brian came to me when he was eight weeks old."

They gave the dog room a thorough sweeping. Ferry was intently curious about the goings-on. Ferry followed them and watched what they did. Heck and Lennox discovered they both liked to play tug. They liked to play tug a lot. Neither of them had ever met another dog who liked to play tug as much as they did. They played tug all afternoon.

"Why do Newfoundlands like to play tug?" Steve asked. He stood by the window, keeping an eye on Heck and Lennox who were out in the yard with a long rope of knots.

"They tow boats. Towing a boat is a requirement for water-rescue titles. Some people hook their Newfs up to wagons and the dogs haul firewood, or Christmas trees, or whatever."

Steve looked down at the dog by his side. Ferry didn't want to tug. She wanted to watch, to see what he and Karen were doing. She watched Karen put the dog blankets and dog towels into the washing machine. She stood up on her back legs to look inside. Her face was wrinkled in concentration.

"Have you ever thought about teaching Ferry to do the laundry?" Steve asked. "I bet she could do it."

After their day of dog chores they stood in her shower. They soaped and scrubbed and rubbed until the hot water ran cold.

"Do you trust me?" Steve asked.

"Yes."

He grinned at her. "Prove it."

"How would you like me to prove it?"

"Prove it by reading or knitting or whatever you do in the living room while I cook dinner for you."

"You cook?"

He slipped into his flannel shirt. "Let me do this for you."

"I like the things you do for me."

He pointed to the door. "Good. Then go do something for yourself and let me do something for you."

She left. She curled up on the couch with a book. She opened it and stared at the pages, but her brain couldn't decipher the words. She gave up and pulled out Katie's shawl. She found her place in the pattern and she began to knit. Lovely dinner smells floated out of the kitchen but Karen continued to knit. The dinger dinged and the oven door screeched but Karen continued to knit. Steve leaned over the back of the couch and kissed her softly on her cheek. She left her knitting and followed him.

* * *

Suddenly she was awake. In the middle of the night, she was awake. Wide-awake. Steve slept soundly, one arm flung out toward her, as if even in sleep he wanted to hold her. She slipped out of bed, careful not to wake him. Lennox, in her rocking chair, watched her every move. When he realized she saw him, his tail revved up to a blur.

"Shhh!" She beckoned to him and he nimbly slipped to the floor. She pulled the quilt off the back of the rocking chair and wrapped it around herself as she padded down the hall into the kitchen. Lennox decided this was a great new kind of adventure. Karen poured a glass of water and drank. She poured fresh water in the dogs' bowls and Lennox drank. "You're a noisy drinker," she told him. He was so pleased she noticed.

Karen opened the back door for him. The biting wind whipped at her quilt and smacked her naked legs. She shivered at the door. Lennox trotted out, did his thing quickly, then took the steps two at a time in a dash for the door.

"What a big wuss," she told him as she gushed over him. This dog had brought great change to her life. This dog and Steve, she corrected herself. She scanned the kitchen. She saw Steve's favorite mug in the sink, a boxing magazine tossed on the counter, his boots sprawled on a mat by the back door, his jacket hung on a hook by the door, his clump of keys on the table, a small bottle of his hot sauce shoved against the napkin holder, and a hastily scrawled note on the pad by the phone in his distinctive handwriting. She wandered into the living room. She found his sweatshirt dumped on a chair, a stack of his books dumped on the dining room table, a pair of his socks stuffed under the couch, his toolbox in front of the fireplace. In her bathroom, the bathroom they shared, she knew she'd find his toothbrush, his soap, his shampoo, and towels that were not her pastel-colored ones. Shirts of his hung in her closet, his jeans were tangled with hers in the washing machine. Even Lennox had moved over some of his toys, including two bowling balls. Two, Steve explained, because she had a very big backyard. But the single biggest sign of Steve was his coffeemaker, set on a timer, and the smell of coffee that greeted her every morning.

She sat on the couch and pulled Lennox up with her. She adjusted the quilt so it covered her toes. She and Steve cuddled up on this couch the night he told her about Caroline, how he failed at marriage. She told him one person alone couldn't fail at something that required two people to do. She loved him for his refusal to speak badly of Caroline.

Their lives, hers and Steve's, were combining, woven together with dirty blue jeans and coffee beans, the little details of everyday life. She rubbed Lennox's ears. He rolled over on his back. They both made compromises. She switched to an electric alarm clock because he didn't like the ticktock of her windup Baby Ben. He learned to check plates even straight out of the cupboard for stray dog hairs.

"I like him here," she told Lennox.

Lennox groaned and wiggled to work himself deeper into the couch.

"You are a very mushy dog," she told him.

"Katie told him the same thing before she left."

She whipped her head around. "You startled me," she said.

He climbed over the back of the couch to cuddle under the quilt with her.

"Why are you awake?" she asked. She wrapped her arms around him. The feel of his skin was something else he brought with him. She nuzzled her nose in his neck. Her nose was cold. His neck was warm.

"You weren't there," he said. "What were you doing out here without me?"

"Thinking."

"About what?" He rubbed his cheek against hers.

"I was thinking about all of your things that are here in my house."

"Is that a problem?"

"No."

"Then why were you thinking?"

"I was thinking about how our lives were changed by being together. You spend so much time here with me it feels like you're moving in bit by bit."

"Does that bother you?"

"No. It doesn't bother me. But once our lives start to twist and twine around each other, it's more difficult to sort them out."

He thought about this. "Do you want to sort them out?"

"No!"

"What do you want to do?"

"I don't want to do anything. I'm just thinking about it."

He frowned.

"What's wrong?" she asked.

"I don't understand why you're thinking about all this if you don't want to do anything about it."

"Hmm. I guess it's just what I do. I think about things."

He nodded. "Oh, yes," he said. "Jessie warned me about that. She said you micro-analyzed. She said it was sometimes annoying." He kissed her. "I'd rather do things." He kissed her again. "Let's go back to bed and do things."

Chapter 32

Sunday afternoon, Steve drove Lennox up to May's.

"How is Karen doing?" May asked. "It's tough to lose a dog."

"She'll be fine," he said.

"I know she *will* be fine. But how is she now?"

"She misses him. After we put away his crate she said the room looked too big."

"She's grieving."

"She says she's processing."

May grinned. "They're sometimes the same thing. Hey, tell me about Katie."

"She's great. She has guts and determination and heart. I think she must be exactly like Karen was at her age."

"She'll only be here for ten days before combat school, right?"

"That's the plan."

"And then you probably won't see her for who knows how long."

"May," he said. "What are you up to?"

"I'm not up to anything."

"Come out with it. Give me your best shot."

"You just don't like jabs."

"Let me have it."

May looked at him, measuring something, he wasn't sure what. "Okay," she said at last. "Here it is. Katie will only be home for ten days and after that you have no idea when you'll see her again. I would think Karen would want Katie to be at your wedding. I would think *you* would want Katie at your wedding." She shrugged. "Punch you wanted, punch you got. But you know I'm right."

"Aren't you jumping the gun here? Just a little?"

She shook her head. "No. I see your face when you talk about her. I hear your voice when you say her name. I've also seen her face when she talks about you, and I've heard her voice when she says your name. It's written in stone. There's nothing you can do about it—except make sure Katie is there."

"No." He held up his hands. "No. You're out of line."

"So what? Just because I'm out of line doesn't mean I'm not right."

"I'm leaving now, May. Thank you for taking care of Lennox for me. You have all the phone numbers: Dr. Winthrop, Jessie, my cell, Karen's cell. Here's his dog food. Here's his favorite bowling ball. Lennox, old guy," he swept his dog up in a great big hug. "I'll see you in a few days and then you'll see Katie."

"Don't waste those ten days," May called, following him out the front door.

"Good-bye, May," he said as he got into his car and closed his door.

May opened it. "You'll never forgive yourself if you don't do it now, when Katie can be there."

"This really isn't any of your business."

"I know. But that still doesn't mean I'm not right." She wrapped her arms around herself and shivered.

He stopped with his hand on the key. "I know," he told his sister. "You're right. But it still might not be the right time."

"Not the right time for Karen? Or for you?"

"I don't think either of us is ready."

May grabbed at his sleeve, like a puppy trying to get attention. "She's not Caroline. She's stronger than Caroline. Karen could deal with the double whammy, if you gave her the chance."

"I don't think so," he said quietly, almost to himself.

"Then," his sister said, "you don't know her at all." May stood up straight. She stepped away from the car. "Have a nice trip. Drive safely. Give my regards to Parris Island."

As he backed out of her driveway, he kept an eye on her, standing in the chilly air. He pulled out into the street and stopped, still gazing at his sister. She had made her opinion known to him. Now she stood straight and still, refusing to even shiver in the cold. It was her way of challenging him to consider her words.

Steve thought about his sister. He thought about Karen. He thought about himself and he even thought about Caroline—but not for more than a second. He looked at the thick low sky. He thought about Karen again, waiting for him at home. When had he started thinking of her house as home? He didn't want to think about that. That was something Karen could think about. She'd probably like thinking about that. He looked at his sister. She stood straight and still to challenge him.

Oh, hell. He checked the street for traffic, then he opened his car door. He climbed out into the cold and faced his sister. He smartly saluted her. It was his way of telling her he accepted her challenge.

They stood straight and still, a car and a driveway and many words between them, but they were still as close as twins could be. They had started their lives together, floating around in the dark next to each other, growing bigger and bigger until they crowded each other out, and still they continued to grow bigger and stronger until they stood here now, as they had stood before, when they felt this strongly about opposing sides. She knew him better than anyone in the world. He knew her so well he would gladly trust her with his life. Maybe that was what he should do now.

Suddenly May broke and ran toward him, crying and holding out her arms to him. She threw herself at him and hugged him and he hugged her. "I love you so much you big dummy!" she said. She pounded him on his arm. "I love you so much I don't ever want to see you mess up your life like you did before. I know this is none of my business, and before, when you told me it was none of my business I believed you and so I stayed out of it, and you were so very unhappy I couldn't stand it! And I know it was your life, but ever since then I've told myself if I'd made you understand what I saw, maybe things would have been different, maybe things wouldn't have . . . maybe you would have had a happier life."

"Maisie May, don't blame yourself for what happened between Caroline and me."

"But I do, Stevie Steve. I do because I saw what was happening and I didn't stop it. I let it happen because I thought it was none of my business and I could shoot myself for that! And now I see you about to make the same mistake, only by *not* marrying someone you should, instead of marrying someone you shouldn't. And if you don't, and you end up unhappy again, I'll be so mad at you I'll . . . I'll . . . well, I don't know what I'll do to you but it'll be really horrible!"

Monday evening, Steve did not go to the gym. After work, Jessie brought over a copy of the new Terry Pratchett book. "To read on the trip," she said. Sally brought over a gallon-sized zippy bag filled with chocolate chip cookies. "For the trip," she said. Melissa brought over a dozen little snack cans of fruit. "For the trip," she said. Sylvie ran over from next door with a bag of marshmallow peanuts. "For the trip," she said.

Even if she didn't have a sister, Karen thought, she had the best friends in the world. "Jessie once said," she told Steve that night, "the five of us were Siamese quintuplets in a former life. Sometimes I think she's right."

At last it was Tuesday. They loaded the car, added the dogs, then stopped off at a gas station on their way to Susannah and Lloyd's. Karen gave the dogs to her dad, with kisses all around. Susannah handed Steve a heavy cooler. "Trip food," she said.

On the way out of town, Karen said, "Can we stop at the yarn shop? For only a minute?" They passed the brazen tree on the corner near Karen's office. The leaves were all gone. As Katie said last year, autumn has leafed and left.

Bridgit greeted them as they came in the door. "She loves to greet people," Connie said.

"I'm glad," Karen said. She hugged Bridgit. Bridgit wagged her tail. "Connie," said Karen, "I need to make socks."

"Socks are good for trips," Connie said. "They're small and they finish quickly."

"I want the brightest colors you have. I want to knit socks that rage and riot and gallop triumphantly. I want lots of yarn to knit lots of socks."

She knitted as Steve drove. She concentrated on her knitting and he concentrated on his driving. They drove through West Virginia, Virginia, North Carolina. When they stopped for the night, outside of Charlotte, Karen held up one finished sock. The colors rioted and raged. She looked at Steve. "Are you okay?"

"Sure. Why?"

"You haven't said much today. I wondered if something was going on?"

"Going on?"

"Yeah. You know. Going on in your mind."

He chuckled. "No, there's not much going on in my mind."

"I don't believe that."

"It's true. You like to analyze things. I like to do things. I thought we'd already agreed on that the other night, when I got to do a lot of the things I like to do."

"You're good at trying to distract me." She cast on sixty-four stitches for her second sock.

"I like to do things to distract you."

She said, "My mom was right. She said you couldn't help but feel hopeful when you were working with all these glorious colors."

Karen finished the second sock as they crossed the South Carolina state line. She pointed out the trees along the highway. They were tall and spindly and bare straight up to the top, where they threw out branches of evergreen. "What odd trees," she said. "Look, is that Spanish moss? I've never seen it before. It's like something out of *Gone with the Wind* or that little old lady in *Great Expectations.*"

"I don't think Spanish moss grows in England."

"I wasn't being literal." She felt like she was entering a different world. Nothing looked like Ohio.

Steve drove past the exit for Beaufort and followed the signs for Hilton Head. The highway was long and wide, with trees and bushes planted all along. Karen noticed a blue sign with white letters. "Evacuation Route?" she asked.

"Hurricanes happen."

Ohio didn't have hurricanes. Tornadoes, but not hurricanes. Karen watched the world fly by. This was where Katie had lived for the past three months. She wanted to know all about it.

They almost missed the motel; it was hidden behind the trees that lined the highway. This was another difference, Karen thought. In Ohio we don't hide our motels. The motel room, however, smelled like motel rooms everywhere, like stale air and old air-conditioning.

Karen looked at her watch. It was late afternoon. Family Day at Parris Island began at noon on Thursday. The letter from the Marines instructed family members not to arrive before then. "We have almost a whole day to wait," Karen said. "I don't think I can stand it!" She put on her new socks and held out her feet to admire them. They were really great socks. She took them off to keep them new for tomorrow. What to do now? Then she noticed Steve doing small shoulder rolls.

"You've been driving for two days while I've been knitting. Come, sit in this chair. Let me rub your shoulders."

"Gladly." He pulled off his shirt.

"I love the way your skin feels," she told him. "Your skin is warm and smooth and firm." She stopped rubbing to drop a kiss on his shoulder. "Your skin feels different from mine."

"I like the way your skin feels," he said. "Your skin is warm and soft."

"Let's take a shower," she said. "We should be all nice and clean before we go out to find somewhere to eat."

"We should buy something for your house," he said.

"What?" She turned around so he could scrub her back. She loved the feel of his hands on her.

"A bigger water heater."

"You want to spend more time in the shower with me?"

"Absolutely."

"Then I'll have to ask Santa for an industrial-sized water

heater." She turned around and slid her arms around him. "Speaking of industrial-sized . . ."

They decided not to go out to eat. Instead, they sat cross-legged on the very rumpled bed and finished Susannah's trip food. They decided to go to bed early. But they did not sleep.

Thursday they drove over to Beaufort to have a late, leisurely, breakfast.

"It's not time yet," he told her. "You keep looking at your watch."

"I'm nervous."

"Why?"

"It's the way mothers are."

He chuckled.

"What's Katie doing right now?"

"She's probably in the squadbay getting ready for Family Day. Soon they'll have lunch in the chow hall. Then they'll go back to the squadbays for one last spit and polish before they're released to see their families."

"Is she nervous?"

"Probably."

"Why?"

"This will be the first time you see her as a Marine."

Karen worried Katie's pendant. "My daughter is a Marine," she murmured. "I still don't believe it."

"You will."

Finally it was time. Karen stared out the window as the world went by. "The houses are different. They're all low to the ground."

They drove toward a bridge. "Look." Steve pointed to a green highway sign.

"Marine Corps crossing," she read. "We're close?"

"Very close." He turned onto a cloverleaf and came to a

stop at the end of a line of cars. "Welcome to Parris Island," he said. He rolled down the window to greet the sentry on duty. The sentry checked their identification and waved them through.

"Welcome to Parris Island," Steve said again, "where we make Marines."

Chapter 33

"I'm going to cry."

"That's okay. Family Day is an emotional time for everyone."

Karen looked around. She saw water.

"Island," he said. "Parris Island. It's an island. We're driving across the causeway." Then, "Calm down. Relax."

"I'm sorry. I'm . . . I'm . . . I can't sit still. I feel like a kid before my parents are awake on Christmas morning."

He chuckled. "We're coming into the main base area," he said.

Tall, leafy, trees sheltered redbrick buildings, none of them more than two or three stories high. "It looks like a college campus," she said.

He stopped at a stop sign and pointed. "New recruits." A group of young men in sweats and black caps jogged down the street. Alongside them was one of the infamous Marine Corps drill instructors. Their breath hung like clouds in the air.

"How do you know they're new?"

"See those yellow bands? Like school crossing guards. That says they're really raw. Just off the bus. Also, they don't know how to jog in formation yet. They'll learn."

She needed to see everything at once, drink it all in, in great big gulps.

The Visitor's Center was noisy and crammed with people.

Karen held onto Steve's hand as they squeezed in. She didn't want to lose him in the crowd.

Suddenly, a young Marine on top of a table hollered, "Secure the noise!"

Like magic, she thought, it was quiet. "Close the doors," the Marine continued. "Don't let all my warm air out into the street. I know you're all anxious to see your new Marines. You will, in a few minutes. But first, there are rules your Marines must obey while you are here."

Karen gripped Steve's hand as she listened to the rules. That young man was a Marine. Katie was a Marine. She tried to put the two together. She tried to imagine Katie up there on that table commanding the attention of a room crammed with parents who only wanted to see their kids. She couldn't imagine it.

"If there are no other questions," the Marine said, and he told them where to find their Marines.

"Katie's in the Fourth Battalion," Steve said. "She'll be at the squadbay."

At last they were outside again, away from the noise and the press of anxious families. Karen buttoned up her coat.

"Cold?" he asked.

She nodded. "I didn't think South Carolina would be this cold."

"Couple of years ago it snowed on graduation."

"Do you know where we're going?" She walked quickly to keep up with him. His legs were longer than hers, and he jogged every day.

"Yes." He tucked her cold hand into his arm. "There it is," he pointed to a cluster of buildings that looked like a college dormitory. "The Fourth Training Battalion. All of the female recruits are here."

"Where's Katie?"

"Don't panic."

"Okay." She stood on her toes and tried to see over the

crowd of excitedly milling families. She heard a collective gasp and caught a glimpse of a group of women in dark olive green. The new Marines were coming down the steps from the building. She threaded through the throng, looking at all the young women in uniforms who were themselves searching. Where was Katie? All around her mothers and fathers were hugging their daughters, but where was Katie?

She felt a tap on her shoulder. She turned expecting Steve.

A young woman stood in front of her. A stranger exuding confidence and poise. Maybe she knew Katie.

"Hello, Mom."

Karen was stunned. Surely this self-assured young woman, it couldn't be her daughter. Not Katie. Katie just graduated from high school and this young woman was . . . was . . . Katie. She threw her arms around her daughter and hugged her tight, laughing and crying at the same time.

"I can't believe it," she said. She held Katie at arm's length and drank in the sight of her. "I didn't recognize you. You look taller."

"I'm me."

Karen knew her daughter wasn't the same. She was someone else altogether. She remembered what Steve had said, Katie would be more herself than she ever had been before.

"Hello, Katie," said Steve. "Congratulations."

"Thank you, sir," she beamed. "I'm so glad you came."

"I would not have missed it for the world."

"We have the rest of the day," Karen said, "until seven o'clock. What would you like to do?"

"Nineteen hundred. We use a twenty-four hour clock. That way we don't become confused with a.m. and p.m." Then she grinned. She still had her million-dollar grin. "I want to show you everything. What do you want to see first?"

"The swimming pool."

"It's this way." But she couldn't find it at first. "I think it's over there," she pointed across a parking lot.

"Let's cut through the parking lot," Karen said.

"No. Mom, we can't. That's a parade ground. We don't walk on it. We walk around it."

Karen looked at Steve. "Is this one of the respect things?"

"Yes. It is."

They walked around, with Katie between them.

Katie showed off the pool. Karen read a sign posted on the wall. "We teach the world's worst swimmers."

"It's not about swimming," Katie said. "It's about surviving in the water. We jump off that tower over there, with all our gear on, and swim across the pool."

Karen looked at the tower. Katie jumped off that? Katie-who-is-terrified-of-heights? She looked at her daughter again. She saw more of this new person.

"All your gear?"

"Over there is all the practice gear; helmets, rifles, boots, packs. We don't get our real things wet, of course. It's really cool. One girl didn't know how to swim. She still can't swim very well, but she can stay afloat in the water with all her gear. You tie your trousers at the ankles and blow them up at the waist. They float." They passed someone in a uniform. Katie saluted. "The rule is, you salute anyone with anything shiny on. Steve, did you bring your uniform?"

He smiled. "Yes. For you."

Katie showed them the rifle range, and the yellow footprints, "All the recruits who came before me, and all of them who come after me, we all began here. Oh. Steve. You must have started here, too."

She showed them the sandpits outside the squadbay. "The sand fleas are nasty, but they die off when it gets cold. Then the sandpits are like a cold litter box."

She took them upstairs to show them her rack. The squadbay was spotless. It was filled with families and their new Marines. "You don't know how we scrubbed," Katie said.

She led them up to a woman who stood at the head of the

room, ramrod straight. She introduced them to Staff Sergeant McNamara. Karen saw the respect in her daughter's eyes as she introduced them to her drill instructor. She'd written to Colleen that this woman was pure evil on a stick.

Once outside, Katie said, "Staff Sergeant McNamara, at first I thought she was the meanest old witch, a real slave driver. But then, I don't know. Something changed. I realized she wanted us to succeed. She's awesome. I have so much respect for her."

Steve had been silent through most of it, but now he spoke. "What was the most difficult thing for you to do?"

"The tower." She led them down the tree-lined road. "The tower was worse than the gas chamber. I mean, in the gas chamber all you have to do is take off your helmet and recite the pledge of allegiance before you pass out from the gas, and when you finally get outside and everyone is coughing up gunk and vomiting and stuff, that's pretty gross. But the tower, you have to jump off the tower. There, Mom. At the end of the driveway."

Karen tipped her head all the way back to see the top of it. "Oh, my!" she breathed.

"It's about seventy feet high," Katie said.

"You jumped off?"

"Well, yeah. On the other side we rappel down."

Karen stared at her daughter. "*You* rappelled down? You actually climbed to the top? And then you rappelled down?"

Katie stood and looked up at the tower. For a while she was silent. Then she said, "From the other side. On this side you climb up to the top, hold onto a rope, and drop. All you have is that rope."

Karen looked up at the impossibly high tower. She looked at her impossibly courageous daughter. She was stunned.

"Marines have to know how to do it, Mom. It's the way we get out of helicopters." Katie sounded perfectly casual, as if it were the most reasonable thing in the world. Then she continued, "When they brought us over here, it made me sick to my stomach to even look up at it. But then, I had to climb to the top. Do you know how small all of this"—she gestured around at the trees—"looks from up there? That was the moment I knew I'd fail. I thought I couldn't do this one thing. I could do all the rest, getting yelled at, not washing my hair every day, screaming 'Yes, ma'am' every other second, and doing push-ups in the sandpits and then sitting in the sand, absolutely still, while the DI yelled at us and the sand fleas got us. Oh. And the rifle stuff, taking it apart and cleaning it and putting it back together again in, like, ten seconds. And running for miles and miles. I could do all that. But I couldn't jump off this tower. It wasn't a Ward Gatti thing. I mean, I wasn't giving up, it wasn't a matter of endurance, I just couldn't make myself do it. I was that scared."

"What gave you the courage?" Steve asked.

"Motivation." She grinned. "One of the DIs motivated me. She said—yelled really, they yell all the time—'Matheson, why aren't you off my tower?' When you're a recruit, everything belongs to them. And I said, 'This recruit is scared of heights, ma'am!' and she said, 'that's the difference between recruits and Marines. Marines don't let fear get in the way of a mission. Now get off my tower!' and I realized I had to stop thinking like a recruit and start thinking like a Marine. I told my fear to go stuff itself, and I yelled, 'Yes, ma'am!' and I did it. I got off her tower. I climbed down that big fat rope. And I didn't slide down either. I climbed, hand over hand, using my feet as a stopper, so I didn't get any rope burns. And, you know what? I know I won't ever let my fear get in the way of a mission."

Karen looked at her daughter, a brand new Katie, standing up straight in her brand new Marine uniform, bursting with pride and confidence and even a little bit of swagger. Her whole attitude said she could take on the world and win.

Karen had absolutely no doubt that she could. "This must have been one of your grandmother's miracles."

"No, Mom. It wasn't a miracle. I was highly motivated. Oh. And then Staff Sergeant McNamara, who was at the bottom, told me I'd done good, and I got all excited and I yelled, 'Yes!' And then Sergeant McNamara came over and yelled at me to get back in line." She chuckled.

"She yelled at you because you did it?"

"No. She yelled at me because I made a fuss about doing it." She looked up at the tower again. "To think that I was afraid of climbing down a rope," she said.

The rest of the afternoon they walked with Katie, and talked with Katie. They listened while Katie talked, and she talked and talked. She overflowed with words. They ate dinner at the base buffet and then it was time to walk Katie back to her squadbay. Walking through the chilly winter night, Katie asked about the dogs, and they told her about how Bridgit needed Connie Wilde, and about Brian and how they planted a baby apple tree with him.

Katie looked up at the lights in the windows of her squadbay. "You had your Crucible, too, Mom," she said.

"See you tomorrow," Karen said as she hugged her daughter close.

Katie reached out to hug Steve. "I'm glad you're here," she told him.

"I wouldn't have missed it for the world."

Katie did not go inside. She stood and stared at them. "So," she said, "Mom. Steve. Are you ever going to tell me?"

"Tell you what?"

"That you're, like, you know. Sweeties."

"Sweeties," Steve muttered to the sky. "Sweeties."

"Yes, Steve," Katie said. "I heard *from other people* that you and my mother are sweeties."

Karen looked at Steve. Steve looked at Karen. "Jessie!" they said at the same time.

"No," Katie said, "it wasn't Jessie. So when were you going to tell me?"

Karen was at a loss. "I don't know. We never discussed it. We hadn't actually decided on a specific time to tell you."

"Now is a good time," Katie said. "In fact, I think now is an excellent time."

"Well," Karen said, "all right. Steve and I have been seeing each other for a while now."

Steve, looking at the sky again, snorted.

"Well then," Karen said, "you tell her."

"Katie," Steve said, "your mother and I . . ."

Karen stared at this man. She had never before seen him at a loss for words. Now he stood straight, in that Marine way of his, and he said, in that voice he used when he told her Marine stories, that voice that told her, more than the words themselves, that he had respect and honor for the story he told; now he said, in that same voice, "Katie, I love your mother."

The brand new Marine, in her brand new uniform, shining and gleaming and sparkling, suddenly erupted into a wild war whoop, with an air punch to boot, "Yes!" Then she ran into the building.

Chapter 34

They watched Katie disappear into her squadbay and then Steve wrapped Karen in his arms and they stood in the dark and listened to Parris Island. They stood until a cold rain drove them to find their car and leave Katie on Parris Island while they drove back to Hilton Head. *Katie, I love your mother,* he'd said. His words repeated over and over in time to the windshield wipers. *Katie I love your mother Katie I love your mother Katie I love your mother.* She leaned her head back against the headrest. *Katie I love your mother Katie I love your mother Katie I love your mother.* The words were engraved forever in her memory.

He unlocked their motel room door and held it open for her and followed her in. "What do you think?" he asked.

Her eyes widened. "What?"

"What do you think?" he said again.

"About what?"

"About what?" Surely he couldn't have heard her correctly. "Yes. What do I think about what?"

"Katie. What else?"

She sank into a chair and stared at him. "What else? What about the mother of all bombs you dropped today?"

"Mother of all bombs?"

"Yes. You know."

"Obviously I don't." He sat down on the edge of the bed. "Is this one of the times you micro-analyze things and I want to do things?"

She hadn't thought of that. She explained. "You told Katie you love me."

"So?"

"So?!"

"Is this a secret? Did you not want her to know?"

She stared at the man she thought she knew so well. She realized she didn't know him as well as she thought she did. Which meant he probably didn't know her as well as she thought he did either. "I guess," she said in a small voice, "I guess I wish you'd told me first."

"Told you?"

"Told me you love me."

"Don't you know that?"

"Now I do."

"You didn't know that before now?" He looked thunderstruck. "How could you not know?"

"You never told me."

In an instant he was on his knees at her side, his arms around her, looking intently into her face. "I tell you all the time," he said. "Maybe you don't listen."

It was her turn to be thunderstruck.

"Maybe," he told her, "you depend so much on words that you don't hear other things."

"What kind of things?"

"Looks, touches, a ramp for Brian . . ."

"Oh."

"The same way you show me without words. Like knitting me a sweater."

"How did you know about that?"

He gave her a look of tolerance. "I spend a lot of time with you. I see you knit. I pick up things for you when they fall out of your knitting bag. It's nice, by the way." He tugged at a lock of her hair to draw her close to him, until she was close enough so that he could kiss her. "I don't always have the words, Karen," he whispered. "I don't always know the right words, but I will always find ways to show you how much I love you."

"Show me now," she said and he did, and it was a good way.

After, she stared up at the ceiling, staring at nothing, processing and micro-analyzing. She thought about Steve and Katie and Roger and her father and mother. She thought about what it means to be the mother of a Marine, or, as May was, the wife of a Marine. She thought of boxing and the way Gatti and Ward had respect for each other. She thought about the dogs. Her life was changing and she was ready to go with it, with where it would take her. She was ready to weed the garden of her ideas and see what new ideas sprouted.

She looked over at the man beside her, the man she loved so deeply. His eyes were open. He was looking at her.

"What are you doing?" he whispered.

"Thinking," she whispered. "What are you doing?"

"Thinking."

"What are you thinking about?"

"Something my sister said."

"What did she say?"

"She likes you."

"I like her, too," Karen whispered. "But you, you I love." And she showed him.

"May was right!" Karen said the next morning. "You are something in your uniform! Wow!"

"They always fall for the uniforms," he teased.

"I fell for what's in it," she teased back.

"Watch it," he warned. "Wrinkles."

They arrived at Parris Island early enough to have time to

walk around before Katie's graduation. The temperature was warmer than yesterday, so the walking was pleasant. "There is something I want to show you."

"Can Katie walk around with us?"

"No. We won't see her until the ceremony."

Karen felt proud of the man walking beside her. He was, to use Katie's word, awesome. "Where are you taking me?"

"Up here," he pointed. "On the right. Look."

Karen gazed at the towering sculpture of the raising of the Stars and Stripes on Mount Suribachi. "It was Marines?" she asked.

"Five Marines and a Navy Corpsman," he said. "Victory after the costliest battle in Marine Corps history; a battle in which more Marines were killed than Japanese." He told her the story of the bloody battle and of the many valiant young men who were part of it.

He took her aside, away from the families taking photographs of the sculpture, to a spot under a tall bare-branched tree. Pulled something out of his pocket and handed it to her. She looked down, and her mouth dropped open.

"This is the Marine emblem," he said. "The eagle is for the nation, the world stands for our worldwide service, and the anchor reminds us of our naval heritage. Every new Marine receives one. Katie has one too, now. This is the emblem I received on the day I graduated from Parris Island. Karen Matheson, will you marry me? I don't have a ring for you, but I have this emblem, which means more to me than any ring ever could. I want you to have it. Will you marry me?"

She was speechless.

"Will you? We can get a ring if you'd rather have a ring . . ."

She stared at him and blinked.

"Say something," he said.

She reached into her pocket and pulled something out. It was small and black. "I was going to give this to Katie today," she said. She put the Marine emblem in his hand.

"Where did you get this?"

"From Katie's father."

"He was a Marine?"

"Yes." And she told him how they'd met. How they'd spent the night together and he'd left, leaving her an emblem and a daughter. She told him all of it.

"You must have been very special to him," he said when she was finished. "No Marine would entrust their emblem to someone else unless . . ."

"Unless it was someone very special," she finished his thought.

"Yes. Very special."

"I didn't know what it was, at first, but Roger told me."

"Your brother?"

"He was the first one to figure out I was pregnant. Mom suspected, I think, but Roger knew. So I talked to him. I didn't tell him all of it, but he's smart enough he probably figured it out. Anyway, he told me this was a Marine emblem."

"So that's how you have one, too," he said.

She shook her head. "It's for Katie. At least, I thought it was. She may not want it, now that she has her own."

Steve glanced around at the gathering crowd. "It's going to begin soon. We should find seats. But first, you didn't answer. Will you marry me? Please."

She smiled. She beamed. She felt like spun sugar. "Yes."

Katie's graduation held all the ceremony he'd promised it would. Karen expected that. She didn't expect the enormous welling up of pride she felt for her daughter. Pride welled and swelled within her, threatening to erupt as she sat in old worn bleachers and gazed down at the parade ground below.

On the parade ground, eight platoons of eighty brand new Marines stood in perfect formation, each one bursting with the same pride and confidence and certitude that comes from the knowledge that they have earned the right to belong to a whole that is greater than the sum of the parts, that they were now one with those who had come before, and with those who would come after; the knowledge that they jumped off the tower because they knew they would not fail. They knew they could do anything, whatever it was, whatever it took. They would not fail. They were United States Marines.

When the drill instructors, facing their new Marines, gave their final command, Karen did not hear, but she saw. Eight platoons of brand new Marines tossed their covers high into the air, and erupted into a cheering sea of joy. Karen felt her own heart soar with them. Beside her, Steve gripped her hand hard. She knew he felt it too.

"Let's go find Katie," he said.

"I have to tell her about her father," she said.

"I think she knows," he said.

Then she saw her daughter coming at a full run into her wide-open arms.

It was time for Karen to tell Katie about her father. She had to do it. She had to climb her tower and jump off and climb down the rope. She had to do it. But first there were pictures to take and Katie's fellow platoon members to meet, and their families, and everywhere she looked there were smiles and proud tears and Marines saluting Steve at every turn.

"Do they all know him?" Karen whispered to Katie.

"No," Katie whispered back. "When you're a new Marine you salute anyone with anything shiny."

Keith's emblem in Karen's pocket grew heavier and heavier on Karen's heart. She had to do this before they left Parris Island. She climbed the ladder. "Let's all go over there," she said. She pointed to what looked like a seawall.

"That's the Atlantic," Katie said. They walked with interlaced arms, Katie in the middle.

Karen stood on top of her metaphorical tower and looked over the side. There was no good way to tell Katie all this, Karen thought, but Katie had to start thinking like a Marine, so it was time for Karen to give up her old fears, too. "Katie," she said, "Steve taught me to cut out the jabs and use my power punch."

"Power punch?"

"Yes. This is really difficult for me, so give me a minute. Katie, I want to talk to you about your father."

Katie nodded. "Okay."

"You sound sort of casual about it."

"Well, I know about him. His name was Keith and you met him after you got in a snit because you and Roger had to stay home while Grandma and Grandpa went to D.C. so you ran away and went to Columbus and met my dad and he was a Marine and you had a lovely night and then he left and you never saw him again but he left you his emblem and then I was born. Then you decided to shrink the heads of young pregnant teenagers for free, which you thought would be a good way to give back to your mom."

Once more Karen was thunderstruck.

"It's okay Mom. I know all about it. I finally figured out why you never told me."

"What do you mean you know all about it? You couldn't possibly know all about it."

"Uncle Roger told me."

"Roger told you?"

"Yeah. You wouldn't. No one would. Not even Grandma and Grandpa, or Tanner, or Jessie. No one. Finally, in fact, it was the day you got Bridgit, I talked to Uncle Roger. He told me."

"I never told him all of it."

Katie looked pained. "Mom, give him some credit. He knows you better than anyone in the world does. How could he not know? Or figure it out."

"About the girls I counsel . . ." she said faintly. "How did you . . . no one knows."

"We're talking about Hartley, here. Small-town America. Not some nameless, faceless city with a terminal case of urban sprawl. Everyone knows it's pro bono."

"I wanted to give back to my parents."

"Grandma and Grandpa?"

"Yes. You see, she was . . ."

"Wait. Are you going to tell me how you and Uncle Roger were born before Grandma and Grandpa were married and Grandpa was in Vietnam?"

"How do you know about *that?*"

"I did that family-tree project in ninth grade. I looked at dates and subtracted. It wasn't difficult. Then I talked to Grandma. She was really cool about it, too." She blinked at Karen. "You mean you didn't know this?"

"Katherine Eleanor Matheson, you are turning out to be quite a surprising person." She pulled Keith's emblem from her pocket. She looked at it one more time, then handed it to Katie. "You should have this."

Katie looked at her father's emblem.

"I can't take it." She handed it back.

"Why not?"

Katie said simply, "He gave it to you." She grinned. "Besides, I already had it for a while."

Steve cleared his throat. "I gave your mother my emblem."

Katie's eyes grew wide. "You did?" she breathed.

"Yes. This morning. I asked her to marry me and she said she would."

Katie screamed and jumped and whooped and danced. She hugged them hard and danced some more. "I knew it! I knew it! Oh, Uncle Roger was right! I knew it! I can't wait to tell him. Mom, do you have your cell? I have to call Uncle Roger."

"Roger?"

"I got a letter from him yesterday. He told me you two were going to get married. He said Grandpa told him Steve was really great, and he thought so, too, and he told you to keep Steve around. He told me you were going to get married. All yesterday, I was waiting for you to tell me."

Karen shook her head. "Let's go home," she said wearily. "I need my dogs."

They drove over to the Fourth Battalion squadbay to pick up Katie's seabag. "Look at all the license plates," Karen said. "There are cars from all over the country. There's Arizona. And Oregon."

"We're here," Katie said as she hopped out of the car. "Keep the engine running, Steve. I'll be right back."

Steve said suddenly, "Katie said something just now, about while your father was in Vietnam . . ."

"Roger and I were born."

Karen watched a strange look grow on Steve's face. "Steve? Are you all right?"

"You're twins? And he told Katie you and I were going to get married?"

"Yes. He always knows when I'm upset, or something like that. I know those things about him, too. We're really close."

Steve shook his head in amazement. Then he began to chuckle. "I don't believe it."

"Believe what?"

"Last night you asked me what I was thinking. I told you I was thinking about something May said. She gets these feelings, too. May and I are twins."

She looked at his grin. Then she got it. "No," she breathed. "She didn't."

"She did. She said we should get married now, while Katie is home on leave."

"Katie has ten days."

"Ten days."

"Hmmm."

Then they saw Katie with a seabag over her shoulder. Steve went to her to take her seabag.

"I can do it," she said.

"I know you can. But I'm a man. I can't let you."

On the way back off the island, with all the other families in all of their cars, Karen had a sudden thought. "Steve, is there a store around here?"

"The exchange. It's right up there. Do you want to stop?"

"Yes. Please."

She dashed into the exchange. A few minutes she dashed back out.

"Gee, Mom," Katie said. "What was so important?"

"I needed something for my car." Karen handed her the paper bag. Katie pulled out a bumper sticker. 'My daughter is a United States Marine,' she read. "Thanks, Mom. I love you, too." Then she added, "By the way, I noticed your new socks. All those colors are terrific."

"Yes," Karen told her. "They rant and rage."

"They scream and yell," Katie said.

"They holler and whoop."

"They rampage and gallumph."

Steve reached for her hand and pressed it. She lifted his hand to her lips for a kiss. "Yes," she said. "They do."

Epilogue

"Mom! Jessie called to say she has a pink and obnoxiousiy frilly bow for Ferry and tux fronts for Heck and Lennox. She'll bring them to the hall. Oh. And she said she'll call Grandpa to tell him. Do you need help up there?"

"No thanks, Katie," Karen called from inside the upstairs closet. "I think I can get it all." Karen's arms were loaded with The Dress in its garment bag as well as a smaller satchel for all the associated paraphernalia she'd need. It wasn't heavy, but it was clumsy. Karen backed out of the closet and blew a lock of hair out of her eyes. This idea of turning into Cinderella going to the ball was complicated. Karen felt she'd almost rather get married dressed as her usual pumpkin self.

She stopped at the top of the stairs and stretched to see over The Dress in her arms. She dropped the satchel and shifted The Dress so she could at least see the stairs if she went down them sideways.

"Let me do that!"

"It's okay. I have it now." The garment bag swished against the wall as she carried it down the hallway and out to the door to the garage.

"Let me get the door." Katie squeezed past her. "Now the car door."

Karen slid The Dress onto the front passenger seat of her van. "Wow! Moving this thing is a major event."

"You think it needs its own seat belt?" Katie grinned.

Karen gazed at her daughter. "I'm going to miss you. I'm proud as anything of you. But I'm still going to miss you."

"I'm going to miss you, too. But let's not get all mushy here. Hey, you keep watch while I get your other stuff."

"Has May called yet?" Karen called after her.

"No. But she'll be here. Don't worry."

Don't worry. What useless advice. Of course Karen worried.

"She wouldn't miss this for the world." Katie set Karen's satchel in the back of the van. "Now. What else has to go?"

Karen considered. "The Dress."

"And the war gear that goes with it" Katie teased.

"Watch it. I'll leave you at home."

"You can't. I'm your honor maiden."

"That's the kitchen phone." Karen hurried to reach it before the answering machine picked up. Katie grabbed it first.

"Matheson's Wedding Chapel of True Love," she said.

Karen rolled her eyes.

"Sure, Auntie May. She's right here." Katie stuck her tongue out at her and held out the phone.

"Hi Karen, I just passed the welcome to Hartley sign. You want me to pick up anything on the way to your house? Something to eat?"

"I don't think I could eat anything."

"That nervous?"

Karen thought. "No. Not nervous. Well, maybe a little bit nervous. Anticipation. I'm sweating like the dickens."

"I didn't know dickenses sweat. Go jump in the shower. I'll plug in my hot rollers when I get there."

Karen closed her eyes and relaxed in the warm water. What a week this had been. Her parents told her they wanted to formally adopt Heck, who seemed quite pleased by this turn of events. Heck liked sleeping on the rug at the foot of their

bed. He also liked sneaking onto their bed and worming himself between Susannah and Lloyd.

Ferry had glued herself to Karen's side. "She's trying to tell
you something," Steve said.

Karen held Ferry's great head between her hands and
looked into the doggy brown eyes. "What are you trying to
tell me?" she started to ask. But then she realized she didn't
have to ask. She knew. She nodded to Ferry. "You're my dog,
aren't you?"

Ferry's eyes twinkled. Ferry swished her tail. Ferry understood. Ferry's only question was why had it taken Karen so
long to figure it out?

Then there had been the issue of *Friday Night Fights*.
"Your house?" Steve asked when Karen asked what time
everyone usually arrived.

"Not my house," she said, "our house."

"I can take the gang to my place," Steve said. "You might
not want to spend your last night as a single lady watching
boxing with a bunch of young people."

"Your place is full of boxes." Karen put her arms around
him and rested her head on his shoulder. "I would feel like I
had to keep packing. I'd rather watch boxing here."

His arms tightened around her. "I love you."

"I love you, too."

Word went out among Steve's boxing crowd that *Friday
Night Fights* were at Katie's house. Jim Tate was the first to
arrive, with a new young lady. "Steve," the young man said,
"this is—"

"Candy!" Karen exclaimed, peering over Steve's shoulder.

"Hi, Dr. Matheson," Candy said.

"You know each other?" Steve asked Karen.

Candy turned to the young man next to her "Jim, this is Dr.
Matheson. I told you about her. She's helping me figure

everything out. You know, about my baby and my life and everything."

Jim's eyes grew round. "Your doc is marrying Steve? Cool!"

Candy followed Karen into the kitchen to help with snacks. "Jim and I live next door to each other," Candy explained. "Oh. He's not my baby's father. But I've known him all my life. He's sort of had a crush on me for a long time."

"How do you feel about him?"

"He's a really good guy. I like him a lot. That's why I have to be careful."

"Careful?"

"I don't want to use him. You know. As a reason to keep my baby."

"You think you might want to keep your baby?"

She shook her head. She smiled at Karen, but her eyes looked old and wise for one so young. "No. I can't give my baby the things I want her to have. I've talked to that adoption agency and they say I can have an open adoption. Where I help choose the parents for my baby, and I can maybe see her sometimes. You know. As she grows up."

"Is that what you want?"

"Yes." She nodded. "It is."

"So where does Jim come into this?"

"We're friends. I told him we couldn't be anything else until after my baby is born and goes to live with her new parents. Then we'll see."

Karen decided watching boxing with a group of noisily enthusiastic young people was fun. She wondered, however, how much boxing Jim Tate saw. His gaze kept shifting to the young lady next to him.

"Mom!" Katie hollered. "You still in there? May says her rollers are hot. And you have a wedding to get to."

Karen started. "I'll be right out," she called. She turned off the water and prepared herself to turn into Cinderella going to the ball.

She wore The Dress and the gossamer web of a shawl Susannah had knitted while Lloyd was in Vietnam. Ferry, ever the diva, posed prettily in her frilly pink bow while Lennox and Heck were tolerant of their tux fronts. The three dogs along with Katie in her dress uniform stood with Karen and Steve as they spoke their vows.

After the brief ceremony came all the picture taking. Ferry assumed all the flashes were for her. Lennox scratched his neck and his tux front slipped.

The hall was bursting with family and friends and food and flashes and an amazing cake baked by Liz from the library. There was hugging and laughing together, dancing, picture taking, happy tears.

Karen spotted May and Jessie huddled together in a corner, whispering. She nudged Steve and pointed. "They're up to something," he said.

Katie came up and handed each of them a cup of lemonade. "You must be really special because Sylvie brought you the very last of those ice cubes with the violets in them. Hey, Steve, didja tell her yet?"

"Tell me what?" Karen asked.

"We got a phone call," Katie said. "After you and May left. Steve came to pick me up and we got a phone call. You tell her, Steve. I'm going to go dance." She disappeared into the crowd.

"Phone call?" Karen prompted Steve.

"We have to go to Toledo tomorrow."

"Toledo?"

"Yeah. We got a call from the rescue coordinator. Seems a dog warden over in Toledo found a young Newfoundland wandering around downtown Toledo. The warden took the dog to the pound and called Newf Rescue. She called us. I told her we were getting married today, but we'd pick him up tomorrow." He grinned at her. "Katie and I set up a crate for him in the dog room. She ran me through the new foster dog drill."

Karen's eyes filled. "I love you, too," she said. "I love you, too."

Discover the Thrill of
Romance With
Kat Martin

___Hot Rain

   0-8217-6935-9   **$6.99US/$8.99CAN**

Allie Parker is in the wrong place—at the worst possible time . . . Her only ally is mysterious Jake Dawson, who warns her that she must play the role of his reluctant bedmate . . . if she wants to stay alive. Now, as Alice places her trust—and herself—in the hands of a total stranger, she wonders if this desperate gamble will be her last . . .

___The Secret

   0-8217-6798-4   **$6.99US/$8.99CAN**

Kat Rollins moved to Montana looking to change her life, not find another man like Chance McLain, with a sexy smile of empty heart. Chance can't ignore the desire he feels for her—or the suspicion that somebody wants her to leave Lost Peak . . .

___The Dream

   0-8217-6568-X   **$6.99US/$8.50CAN**

Genny Austin is convinced that her nightmares are visions of another life she lived long ago. Jack Brennan is having nightmares, too, but his are real. In the shadows of dreams lurks a terrible truth, and only by unlocking the past will Genny be free to love at last. . .

___Silent Rose

   0-8217-6281-8   **$6.99US/$8.50CAN**

When best-selling author Devon James checks into a bed-and-breakfast in Connecticut, she only hopes to put the spark back into her relationship with her fiancé. But what she experiences at the Stafford Inn changes her life forever . . .

Available Wherever Books Are Sold!

Visit our website at www.kensingtonbooks.com.